THE HOLYWELL DEAD

THE HOLYWELL DEAD

CHRIS NICKSON

The
Mystery
Press

For all the plague victims who lie nameless.

Cover photograph: © iStockphoto.com

First published 2017

The Mystery Press is an imprint of The History Press
The Mill, Brimscombe Port
Stroud, Gloucestershire, GL5 2QG
www.thehistorypress.co.uk

British Library Cataloguing in Publication Data.
A catalogue record for this book is available from the British Library.

ISBN 978 0 7509 7995 5

Typesetting and origination by The History Press
Printed and bound by CPI Group (UK) Ltd

CHAPTER ONE

May 1364

'Do it like this,' John the Carpenter said. He worked the chisel into the wood and eased it back out, then felt the straightness of the cut with his finger. The boy watched, absorbed, following each small movement. 'Now you try it.'

Alan wriggled closer, so he could look down into the joint. He tested the sharpness of the tool's edge with his thumb. Satisfied, he took a breath and began, aware of the line marked on the wood, knowing he couldn't go beyond that.

'Very good,' John told him once he was done, and the lad beamed. Alan had just turned eight, still without the strength to do many things, but he was learning quickly. John had agreed to take him on, to teach him, because the boy had the feel for wood; it was deep in his nature. That was a rare gift. It spoke to him, told him what it needed. In time he'd be able to make a living from this, the way John did. For now, though, he needed to learn, to work his apprenticeship. The carpenter brushed the sawdust off his hose and shirt. A day's work, well done.

Alan was mute. He'd never said a word since he was born. But he was quick, eager, with a sharp mind for his age.

The carpenter tousled the lad's hair.

'Come on, it's late. I'd better get you home or your mother will wonder where you are.'

The shadows were starting to lengthen. Late May already. After a wet spring, where water puddled deep in the lanes and the fields and the world seemed filled with mud, the weather had finally turned warm and dry.

The crops would be late. Some were starting to grow, although much of the soil was still heavy. The farmers were worried. John had heard them at the Saturday market in Chesterfield, muttering and grumbling and shaking their heads.

But everyone was on edge. The dampness meant illness and bad humours. And a return of the plague. Already rumours had fluttered around of cases in towns away to the south or off to the north. Just talk, he hoped; there'd been nothing close to home. Pray God all the words were wrong. His father, a carpenter, had died in agony during the year of the great death, when John was just the same age as Alan.

No more of those horrors. Never again.

Alan was a fine worker, already cleaning the tools with an oiled rag the way he'd been shown. Slow and steady until he finished, putting everything away in the battered leather satchel.

This wasn't a big job, just a pen large enough to hold twenty sheep. But it meant five pennies a day, the wage of a skilled man now. One of those went to Alan. From the way the boy picked things up so quickly, a few more years and he'd be off seeking his own jobs.

Soon enough it would be evening and the road into Chesterfield was already empty, all the traders and travellers gone for the day. Just their own footsteps raising dust. He'd be glad to be home, to see his wife and his daughter, Juliana. She was almost a year and a half old and more beautiful than he could have imagined any child could be. He'd hoped for a boy but as soon as he saw her it didn't matter; she was so delicate and so full of life. It terrified him to think that the plague might return and take her. Or his wife, Katherine, her sisters, her brother. Even Dame Martha, the neighbour who'd moved into their house the year before, slowly growing too infirm to manage on her own. They were all his family. He wanted to protect every one of them.

John felt it as soon as they entered the town. Something was wrong. The place seemed too hushed, as if it was covered in a pall of sorrow. John escorted the boy to his house, then hurried home.

• • •

He held his breath as he opened the door and stepped into the hall. Jeanette and Eleanor, Katherine's sisters, sat at the table with Dame Martha, practising their writing on pieces of slate. No sign of Walter, his brother-in-law, but that was no surprise; the lad would still be off somewhere delivering messages or with his friends.

Katherine was on a bench, nursing their little girl.

Everything was so ordinary, so normal. Had he imagined things?

'John,' Martha began. Her voice was a worried croak. 'Have you heard?'

'Heard what?' He slipped the bag of tools from his shoulder, looking first at her, then to Katherine. 'What?' It was no mistake; he could feel the fear crawling up his back.

'You know Jack the Fuller?' She put her arms around the girls, drawing them closer to her.

'Yes, of course.' Always smiling when they met, full of bad jokes and a large laugh.

'Two of his children, the youngest ones.' She hesitated for a moment, as if not speaking could unmake it all. 'Plague.'

He crossed himself, offering up a small prayer as he looked at his wife. Such helplessness on her face.

'Sweet Jesu.' But even as he spoke, his mind was working. Jack and his family lived down the hill, at the bottom of Soutergate, close to the bridge over the River Hipper. The air was always damp there, the ground boggy, especially after the wet spring.

Maybe it was the miasma in the air by the water. Maybe it was God's will. He knew that in the end the reason didn't matter. A man was going to lose two of his family, probably more. All the people around would be holding their breath and offering up their prayers to live.

Here, at the top of the hill where the air was clearer and the wind swirled around, would they escape? He knew, he remembered all too well what it had been like when he was a child. No one could forget. The black lumps in the armpits and the groin. The empty cries for help that nobody could give. And finally the stench of hell when they broke, then the sweet relief of death for the sufferers. Half the world had died, and many of those left alive and bereft wished they could be gone, too, because it seemed better than the devastation that surrounded them. Were those days returning? How could he keep his family safe? He reached out and took Katherine's hand, looking down at Juliana. Her eyes were closed. She was content, oblivious to all the pain and panic in the world. Let her live, he thought. Let them all live.

• • •

Supper was quiet, everyone subdued and reflective. Walter came home, but he had no fresh word. No one else struck down, Jack's children holding on to life.

Later, up in the solar, John stood by the small bed he'd made for his daughter, staring as she slept. He didn't even hear Katherine approach until her arms were around his waist. The girls were asleep, with their soft snuffles. Walter was curled up, snoring. Downstairs, Martha moved around quietly; these days she needed little rest, it seemed.

'It's in God's hands, you know,' Katherine said softly in his ear.

'Yes.' But how could he put all his faith in someone who had allowed so many to die in agony just a few years before? Better, he thought, to fear and try to fight. Not that anyone could battle this. 'I know.' He turned and held her tight.

• • •

For three days, life in the town seemed to be suspended. No new cases and Jack's children clung to the world. Each morning John collected Alan and they'd march out along the road to Unstone until they reached the farm where they were working. John kept an ear cocked for any gossip from travellers on the road. With evening they'd return to town, to the quiet and the desperate prayers for the future.

Then, on the fourth day, it changed. The news passed rapidly, not long after dawn: Jack's children had both died, and there'd been another case in the night: Will the Miller's widow, a woman who also had her home down by the river. Come evening, two more – Jack himself and a labourer with a tiny cottage on the other side of the Hipper.

No one from up the hill.

Yet.

No one said the word. No one dared breathe it. But all of them thought it.

John tried to concentrate on his work. It would keep everything else at bay. But whether he was using the chisel or the saw, the hammer or the awl, his mind kept wandering. Juliana, Katherine. Jeanette, Eleanor, Walter, Martha. Spare them all.

Twice he almost cut himself, then he had to stop himself shouting when Alan made a mistake, watching the boy flinch.

'I'm sorry.' He pulled a small wooden mug from the satchel and filled it with watered ale from a barrel before handing it to the lad. 'It's just my mood. Pay me no mind. I don't mean it.'

In the middle of the afternoon John stopped and began to clean the tools. Alan gave him a questioning look, but the only answer he could offer was a shrug. He needed to be at home. He had to be with his family.

John stamped the dust off his boots and slipped the worn leather jerkin over his shirt. His hose needed to be darned at the knee again, he saw. But that came with the job, so much moving and crouching and kneeling. He hefted the satchel on to his shoulder and grinned at the boy. Alan beamed back.

They'd barely set foot on the road when he heard it. The slow toll of the bell from St Mary's in town. Burying Jack's children. The first of the Chesterfield dead. He'd spotted the gravediggers when he left that morning, working in an empty corner of the graveyard. How long before all that space would be full? How many more would die in the coming months?

It was only May. Summer, the worst season for the pestilence, hadn't even arrived yet. This could linger, it could worsen. But surely it couldn't be as bad as the black visitation they'd had before? Surely not…

A small elbow nudged him and he looked down. Alan was making quick signs with his fingers. It was a language of sorts they'd worked out between them. John watched, frowned, then watched as the boy repeated it all.

'I don't know,' he said. At least Alan heard with no problem; it was just his speech that God had forgotten. 'Believe me, if I knew when it would all end, I'd gladly tell you.'

• • •

Sunday morning and everyone gathered in church. Dame Martha stood off to the side with the other old goodwives. She always leaned on John's arm when they walked now, but her smile lifted as soon as she saw the women she knew so well, all of them with their snow-white wimples and wrinkled faces. A chance to gossip and compare their aches and pains.

Katherine held Juliana in her arms. By now the girl could toddle well enough before falling over. Each time she tumbled, though, she cried as if the sky had fallen on her. Better to keep a grip on her here and let her gaze around, curious at everything.

The service was short. The priest, Father Crispin, seemed distracted. He was still new, in charge of the parish less than a year and they were still weighing him up, not certain yet what to make of him. Plenty of grey in his hair and today his eyes seemed to be full of fear. Just like his congregation, John thought. They all needed to feel God's blessing today.

After the echoes of the final amen had faded, people gathered outside, sun dappling through the tall trees. Hardly a cloud in the sky but the air still felt close, as if it was pressing tight against his flesh. Not a good omen, John decided. He looked around, waiting for his wife as she talked to some of the other young mothers.

Then the coroner beckoned him over.

De Harville, preening like a peacock in a tunic of red and blue, his parti-coloured hose reversing the colours, all with boots the colour of dark wine. His wife was already on her way back to their house on the High Street, their young son at her side and a servant trailing after. He was the King's Coroner here, and he wore the title with pride. Twice John had helped him find a murderer.

'It's not good news, Carpenter.' His face was grim and his eyes tired. 'Two in the ground and five more confirmed.'

'Five?' John brought his head up sharply. 'I'd heard of three.'

'Two more this morning. Someone came to tell me as I was walking here.' At his side, Brother Robert, the old monk who served as the coroner's clerk, began to mutter a prayer.

'It's in God's hands.' John echoed the words his wife had spoken, empty as they felt. He knew de Harville. A hard man when he chose, but he'd be as scared for his family as every other father in Chesterfield. Ready to cling to any hope, no matter how ridiculous or strange.

'I'm worried about that priest.' The coroner rested a hand on the hilt of his dagger.

The words took him by surprise. 'Crispin? Why?'

'In case he decides to run off. Didn't you see him in there? He has the look of a coward.'

Maybe he was right; perhaps the priest was a frail man. Taking holy orders couldn't change someone's nature. It didn't bring patience or courage or saintliness. He'd seen that during the two years he worked in York, a city full of men who claimed they were dedicated to God. But in the end they were all human. Some were tempted and fell. Some were venal. And a few were good.

'Let's hope not,' he answered. They'd need someone strong to bind them all together. And someone to say the service of the dead.

'We should go, husband.' Katherine linked her arm through his, smiling. De Harville might possess rank but that didn't mean he had her respect. She'd never cared for him and the way he used John to solve killings in the town.

The girls had scampered on ahead, Walter lumbering after them like a monster and delighting in their shrieks. God be praised, John decided, he was a lucky man to have all this. He just hoped it would all still surround him at the close of the year.

• • •

Evening. It was light outside, but the shadows were growing and the warmth of the day was beginning to drift away. Walter was playing nine men's morris with Dame Martha. Katherine was darning and mending clothes, the girls sewing and cutting at her side. Juliana lay asleep, eyes closed, at peace with the world.

John sat with a mug of ale, lost in his thoughts, content. He sat up quickly at the knock on the door. Who could want him at this time? He looked at his wife. Her eyes were wide and frightened.

'Brother,' he said as he opened the latch. 'Come in.'

Robert shook his head. He was breathing hard. These days walking even short distances seemed to exhaust him.

'Father Crispin has gone. He wasn't at the service tonight and he's not at his house. The coroner wants you to help search for him.'

'Me?' He didn't understand. 'That's a job for the bailiffs.'

'He wants everyone looking, John.' Brother Robert's chest moved more slowly, the redness starting to disappear from his face. 'He's out there himself. You heard what he said about the priest this morning.'

He remembered, and it seemed as if he'd been right. But this wasn't like the coroner.

'What do we do if we find him?'

'Bring him back.' Robert lowered his gaze, staring at the ground. 'He says a priest shouldn't run away and he'll be damned if he'll let him.' As soon as he spoke he crossed himself.

Those certainly sounded like de Harville's words. He could hear the man's voice and see him plunging his dagger into the scarred wood of his table as he spoke.

'I'll come,' he agreed. A quick word, pulling on his boots, the hooded tunic and the old jerkin on top, and he was ready.

• • •

Full night arrived and they had to stop. They'd simply be blundering around in the dark. Even if the priest was there they'd never see him.

Dame Martha was still awake when he returned, sitting by the soft light of a tallow candle.

'Did you find him?'

'No.' With a weary groan he lowered himself on to the bench. 'He could be in Sheffield by now or halfway to Lincoln.'

'His duty is here, John. In the parish.'

'I know.' Yet how could you force someone to stay? He took Martha's hand. Her skin was like parchment, old, mottled with brown spots. Each year she seemed to grow more frail, her bones more brittle and her step less sure. But her mind was agile, and her tongue could be tart when needed.

'Perhaps he'll see sense,' she said. 'Maybe God will open his eyes.'

'Let's pray He does.' He kissed her cheek and climbed up to the solar. He needed his sleep; the morning would arrive all too soon.

• • •

No word on Crispin as John walked over to collect Alan. A shower had passed through before dawn, enough to dampen down the dust for an hour or two. Fluffy, high clouds skittered across the sky, passing in front of a pale sun.

Not as warm today, he thought as they walked out towards Newbold. Farmers were on the road to town, ready to set up at the weekday market on the north side of the churchyard. Slabs of fresh-churned yellow butter, chickens in cages, early onions and beans, fragrant heads of wild garlic. He nodded his good morrows, exchanged a word here and there.

He was ready to work. Another day and they should have the sheep pen finished, then there were other jobs waiting, in town and around the area. Alan was learning more with each one. Walter helped when they needed extra muscle and a stout back, but wood didn't call out to him; he was happier delivering messages all around Chesterfield.

The house sat a few yards back from the road. Until February old man Peter had lived there. But he'd died and the place had been empty ever since. Shutters closed, door locked. John noticed the place each time they passed, curious to what it might be like inside.

This morning, though, was different. The door hung wide, open to the sun and shadows. But there was no sign of life about the place, no sense of anyone busy within. Wait here, he told Alan, and handed the boy his bag of tools. Cautiously he approached the house. His hand gripped the hilt of his dagger, ready, just in case.

'God's peace be with you,' he called out, but there was no answer. Just the birds singing in the branches. Inside, it took his eyes a few moments to adjust to the gloom, blinking until he could make out something in the corner. He moved closer, his knife out and ready. His palms were damp with sweat.

Then he realised what he was seeing and crossed himself. God save them all.

• • •

'We're searching for the priest and you find this,' De Harville complained. Caught in its winding sheet, it had to be the body of a man. Big enough, broad enough.

'I didn't choose it, Master,' John replied.

The shutters were pulled back and daylight flooded into the room. The bailiffs tried to keep their distance from the corpse, scared it could be another plague victim. Finally, tired of waiting, John stepped forward. If the man had died of pestilence, no one would have covered him so thoroughly. They'd have stayed far away.

Pray God he was right.

John knelt. The knife blade slid through the heavy cloth and he tore it further, ripping and shredding the fabric. For a moment he felt he couldn't breathe. Then he stood and turned to de Harville.

'Now we know what happened to Father Crispin.'

CHAPTER TWO

De Harville stared, saying nothing for a long time.

'Slit it all the way open, Carpenter,' he ordered finally. John sliced the heavy sheet until the body was exposed. Crispin was dressed, arms crossed over his breast. For all the world he looked like a man at peace, quiet and content in his death.

No wound that he could see, no strange smell of poison as he lowered his face towards the man's mouth.

'Well?' the coroner asked.

'I don't know.' He rolled the corpse on to its side. There it was, the small dark patch of blood on the back of his cassock, the tiny stain on the sheet beneath. 'This is it.'

Whatever had made the wound was thin. Not a knife. Smaller, more like one of the needles the goodwives used. Yet bigger than that, longer, and very sharp, he thought, to pierce clothes and skin and to kill.

De Harville squatted, moving around to view the body from different angles, tongue between his lips.

'Examine him properly, Carpenter. See what the body can tell you, then have the bailiffs take him to be buried.'

'I have work to do—'

'You have work to do for me.' The man's eyes flashed. 'You were the first finder. That means a fine, returned when the murderer is found. A shilling.'

'I have money at home.'

'You've found killers for me before, Carpenter. You can do it again. Four pence a day.'

'I usually make five. And my ale.'

'Four's my offer.' His mouth curled into a smile. 'Don't try my patience. Or I could put you in jail until we find the killer.'

John stared at him. 'That's not the law.'

'Carpenter,' de Harville reminded him slowly, 'I am the law.'

Beaten without even a battle. He knew it. A carpenter was nobody in this world, not when a man with rank and several manors to his name desired something. John had no power; he never would. He nodded his agreement.

'Come to my house when you've finished.' The coroner looked around. 'Why does Robert have to grow so old? I need my clerk with me.'

'You should get someone younger. Let the brother go back to the monastery.'

'Not with plague all over the land. It's safer for him to stay with me until it's passed.' He glared.

John waited until he was alone in the house before cutting through the priest's clothes to expose his skin. Stabbed in the back, but it didn't go all the way through; his chest was unblemished. Whoever did it must have pierced his heart. There was no sign of any other injury. The killer had even taken the time to close Crispin's eyes as he wrapped him in the shroud. Someone who knew what he was doing, someone deadly and calm who felt no hurry or panic.

John paced around the room, examining the floor, pausing to feel the packed dirt with his fingertips. No trace of blood. The dirt was too hard and dry for footprints, but a path from the door could have been roughly swept, he decided, after the body had been dragged. Hard to be certain now, though; so many feet had walked over it.

The priest still wore a wooden cross around his neck, and a leather scrip hung from his belt. There was little inside, just a few coins and an old comb made from bone with some of the teeth missing. Not a robbery. Murder, pure and simple.

Why?

What did he know about Father Crispin? The man had arrived the summer before, after the parish had spent a twelvemonth with no one at the church, just a curate who travelled from Clay Cross to give communion twice a month.

Crispin was older, grey in his hair, so he must have spent time elsewhere. But he'd been a shy man, not given to small talk or idle chatter in the marketplace. No friends as far as John knew.

'You can take him,' he told the bailiffs as he left. They were waiting outside. Rough, hulking men, but good in a fight. 'The church will look after him.'

• • •

De Harville had his feet up on the table, dictating to Robert who tried to keep up with his voice. They both stopped as the servant showed John into the room.

'Well, Carpenter? What do you have to tell me?'

'Very little, Master. It was carefully done and it didn't happen where he was found. Nothing taken from him and that body was prepared. It was a very deliberate killing.'

'Go on.' The coroner stroked his chin.

'I need to know more about the priest. Who he was, where he came from, what he'd done before.' John shrugged. 'It could be an old grudge.'

'Brother?' De Harville raised an eyebrow and looked at the monk. 'How did he come to us?'

'We wrote to the bishop to ask for a priest to replace the old one. After six months of begging he sent us Crispin.'

'Did you know him at all?'

Robert shook his head. 'I tried to talk to him, but he smiled and passed me by. It always seemed to me as if he didn't have too much time for anyone here, as if in his heart he wanted to be somewhere else. He performed his duties and retreated home again.'

'I'd like to look in his house,' John told de Harville. The man gave a short nod.

'I'll come with you. I was there yesterday when we started hunting for him.'

It was a small stone building on the far side of the churchyard, with a door to the street and two expensive glazed windows, one for the hall downstairs and another for the solar above. The coroner chose a key from a heavy ring and turned it in the lock.

The room smelt musty and unloved, as if the inhabitant had been here reluctantly. John moved around, trying to fill himself with the sense of the priest. All he could feel was a man who lived a small life. Someone who wanted to be unremarkable, unnoticed. Hidden.

There was nothing of Crispin in the hall. Just the usual furnishings of any priest's house – a table, a bench, a prie-dieu, candles in their holders, a Bible on the table. Above, in the solar, no more than a bed of old straw and a chest. Locked. He turned to de Harville. The coroner nodded.

He forced the hasp with his knife, pushing back the lid. A thick winter cloak of good wool lay on top, carefully rolled and scented with herbs to keep off the moths. It looked well-worn and old, John decided as he lifted it out, the nap of the cloth worn smooth. A pair of boots lay beneath, with heavy, solid soles, the uppers made from soft, expensive leather. He set them aside and returned to the chest.

It didn't seem possible. John glanced at de Harville.

'You need to see this, Master.'

A pair of knives, beautifully crafted, in heavily worked leather sheaths. A short sword in its scabbard. Not the tools of any holy man that he'd ever met.

'What do you make of it, Carpenter?'

John sat back on his heels, still staring at the weapons in the chest.

'I don't know.' In York he'd once heard of a soldier who'd become a monk. But never one who'd taken a priest's vows. He glanced up at the coroner. 'It seems that Crispin has a past. But there's nothing here to let us know who he really was.'

De Harville drew out the sword, weighing it in his hand and making a few tentative cuts.

'It's a fine piece of work,' he said admiringly. 'Not cheap.'

John stood, his eyes roving around the solar. It was the same as the hall, nothing else of Crispin's around, nothing that marked his presence here. What tiny life he had was all in that chest, and it didn't speak of a peaceful man.

He tossed the straw of the bed, in case the priest had hidden anything. Then a closer search in the hall. Nothing. Maybe he simply had nothing to hide, no other possessions.

Outside, people moved around and the world seemed normal. The May sun shone and he felt the warmth on his face. The priest's house had seemed chilly, as if spring had never quite reached the place.

A goodwife passed, clutching her basket, giving him a curious stare for a moment before turning away and forgetting him in an instant. John turned his head and looked back. A carrion crow perched on the roof of the house, its beak bobbing and pulling at something. Was that an omen?

'What now, Carpenter?'

'I don't know. How can we find out who killed him if we don't know who he'd been when he was alive?'

The coroner gave a tight nod. 'I'll write to the bishop. Meanwhile,' he ordered, 'I want you to start asking questions in town.'

• • •

Juliana pushed herself to her feet as he entered. She began to smile and tottered towards him. John scooped her into his arms, ducking to kiss Jeanette and Eleanor on the tops of their heads as they sat and span wool.

Dame Martha was working with Katherine in the buttery, brewing a fresh batch of ale. She assessed him with old, wise eyes.

'Coroner's work again, John? It's all over town.'

He nodded, seeing his wife frown.

'There's not much to find so far.' He reached out and squeezed Katherine's hand lightly, an apology. But she knew he had no choice. If de Harville ordered, he had to obey. It was the way of the world. 'What did you know about Father Crispin?' he asked Martha.

'Very little, I suppose,' she answered after a moment as John tickled Juliana under the chin until she giggled; death and joy side by side. 'He said the mass well enough but I don't remember ever speaking to him.'

'Could you ask the other goodwives? They might know something.'

'I will.' She gave him a pointed look. John let his daughter slide down his body. Martha took her by the hand and led her back into the hall.

'I don't want to do it,' he told Katherine.

'I know.' There was a bitter undertone to her voice.

'I found the body.'

'And now you have to neglect your own work to do the coroner's job?'

It was the same argument they'd had before. But they both felt the same, and the words were no more than her resentment at the way the coroner used his position. Finally he stroked her face.

'I'm sorry,' he said, 'But I don't think there'll be much I can do. I don't think the answers to this are in Chesterfield.'

'There was another case of pestilence today,' she told him, and suddenly he felt guilty. The priest's body had driven everything else from his head.

'Who?'

'Elizabeth, the drover's wife.'

The woman's face sprang straight into his mind, round and red and cheery. They had five children, the oldest twelve, the youngest two, and she herded the little ones in front of her like a flock of sheep. Two of them worked but the youngsters kept close to her skirts. With her husband gone most of the time, taking his horse and cart between Sheffield, Derby and Nottingham, what would happen to them all?

The family lived close to the bottom of Soutergate, no more than a dozen yards from the bridge across the river. Praise God the plague hadn't begun to climb the hill yet, he thought, then crossed himself.

'Go,' Katherine told him. 'It'll be dinner soon.'

• • •

He spent the afternoon asking questions around Chesterfield. But people had other things on their mind than Father Crispin. The new plague case brought more worry and fear. They drew into themselves and pulled their families close.

They were wary of any stranger, and John had only been here for three years. He'd need more time to be trusted.

Still, no one had anything bad to say about the priest. He'd done his job well enough, yet none seemed to know him. Crispin had been remote, he'd made no attempt to be a part of the town.

Maybe it was simply the man's nature, John thought later. He was sitting in the garden, holding a mug of ale, taking occasional sips. The priest had been a fighting man at one time. A successful one, to judge by the quality of his weapons. Perhaps it was that part of his history which made him wary of people.

'John?'

He hadn't heard Walter approach. But Katherine's brother was light on his feet. He was taller than John now, fifteen years old and still growing like a weed. He earned a living by delivering messages and packages all over Chesterfield, reliable, swift, honest.

Some thought he was simple. When he was younger, someone had hit him hard on the head. Since then he'd spoken slowly, and sometimes he stumbled over words. But there was nothing wrong with his reasoning. Or his courage. John had learned that all too well.

'Any more word on the victims?' John asked.

The lad shook his head, the thick mop of hair dancing from side to side. The dust of the day still clung to his hose and tunic. 'Do you need help looking into Father Crispin's death?' Walter had worked with him before. Saved his life, too, and put himself into danger. But the lad relished it. He liked the adventure and the excitement. His eyes glittered hopefully. He was young, he was immortal.

'Not yet.' He saw Walter's face fall and told him what little he knew. 'I don't even have any idea why anyone would want to kill him.' John eyed the young man. Walter was observant, so much a part of Chesterfield that people rarely noticed him. 'What about you? Is there anything you can tell me about him?'

'I-I-I saw two men at his door last month,' he answered after a long pause.

'Who were they?' He could feel his heart start beating faster with the sense that this was something.

'I don't know, John,' Walter answered. 'I couldn't see their faces.' He hesitated, drawing the picture into his mind. 'I think they were big men.' He smiled quickly. 'They had mud spattered on their legs and on their boots, as if they'd ridden.'

John was always astonished by the lad's memory. He could conjure up images, still see things that had happened long before and pick out the tiniest details. That men had visited Crispin was interesting. If they'd ridden to town, then they would have stabled their horses somewhere. In the morning he'd discover more.

John chuckled. 'You've helped me already.'

Walter frowned. 'But I haven't done anything.'

'You have. You've done more than you know.'

• • •

In the darkness he sensed Katherine was still awake. Her small shifts in the bed, the uneven breathing even as she tried to be quiet.

'Tell me it will be all right,' she said softly.

Very gently, he squeezed her shoulder and pulled her closer. But he said nothing; he couldn't lie to her.

• • •

'Last month?' The man stroked his chin. His clothes were filthy and stained. The whole stable reeked of manure. A boy moved a pile of it around with a besom, pushing it against a wall where it quickly gathered flies. 'Aye, I remember now.' He smiled, showing a mouth almost empty of teeth. 'Didn't stay half a day but they still expected the horses properly groomed and fed. Haggled over the price, too.' He spat with disgust. 'And then they didn't want to pay.'

'Where did they come from? Did they say?'

He shook his head. 'Said no more than they had to. I'll tell you something, though: they had money. Both of them on good beasts and better clothes than you'll see round here.'

'What do you mean?' Strangers with money and good clothes? It seemed surprising that more people hadn't noticed them. Men like that stood out and gossip was like gold.

'Fine beaver hats and jackets with stitching on them.'

'Stitching?' John could feel his hopes rising. 'A coat of arms?'

'No.' The man shook his head. 'Not that. What do you call it… patterns.'

Embroidery, he thought. So much for that thought. Still, dressed like that they weren't scraping for pennies. Men with some status.

'No badges? No marks?'

'No, nothing.'

Impossible to tell whose men they were. 'How were they armed?'

The stableman grinned widely again. 'I noticed that, right enough. A sword each and they both carried daggers. Hilts bound in leather and silver on the pommels.'

'Silver?' John asked sharply.

'Sure as I'm standing here,' the man said with a nod. 'On the bridles, too. Like I said, fine animals and well-tended.'

'What did they look like?'

'They were big. Broad,' he replied after a moment. 'Hard eyes. They looked cruel. Arrogant, that's it. One of them had a scar on his face. I'll tell you this, Master, I'd not be wanting to go up against them.'

John slipped the man a coin, watched it disappear into his scrip, then said his farewells. It was a little more information. But did it help, or did it simply raise more questions than it answered?

What else could he do, though? He'd followed the only track he had, and that had come to nought. Until he knew more about Crispin, he was stuck. Finally he returned to the house, noticing a shutter that was just beginning to sag, kissed Katherine and picked up his bag of tools.

'I'll be back this evening.'

She looked surprised but happy. 'No more mystery, husband?'

'Not today, at least.' He smiled, then his face turned serious. 'No more word? No victims? I didn't hear anything.'

'No, praise God.'

But he knew it wasn't over. Jesu save them, it had hardly begun.

• • •

Alan beamed to see him, pulling at his mother's sleeve as she opened the door.

'He's missed you,' she said. 'I tried to explain but all he wants to do is go to work.'

'That's what we're doing.' He ruffled the boy's hair. 'A half-day's labour. Are you ready?'

As they walked, Alan moved his fingers so quickly that John kept stopping him; he couldn't understand it all.

'Slower, slower.'

The boy was concerned that they might not work together any more because of the carpenter's job with the coroner. He wanted to learn, he was eager; it was the first thing in life he'd ever done well, the first thing that had come as naturally as breathing.

'Don't you worry,' John told him. 'There might be interruptions but I'm not giving this up. It's what I do. It's what I've always done. You as well.' As he spoke Alan nodded gratefully.

Only half a day's work, but they filled every moment. More often now the boy could start on a task without being told; he realised what was needed and set to it on his own.

CHAPTER THREE

The days passed with work and the tolling of the church bell for the dead. New victims appeared in dribs and drabs. One, then nothing, two more, a gap just long enough for the town to begin to believe it might have passed, then another. So far all the victims lived close to the river; it was a single ray of hope.

John finished two small jobs. The next one was in town, shaping and erecting the framework of a kitchen behind one of the grand houses out past West Bar. A fire had destroyed the old one, and heavy, charred beams still lay on the ground, stinking of the blaze. It was simple work, cutting and putting up the wood before the mason came to lay the stone of the walls. He'd done it often enough before, here and in York. Most of the job was just sawing and shaping. Slow, repetitive, and with plenty of time to reflect.

There'd been no word yet from the bishop in Lincoln; he was certain that the coroner would have sent for him if any letter had arrived. John kept asking questions around the town, but it seemed as if no one in the flock had ever properly known their priest. A few had talked to him, arranging for weddings, for funerals, but none could say much about him. His past remained a mystery, and no one other than Walter seemed to have noticed his strange visitors.

Alan was cleaning the tools, wiping them with the oiled rag, when John heard the footsteps. Someone running. He turned, right hand ready to reach for his knife but it was Walter. For a terrifying moment the blood went cold in his body. Not plague at home?

'Th-the coroner wants to see you, John,' he said.

The carpenter took a long, deep breath. Small mercies. God be praised. 'Thank you.' He turned to Alan. 'Finish the tools.' He hesitated for a long moment, then said: 'Take them home with you. Make sure you look after them.'

The boy smiled as if he'd been given the greatest gift in the world, making swift signs. Thank you, he'd take good care of them.

'I know.' It would be the first time since his father died that John hadn't kept the tools close at night. He was surprised to realise that he trusted the lad so much.

• • •

De Harville was pacing angrily up and down the hall, his hands clenched into fists. Brother Robert sat at the table, pain flickering in small waves across his face.

'What is it, Master?' John asked.

The coroner looked at the monk and nodded.

'We've heard from the bishop's secretary,' Robert began gravely, then started to cough. He held up his hand as John started towards him before taking a sip of ale to clear his throat. 'He says that the bishop's office is willing to tell us more about Father Crispin. But we need to go to Lincoln and have an audience with them.' The words came out as a breathless croak and he drank a little more.

'See them?' He didn't understand. 'Why can't they say it in a letter?'

'I don't know, Carpenter.' The coroner held a pewter mug so tightly that his knuckles were white. 'And now we have to go all the way to Lincoln to find out.'

We. 'You know they'll listen to you more than they would to me, Master.'

'Of course.' De Harville nodded, taking it as his due. 'But I want you to come with me.' He gave a dark, wolfish smile. 'You can be good company on the journey and hear what they have to say.'

'I can't. I have work waiting here.'

'Then it will just have to wait longer.' He waved it all away. 'We leave first thing in the morning.'

• • •

'No,' Katherine told him. She stood with her hands on her hips, the fire blazing in her eyes. 'He can't do that.'

'He's already done it.'

'Stand up to him, John. Tell him no.'

'I did. He told me it wasn't my choice to make. Like it or not, I was accompanying him.'

'Then I'm going to see him.' She started for the door, but he caught her arm.

'No, please. I can fight my own battles,' he said softly.

'It sounds like you surrendered on this one. Or perhaps you want to leave us for a few days?'

John stared at the ground, biting his lip.

'You know I don't want to go anywhere. Not now, with Juliana so young and pestilence all around town. But we both know I can never win against de Harville.'

She was about to answer when Eleanor dashed through the house. Her eyes were wide and her face was pale.

'I think there's something wrong with Dame Martha.'

Everything else was forgotten; their argument no longer mattered. The old woman was lying on her bed, eyes closed. John placed a hand on her neck. A strong, steady beat. She was alive.

'Martha,' Katherine said. A whisper at first, then repeating it more loudly until she stirred, eyelids beginning to flutter.

John took her hand, pressing it between his palms. The flesh was chilly and clammy, although the evening was warm. Martha moved her head, looking from one to the other of them, and the girls waiting by the door.

'What is it? What's happened?' she asked. Her voice was thick, the words slurred but growing clearer as she spoke.

'We were worried about you.' Katherine smiled. 'You didn't want to wake up.'

'I must have fallen asleep.' Martha closed her eyes again for a second, then opened them wide. 'I don't remember.'

John helped her to sit and sent Janette for a tumbler of ale.

'Don't fuss,' the woman said as he held it to her lips. 'There's no need. I'm not an invalid. I just fell asleep for a little while, that's all.'

John took a breath. 'Eleanor, why don't you stay with Martha?'

Katherine followed him up to the solar. With quiet voices, no one would overhear their worry.

'She wasn't asleep,' he said.

'I know. She…' after a moment Katherine shook her head. She didn't have the words for it. Neither did he.

'I need you here, John. You can't go, not when this has happened.' Not pleading, not a demand. It was simply how life had to be.

'I'll go and talk to him now.'

Martha rested on the settle, more colour in her cheeks, chattering brightly to the girls, telling them a story about a knight who pursued the hand of a beautiful maiden. John stood, listening and watching, caught in the tale and the telling.

He roused himself and slipped out of the door. Past Martha's old house on Knifesmithgate, leased now to a merchant and his family. Since the first cases of plague there were fewer people on the streets; it felt safer to stay behind closed doors and keep company at bay. No greetings now, they turned their faces away as if they were scared to show their fear.

He had to wait to see the coroner. The man was in his garden, watching the nurse play with his son. Finally he returned, striding into the hall.

'Well?' he asked. 'What is it? I thought we had everything settled for tomorrow.'

'Dame Martha isn't well. I need to stay in Chesterfield.'

De Harville stared. His eyes were hard, and John could read the doubt in the man's face. Martha was well-regarded in Chesterfield. The coroner could insist, but if word passed around town about his insistence and Martha died while they were gone…

'How bad is she?' he asked.

'It was just a spell. But at first we couldn't wake her. There might be more, we don't know.'

The coroner ran a hand through his hair. He was weighing everything. The plague, the journey.

'Very well,' he agreed finally. 'Stay here, then. But keep looking into this death. Someone here knows what happened.'

'I will, Master.'

Outside, he felt stunned. He'd never expected the man to give way so readily; he couldn't remember that it had ever happened before. But it was all for the good. And it was true.

He did need to be here, to try and keep his family safe from the wolf that was stalking the land.

• • •

The days passed in hope and sorrow. Only one more victim, a child of five who took the pestilence and died in two days, buried with the others in the corner of the graveyard. No longer empty, but like everyone in the town, he prayed it wouldn't become full. Vain, foolish wishes; it was out of his control.

Each day he worked with Alan on the new kitchen building. Walter joined them to help to raise the beams until the frame stood firm and ready for the masons. It was solid work, John decided. He walked around testing every joint. They'd done the job well.

'John, I-I heard something,' Walter said as they strolled home.

'What?' He turned his head. The lad looked serious, as if he was trying to arrange his thoughts into order.

'I had to go out to Newbold earlier. On the way back I passed two men. One of them said, "Now the priest's gone, there's one less of them to worry about."'

'What?' He stopped suddenly and turned, his hand on the lad's arm. 'Are you certain they said that? Those exact words?'

'Yes, John. I know they did.'

They began to walk again.

'Who were they? Had you seen them before? Was it the same pair you saw last month at the priest's door?' He had a rush of questions in his mind, but he needed to ask them slowly and steadily.

'No, they were different. They weren't from here,' Walter answered with certainty. The carpenter believed him. Walter was all over the town, he knew every face. 'They looked as if they'd come on the road from Sheffield.'

'What did they look like? Were they riding?' He could feel the blood roaring through his limbs, a taste of iron in his mouth.

'No, they were walking. They just looked ordinary. One of them had dark hair. The other…' he ran a hand over his scalp to illustrate, '…his hair was going back.'

Receding. He managed to pry out a few more details. The man with dark hair had a thick beard and was tall and thin, the other shorter and stockier.

'Which way did they go?'

Walter pointed. 'I followed them to Soutergate. They went down the hill and across the bridge.'

Only travellers. Strangers on their journey somewhere. Men who'd heard the news perhaps, or men who disliked priests. That was interesting, at least. But he wasn't sure if it told him anything he could use. He considered what he'd just learned: it probably meant nothing useful.

In York he'd heard whispers about men who condemned the Church and its wealth. With all the plate and the hangings, the money in the coffers while so many went hungry, it was easy to understand. The cost of making an archbishop's cope could feed a village for years.

But while men might resent the Church and its wealth, they didn't kill priests. That meant eternal damnation. Talk came easily but they'd never act. Yet someone had.

'Come on,' John said. 'Your sister will be expecting us.'

• • •

By the time the coroner returned from Lincoln, John had been unable to learn anything more. No one in Chesterfield recognised the descriptions of the travellers Walter had seen. They were only passing through. Another hope crumbled to dust.

He'd given up and returned to his work. It was only building a new gate to a field up towards Whittington, but the money made it worthwhile. The miles were hard on Alan's small legs, but he refused to show it, doing more than his share of the labour.

John let the boy take the lead on the gate, measuring everything and laying out the wood. He offered suggestions, ideas to make it easier, but it was good for Alan. He'd learn more this way. Praise helped, seeing him smile with pleasure, answering the questions his fingers asked. Then checking his measurements and cuts.

They walked the distance back together, weary and hungry. No tolling of the bell today, God be praised. Each day without a burial came as some small victory.

There had only been one more case of plague in the last four days. Perhaps the worst had already been. He hoped and prayed with everyone else in town, but deep inside he knew the truth he was reluctant to admit: the pestilence hadn't vanished. It was there, biding its time, and it would take many more deaths before it was sated.

• • •

'Brother Robert came after dinner,' Katherine told him. 'He sat with Martha for a while.'

They'd kept a close eye on the woman but she'd had no more problems. John had cut her a stick of strong hawthorn, smoothing the nubs and rounding the top so it fitted in her hand. She shooed it away at first, but he persisted until she finally gave in. It seemed to help, keeping her steady as she walked.

'Just a visit to pass an hour?' he asked doubtfully.

'He brought a message from the coroner. He's back. He wants to see you.' She made a dark face. 'Robert was so out of breath that I made him sit for a few minutes and drink a mug of ale until it passed. He doesn't look well. He ought to be at the abbey.'

'I asked. De Harville won't let him go. Not until the plague has passed, he said. He feels it's too dangerous for him to leave.'

'Selfish man.'

• • •

The coroner was travel-stained, dirt and dust still clinging to his hose and boots. He stared at the thick glass of the window, gently swirling a cup of wine in his hand.

'I've been here for hours, Carpenter. I expected to see you earlier after I sent a message.'

'I wasn't at home, Master. I was working,' he added pointedly. 'What did the bishop tell you about Father Crispin?'

'I never saw him.' De Harville frowned. 'Only his secretary. And that man has too many airs above his station.'

'Was he able to tell you much?'

The coroner sighed and took another drink. 'Crispin came late to the Church. He was only ordained five years ago. Before that he was a soldier.'

From the weapons they'd found in the priest's chest, that was no surprise. They'd guessed as much. Something the man had never let go completely, it seemed.

'Whose service was he in?' With so many lords in the land, all of them with their own retainers, it might have been anyone.

'He served the king directly.'

John breathed in slowly. That made Crispin a man of some importance.

'Did you find out why he left?'

De Harville shrugged. 'The secretary didn't say. Very likely he didn't know.'

'Did he tell you where Crispin was before he came here?'

'He was willing to say that much. The priest spent time in two different parishes.'

'Two? In only five years?' Usually a man would stay somewhere for life unless there were problems.

'Yes. I asked why; he refused to tell me.'

And a bishop's secretary was a man even a coroner couldn't bully, John thought wryly.

'Where was he? Did he at least say that?'

'In Lincoln first, at the cathedral.'

It would be easy to keep an eye on him there, to make sure he understood his duties and train him properly.

'Where did he go from there?'

'Castleton.'

The name sounded familiar. He'd heard it before, but he didn't know the place.

'It's almost twenty miles from here, perhaps a little more,' de Harville explained. 'There's a castle there, Peveril. I don't know who owns it now. The king, probably, or a duke. Someone far above our stations, Carpenter. It's been little more than a hunting lodge for years, though. Crispin came here from there.'

It seemed as if the priest had been moved all over, barely given a chance to settle, John thought. Why?

'Did he tell you anything more?'

'No.' His voice had a frustrated edge. 'He claimed he didn't know, but he had a smirk on his face as he said it.'

'Why? Don't they want his murder solved?'

'In truth, Carpenter, I wonder. For all the help that secretary gave, I'm not sure.'

It seemed impossible to believe. Justice was vital, it bonded the kingdom.

'What do we do, then, Master?'

'I need to think about that.' De Harville stared out through the glass again. 'But I won't let it drop. Not now. I don't like people thwarting me.'

• • •

'He's a stubborn man,' John said as his family sat at the table to eat. Juliana was already sleeping, peace and contentment on her face. 'He'll keep gnawing away at it until he finds an answer. The trouble is, it could be a dangerous one.'

'He'll keep using you, too,' Katherine told him. 'That's how he works.'

'He was always like that.' Dame Martha held the bread awkwardly. Her hands were twisted with age; grasping anything was difficult for her. 'He's headstrong. Even when he was a boy. He always wanted his own way. I remember his father had to whip him often.'

'Not often enough.' Katherine's voice was tart.

'Did you tell him about the men, John?' Walter asked, then explained for the others.

'No.' He hadn't seen the sense in it. The pair passing through Chesterfield seemed nothing and the coroner had been in no mood to listen. He'd found no more on the richer men who'd visited the month before.

'He'll say what he wants soon enough,' Katherine said. 'I'm sure it will involve you, husband.'

'Yes.' It wasn't as if they had no other worries. In the shank of the afternoon word had spread that the son of Richard the butcher had the pestilence. It had finally travelled up the hill from the river, all the way to the Shambles. Now nobody in Chesterfield could feel safe.

• • •

In the morning he walked out to Whittington again with Alan. For once, the boy's fingers were still and he looked thoughtful. In the field he set silently to work on the gate, picking up where he'd left off the day before.

Slow and steady, but John could see that the boy's heart wasn't in it. He wasn't surprised; fear and work never sat well together, and fear was strong in the town now. Alan was far too young to have experienced the desperation that existed when the Great Pestilence arrived all those years before. He'd never seen the world collapse. Pray God he'd never experience it.

John worked with him, trying to make the simple tasks fill his mind. But too many thoughts jostled for room in his head. Of death and of mysterious priests and strange men on horseback.

He knew what de Harville would want. The man would send him to Castleton. Just a single night away, not all the days to Lincoln and back. The coroner would push and cajole and order until John couldn't refuse. But he'd wait until that happened. Let the man come to him; he wasn't about to offer. At least Martha had been well; they watched her carefully. No repeats of her short spell away from the world, nothing even close. Yet that meant he had no argument against going.

By the middle of the afternoon the gate was hung, strong and sturdy. It swung freely and fastened stoutly. The steward was pleased, gladly passing over the coins as Alan carefully cleaned the tools, rubbing until he was satisfied, sharpening the edge of a chisel with the whetstone.

It was coming time that the boy had tools of his own and those didn't come cheap. John's had belonged to his father, all the man had to leave behind, the only gift he had to give to his son.

But tools were a matter for another time, he decided as they strolled. In the morning they'd start on the next job. It was just in Brampton, not much more than a mile from home.

The spire on the church guided them back into Chesterfield. It stood tall, the oak tiles glowing in the sun, a beacon to everyone around. And only its own weight kept it firm on the tower, almost like a miracle. There were some nights when the fierce winds blew that he'd felt certain it must topple. Yet it remained, high and proud and visible for miles.

• • •

'Any more?' It was the first question as he slipped the satchel from his shoulder.

'Two,' Katherine told him. Her eyes were still red from crying. 'One of them is Margaret's baby.'

Isabella. She'd been born just a few months after Juliana. The mothers had become good friends. Another one from the Shambles.

He looked at his daughter. She was playing with the girls, innocent and oblivious. The best way. If only he could still be like that his world would be a simpler place.

John held his wife tenderly. A few survived the pestilence. Miracles happened. But they were very, very few, and no one knew why or how they were spared. The young and the old, the weak, they usually died quickly. The first signs became the death sentence.

He couldn't take away Katherine's fear. How could he when his own lurked, black and deep in the pit of his stomach? All he could do was hope, and pray to a God he wasn't certain existed.

CHAPTER FOUR

Far fewer had come to the Saturday market. John stood by the top of the square and watched as people moved slowly around from stall to stall. Normally it filled the square, packed each week with traders and people from the town and the villages all around. Today it felt empty.

Too many frightened people, both buyers and sellers. Where did people decide that the balance tipped between profit and danger, he wondered?

'John?' Walter asked. It was their routine; each Saturday morning they came here together. This time, though, the lad looked fretful. Normally he was eager to plunge into the crowd, to discover everything on offer. 'What's going to happen to us all?'

'I wish I knew,' he answered. 'Everything is out of our hands. Come on, we might as well see what's for sale.'

They slipped through the stalls. Usually the smith from Apperknowle was here with the good iron nails that John favoured. But today he hadn't come. Those trading were mostly the ones who couldn't afford to stay away.

John circled around the market but there was nothing on sale to interest him. Walter was talking to a youth near his own age. There was no sense in staying, no pleasure to be had. He was close to the High Street when he heard the coroner call his name. For two days he'd heard nothing at all from the man. The message to go to Castleton had never arrived.

'Master?'

De Harville was wearing green hose and a dark leather jerkin. A sword hung in its scabbard from his belt, and his boots were polished to a high gloss.

'I want to talk to you after church tomorrow.' He surveyed the square. 'I'm surprised we have this many.'

'The fear may pass in time.'

'In time.' De Harville nodded glumly. 'But who knows how long that will be? Or how many will survive? Look to your own, Carpenter. In times like this it's all we can do.'

• • •

The service ran late. With no priest, they had to wait for a curate from Clay Cross to arrive and hurry through the prayers.

'I need to stay,' John said to Katherine as they came out into the sunshine. 'De Harville wants to talk.' He bent and kissed his daughter's head. Her hair was so soft under his lips and she smiled at the touch.

'Why?'

'I suspect he wants me to go to Castleton.'

'John,' she began, then gave him a bitter look and shook her head before calling the girls and stalking off. He caught a movement from the corner of his eye. The coroner, with Brother Robert hobbling awkwardly behind him.

'You need to keep your wife under better control, Carpenter. That woman has a temper on her.'

He bit his tongue and said nothing.

'Has Dame Martha had any more problems?' de Harville asked.

'No.' The honest reply was the only one he could give.

'Then tomorrow I want you to go to Castleton. Talk to the reeve and whoever else you can find. You can walk there in a day and be back here on Tuesday.'

'And if I say no? With the plague around, no one will welcome travellers.'

'You'll go, Carpenter.' De Harville paused. 'I know you, you're a man who likes answers to his problems.'

John nodded and walked away. It was a pity; the coroner was right.

• • •

He lifted his daughter, rubbed noses with her, then saw her toddle off giggling as he hefted a small pack on to his back. Katherine held him at arm's length, searching his face for something, then pulled him close and kissed him. At the far end of the hall, Dame Martha waved.

'Be careful, John,' his wife whispered. 'Please, always be careful.'

'I will.'

The journey was slow and wearying. The sun arced hot overhead, with barely a cloud in the sky, as if the weather was atoning for the dampness of early spring. He followed a cart track across the moors and between the old, strange rocks down to Hathersage, breaking the journey at an inn there with bread, cheese and ale.

The village lay at the bottom of the valley, with a straight, even walk ahead of him, a stream making its merry music close by. He stopped often, cooling himself with handfuls of water over his head.

Then, finally, John could see the pale stones of Peveril Castle in the distance. It stood at the peak of the hill, high above the village, commanding the view for miles along the valley. God help anyone who wanted to take that, he decided; it looked impregnable. How had they managed to haul all the materials up there?

Castleton itself was no more than a hamlet of small, dark houses strung along the side of the road, always with the sense of the castle looming above them. The church stood by a bend, small, built from cut stone. In the far distance the track rose to disappear between two steep, jagged hills. On the third side there were fields, men bent at their work, then the landscape lifted abruptly. This was wild country, open and unforgiving. It was no place for any man in a bad winter.

John spotted an alehouse by the stream, marked by a green branch hanging over the lintel. Inside, it was cool, with deep shadows falling in the corners. The woman who came with his drink eyed him warily.

'Are you going far?' She had no welcome in her voice. But in times like these who wouldn't be suspicious of strangers?

'I'm looking for the reeve.'

She was older, with plump forearms, grey hair caught under a stained wimple, her face pink and perspiring in the heat.

'What do you need him for?'

'A few questions.' He drank and smiled. 'That's a good brew, mistress.'

'Don't try to flatter me.' She put her hands on her hips. 'Where are you from?'

'Chesterfield.'

'I heard they have the plague there.'

John dipped his head, acknowledging the truth, and she crossed herself. She was old enough to remember the Great Pestilence; she probably lost family to it.

'Then drink up, Master, please, and be on your way. He lives in the last house, just past the end of the village.'

She watched until he left, closing the door behind him with a sharp click of the latch.

On the way John picked a handful of wild parsley and chewed the leaves to sweeten his breath. The reeve's house stood apart from the others. No bigger, but a little more solid. Well-kept, even some flowers growing under the window and a large garden behind the building.

The man who answered his knock was small and squat, as solid a figure as John had ever seen, with thick arms and powerful shoulders. A dark beard covered most of his face, and pale eyes stared up at him.

'God be with you, stranger. How can I help you?'

'I'm John the Carpenter from Chesterfield. I do some work for the coroner there. He sent me down to ask about Father Crispin who used to be the priest here. The alewife said you're the reeve.'

For a long moment the man didn't reply.

'You've come to the right place. I'm the reeve. Elias.' He didn't extend his hand, but these days no one would; there could be death in a simple greeting. 'The word is that you have plague there.'

'It's the truth,' John admitted with a frown and a long sigh. 'A few dead, a few more dying.'

Elias lowered his head and crossed himself. Peace for those who'd gone, protection for the living.

'Crispin, you said? Has something happened to him?'

'He was murdered.'

The reeve raised his eyebrows in disbelief and crossed himself once more. 'Murdered? Sweet Jesu. What happened?'

John recounted it all as they walked down the lane to the church.

'To leave him like that…' Elias shook his head. 'He served us well enough until he was sent to you. You can see for yourself, not many people live here.' He pointed to a distant hill. 'The people from Edale over there, they come for services and funerals. A few more from the farms in the hills.'

'He did his job well?'

'Well enough, I suppose. Kept himself to himself, though. Not like old Father Timothy. He'd always help in the fields, be there with his sickle every harvest, working with the rest of the village. We were sorry when he died. Crispin didn't try to become one of us, if you understand.'

'I do.' It was exactly the way the priest had been in Chesterfield. There, but never part of the place. 'Did you know much about him?'

'He'd come from Lincoln, if that helps. He told me that much when he arrived, and he made it sound as if being here was a step down the ladder.' He shrugged. 'That didn't make us warm to him.'

'Has anyone else been here wanting to know about him?' John asked, but the reeve shook his head.

'Did he say anything about his past at all?' John wondered.

'Not that I ever heard. It's a man's own business, isn't it?'

'Did anyone here get to know him?'

The reeve played with his beard, tugging gently at the hairs.

'There's old Hilda,' he said after a little while. 'She's a widow. Crispin would go and sit with her sometimes. But I've no idea if he ever told her much about his life.'

'Could I speak to her? I've walked a fair way.'

'You can try. I'll warn you, though, most of the time she doesn't talk that much. Had a palsy a few years ago and speaking isn't easy for her. Sometimes she'll be fine, but usually…' he let the sentence drift away. 'I'll introduce you. She knows me, I've lived here all my life.'

'It must be isolated here in winter,' John commented.

'We get by,' Elias told him with a smile. 'Always have, always will.'

• • •

Someone kept the small house tidy. Inside, the floor was swept clean, with new rushes on the dirt, and the shutters were open wide to let in the warmth and the light. Smoke rose from the cooking fire in the middle of the floor, and a pot bubbled lazily over the flames.

Hilda looked even older and more frail than Dame Martha. She sat on a high stool, hands cupped over a stick, watching them with careful eyes. When Elias spoke she nodded and turned her head to John. He squatted, close to her.

'Mistress,' he began, 'the reeve says that Father Crispin used to spend time with you.'

'He did.' Her voice rasped and twisted harshly in her throat, but her face wore a sweet, gentle smile.

'He's dead, and I'm trying to find out about him.'

She breathed for a long time.

'Mostly we just sat,' she told him finally. 'But he told me once he'd been a soldier.'

'For the King?' John asked.

She nodded. 'Up on the Scottish border.' Speaking seemed to tax her, but she continued. 'He told me once that he did something bad. That's why he became a priest. He said it was his penance.'

John could feel his heart beating faster. Finally, here was the meat on the bones of Crispin's tale.

'Did he say what he'd done, Mistress?'

'He killed a powerful man and his sons wanted him dead.'

He hardly dared to ask: 'Who was it, Mistress? Did he say?'

'No. He said that much, but he didn't want to tell me more. All I did was listen.' She gave her smile again. 'I listen well, people say.'

'Did he say anything else about himself?'

'He was born near York. I remember that. A grand house, he said. But nothing more.'

John squeezed her hand gently. 'Thank you.'

'Did that help?' Elias asked once they were outside. He scratched his scalp. 'That's more than I ever learned about him.'

'It did,' John said. 'I don't know what it means yet, but it was worth the journey.' He looked around. 'Is there somewhere I can sleep tonight?'

'Folk are usually generous around here. But with the plague in the air…'

He understood. People looking after their own families and keeping strangers from their door.

'Of course.' He smiled. 'Thank you again.'

CHAPTER FIVE

He found a patch of bracken close to the river, well out of sight of the road. A few years had passed since he last slept outside. He'd become soft, John thought wryly, too used to the comforts of home and a bed with a loving wife in it. But the night felt balmy and sweet, the ferns made a soft pillow, and he was tired to his bones. Thoughts whirled in his head as he lay under his cloak, until the lulling sound of the water finally calmed them.

He woke while the light was only a faint glimmer on the eastern horizon, and stretched out the aches in his body. Cold, clear water to wake him then he was on his way. This was the best time to be on the road. The air was still fresh and the world felt new-made.

He broke his fast in Hathersage, following his nose to a baker's shop, then eating as he climbed slowly up the long hill from the village, stopping to catch his breath and gaze back over the valley.

The last miles were the worst. No clouds in the sky to shade the sun. He was weary and his feet ached inside his boots. Finally, though, he could see the church steeple in the distance; the sense that home was close urged him on.

It was better to stop and make his report to the coroner first. John knew that once he was inside his own house he'd be too weary to leave again. De Harville had gone hawking for the day but Brother Robert sat in the hall, coming awake from a doze as John entered.

The monk listened closely to what John had learned. Between words the carpenter gulped at a mug of ale.

'What do you think, Brother?' he asked when he finished. 'What do you make of Crispin?'

'He sounds like a man with a great deal to fear,' Robert answered. 'He killed a powerful man?' The monk thought about that for a long time. 'It would be a good reason to vanish, if the family wanted revenge.'

'It seems that he couldn't hide well enough.'

'Or perhaps it was chance. Someone passing recognised him and sent word.'

That was possible. If Crispin had done his killing on the king's orders, though, surely the Crown would want this death investigated fully; they'd want to discover the murderers and make them pay with their lives. But if things had been personal, the protection wouldn't extend that far. He needed to think about it and also puzzle out the meaning of the mounted men who'd visited the priest the month before.

'Will you tell the coroner when he returns?'

'I will, John,' the brother promised. 'Now go and see Katherine and Juliana.' His face brightened. 'No new cases while you were away, God be thanked. And no more dead.'

That was a blessing he thought as he trudged the last few yards to his door. Inside, Katherine and the others were gathered around the table for supper. She had Juliana on her lap, feeding her with the small wooden spoon he'd carved.

Home. And he was content. The place overwhelmed him.

John had to tell his story twice; there were too many questions the first time.

'What's Castleton like?' Eleanor asked when he'd finished. He smiled as he described it and tried to put all the wild country into words.

'Do monsters and dragons live in the hills?' she wanted to know.

'No.' He laughed. 'They don't exist, not any more. Only in stories. They were all killed long ago.'

With a serious look the girl nodded, satisfied.

He held Juliana until she drifted into sleep, and watched as Katherine changed the clout around the child. Another piece of cloth to wash in the morning.

• • •

John remembered Katherine's arms around him. The next thing he knew he was waking with light showing through cracks in the shutters. Down in the hall the house sounded alive, voices and laughter, then the cry of an infant.

He rubbed his teeth with a willow twig and washed himself. Poor Alan would wonder what had happened to him.

The boy came dashing out at his knock, fingers moving in eager questions as they walked to Brampton. John answered the best he could, ready to be working with his hands again, to feel the wood talking to him, for life to be as it should.

After this job was complete, they'd begin work on a new door for a house on Saltergate, only five houses from his own home. Simple enough, but it needed to be exact to fit well and keep out the weather. Already he was thinking ahead, letting his mind drift.

Solid labour and honest sweat. It made him happy and put pennies in his purse. John sat on his haunches and watched Alan measure a length of wood then mark it, turning for approval before taking out the saw and cutting.

The boy definitely had the feel. It was such a rare thing, a gift. Some masons possessed it with stone. He'd seen that in York as they wielded their hammers and chisels to create the delicate, powerful tracery which adorned the churches.

By the end of the day things were almost complete. Another hour or two in the morning and everything would be finished. None of this stretched his skills, but it was still satisfying. And to be able to pass on what he knew brought true joy.

He'd escorted Alan to his house and was walking home when he heard hooves, and the coroner barking out his name. John shifted his satchel on his shoulder and turned, shielding his eyes against the late sun.

'You've had time to think about Crispin, Carpenter?'

The man sat well on his horse, back straight, at ease above the ordinary people.

'Yes, Master.' He'd had the time, true enough, but the dead priest hadn't entered his mind.

'What do you make of him now?'

'I think we might never know the truth.'

De Harville shook his head. 'He was killed here. The King appointed me to investigate deaths. I want to know who did it.'

'You're the King's man. Crispin was the King's man once. Wouldn't the King's household tell you about him?'

'I've written to them.'

Who knew how many weeks before an answer came, if at all? They might all be dead of plague by then.

'The little we've learned so far doesn't help us much,' John said. 'We've no idea who he's supposed to have killed, or who they served. We know two men were here on good horses, with weapons. But that's all we know about them. And there's one other thing.'

'What?' The coroner listened intently.

'The people behind this are very likely powerful men. They won't take kindly to questions.'

Start poking in places like that and he might be disturbing a wasps' nest. If the men who'd given the orders were lords or barons or earls, no mere coroner would have the rank to protect him.

'Justice, Carpenter,' de Harville said firmly. 'The law demands justice.'

'And how many are above the law, Master?'

It was a question without an answer. Rank, money, influence, so many things put a man out of reach of the courts.

'You find him and I'll take care of that.' He pulled on the reins and turned away.

Find him? How?

• • •

At home he let it all go. He was surrounded by people he loved and they were all well. John played with Juliana, games of this and that. During the long nights of winter he'd carved pieces of wood into blocks she could stack like stones, another into the shape of a horse, but with wheels that she could pull along with a piece of twine. Nothing special, but he delighted in sitting on the floor and spending time with her as she concentrated, placing one piece of wood on another, higher and higher, until it toppled to the ground.

Sometimes it felt impossible to believe that she was part of him. Each day she seemed to grow a little bigger, with some new skill like a miracle. When she walked for the first time it had terrified him until he came to understand that from then she'd be growing away from them all, becoming someone who would live her own life.

• • •

The next day word spread: two more cases of plague in the Shambles, a mother and her son. The morning after, another three. The houses were squeezed so tight in there, the air so full of the stink of dead animals from the butchers' shops, that everyone knew it would spread.

The fear returned. The goodwives would no longer visit to shop for their meat. Just to set foot in the small streets of the area was courting death. Safer to go without than that. The pestilence was close, and it was growing stronger.

How did you fight an enemy you couldn't even see? And if all these deaths were God's will, what did that mean for the world?

• • •

Faces grew even tighter. Tempers flared. People stayed behind their doors as much as possible. But he couldn't do that if he was going to earn money.

Alan's mother was reluctant to let her son go with him. He understood. But the plague was already here. It would find them or it wouldn't. Whatever they did would make little difference in the end. All the prayer in the world, all the belief, all the nostrums; none of them seemed to help.

• • •

John tested the smoothness of the wood with his palm then squinted down the line. Exactly right. He nodded and a broad smile creased Alan's face. The boy was so gifted that he hardly needed to check his work.

It was the last thing they'd do today. He told the lad to start cleaning the tools then stood and stretched his back. The boards were for the new door, so they needed to be even and soft as silk.

He laid them with the others and covered them. It was tedious work, but necessary, and good practice for Alan. John turned as he heard the sound of feet on the dirt.

One of the bailiffs, breathless and red-faced.

'The coroner says he wants you, Carpenter.' The man bent over, hands on his knees.

'Where?'

'He wants me to take you there.'

'Just a moment,' John told him.

He gave his orders to Alan: finish cleaning the tools then take them home and keep them well until the morning. Pride blossomed across the boy's face, trusted for a second time with the satchel.

'Where are we going?' John asked. He followed as the bailiff strode out briskly, a sword banging against his leg. What was the man's name? Alfred, he thought, but he wasn't certain.

'The Tapton Road, Master. By the river there.'

He'd walked by the spot several times but he didn't remember it well. Better to follow quietly and see.

They scrambled down the bank, clutching at tree roots and thick tufts of grass to stop themselves from falling. The coroner was waiting, trying to brush smears of dirt off his hose and his silk cote.

A lip of ground ran above the water, just wide enough for a man to stand. Lying there, wrapped in a winding sheet, was a body. Exactly the same as Father Crispin. But out here, away from everything? This was an unlikely place.

John glanced back up the hill. The corpse would be mostly hidden from the road by the bushes that covered the slope. Why *here*? Why not send the body out into the river and let the current take it? The flow was strong enough to carry it away.

'Carpenter.' De Harville jarred him out of his thoughts as he nodded at the body. John took his knife and worked it through the sheet, pulling it back until he could see the face. He looked up, confused. This wasn't any man he recognised. He moved aside so the coroner and the others could view it.

Nobody knew him. A stranger.

'We can't examine him down here,' John said. 'We need more room. A rope to drag him up to the road and back to town.'

'Do what he says,' the coroner instructed.

CHAPTER SIX

The man wore good clothes. A shirt of fine linen under a houppelande, tailored hose that fitted closely and beautifully-worked leather boots. The limbs were stiff and unyielding, but John was able to examine the palms of the man's hands. Some calluses and roughness, but this wasn't anyone used to hard manual work. That confirmed the evidence of the clothes. Whoever the dead man was, he'd possessed money and liked to display it. Forty years old, perhaps, with greying hair and a neatly trimmed beard; close to Crispin's age. In death, at least, he seemed peaceful.

A knife hung in its sheath from his belt, and John could see, close to the left hip, where the leather was worn from a sword and scabbard. No scrip, though, just two leather thongs that had been cut. That was different from the priest.

He looked at the coroner. De Harville's eyes were absorbing every detail. He nodded and John turned the body. He knew what to look for and spotted it immediately, the tiny blossom of blood. Very carefully he sliced through the clothes. It was right there, a small, round hole that hadn't gone all the way through the chest. Exactly the same as Father Crispin.

John stood.

'Well, Carpenter?'

'Let me think.' John began to walk away. The body wasn't going to tell him anything more. De Harville kept pace.

John looked up at the steeple in the distance. 'We have an assassin in the town, Master. Both these deaths were skilfully done.' He looked over his shoulder. 'He must have been there since last night. Why did it take so long to notice him?'

'Does it matter?' the coroner asked.

'It all matters. You don't know him?'

'No.' A curt, frustrated answer. 'I've never seen him before.'

Whoever the victim was, he'd been from de Harville's class. A man like that would be quickly missed. Word would spread like a fire. But he wasn't from this area or the coroner would recognise him.

Then why had he been killed and his corpse left close to Chesterfield? What did it mean? Had something happened at one time that involved him as well as Crispin? But *here*?

One man they couldn't identify, another whose past was a silent mystery. And no one to suspect. Nothing at all.

What about the way it had been done? There was coldness and calculation in that. Even wrapping the bodies in shrouds, as if they were simply awaiting burial. The murderer had planned everything.

'What do you think about the way they were killed, Carpenter?'

'A long, sharp needle,' John answered. It had to be that, he was certain. 'A thick one. He knew what he was doing. It was precise, all the way to the heart but no further.'

'How do we find him?'

'I don't know,' he said with a long sigh. 'I really don't.'

• • •

The church bell began to toll as he approached the town. More plague dead going into the ground. The curate from Clay Cross would say the service next time he was here. The important thing was to bury the corpses as soon as possible.

A questioning glance at Katherine as he entered the house on Saltergate. She shook her head: no new victims that day. His family was safe. Perhaps it wasn't much, but he asked nothing more than that.

Treasure what he had, because it could all vanish in a moment. He'd learnt that when he was young. Parents and children died together, and for a year or more those who remained alive survived in a wasteland, abandoned by God. A return to those times could happen so easily.

He picked up Juliana, tickling her until she screamed with laughter. The sound rolled over him, filling him with joy until he was laughing too.

• • •

Later, with Juliana and the girls asleep in the solar, they sat around the table with a rushlight burning as John told them about the new body.

'What I don't understand is the weapon he used,' he said. 'It seems like a needle. Like the ones for darning, but thicker and longer. I've never seen anything like it.'

Katherine and Walter listened closely. Dame Martha seemed to stare at nothing for a long time, staying so quiet that he wondered if she was having another spell.

'Nalbinding,' she said finally.

The word meant nothing to him. Martha rose, leaning on the stick he'd cut for her, and hobbled off into her room. John looked at his wife. She shook her head and went after the older woman.

'What does she mean, John?' Walter asked.

'I don't know.'

Fully five minutes passed before the women emerged. Martha was clutching something in her crooked hand, and dropped it on to the table where it glistened in the light.

'For nalbinding,' she told them. It was a needle, a handspan long, pointed at one end then growing to the thickness of a small finger, with a hole at the other end to thread yarn. 'My mother taught me how to do it when I was a girl,' Martha explained. 'I've forgotten now, but you can make things with it. Clothes.' She sat back with a satisfied smile.

John picked it up and rolled it in his hands. She was right, a needle like this might have been the weapon. It would only take a little work to sharpen the tip until it could pierce flesh. It was small and thin, but still long enough to reach the heart. Easy to conceal up a sleeve and deadly in the right hands.

'May I borrow this?'

'Of course,' she told him with a smile. 'That's why I brought it out.'

• • •

'Dame Martha thought of that?' De Harville asked in surprise. In the corner, Brother Robert lowered his head to hide a smile.

'She did,' John said. 'She's right; something like this would be a perfect weapon for a trained assassin. It would leave very little blood, and anyone could carry it without suspicion.'

'Nalbinding?' The coroner ran the unfamiliar word slowly over his tongue. 'What does it mean?'

'I've no idea.' That had probably been lost over the years. 'Does it matter?'

'No. I don't suppose it does.' He held the needle and mimicked a stabbing motion. 'Yes, I suppose this could work. Now we can guess how it was done, but it doesn't help us find the murderer. We can't search every man in town to see if he's carrying a needle like this. The killer would just hide it somewhere. How do we find him?'

'Perhaps we need to look for strangers,' John suggested.

'Not too many of those in times like these, Carpenter,' de Harville said. 'You ought to know that.'

'Perhaps we should look for those who came after Father Crispin arrived, God rest him,' the monk said.

'That's possible,' the coroner allowed. 'Think of some names.'

Who? It wasn't too long since he'd been new here himself, watched constantly and suspected. No faces sprang into his mind but surely there had to be a few.

'I can ask Walter. He should be able to tell me.' Going back and forth delivering his messages, he saw everyone in Chesterfield. With his memory he would be able to pick people out.

'Your wife's brother?' the coroner asked. 'As good as anyone. Find some people and look at them.'

'Yes, Master.'

• • •

With nothing more to do until Walter came home that evening, he collected Alan. Better to earn a half-day's pay with some honest work. The boy stumped along with the satchel on his shoulder, proud to carry it. It dragged him down, but he wasn't about to stop.

Was that how he'd been, John asked himself? Eight years old, his tools the only thing in the world that he owned. He'd kept moving, from village to town, one small job on to the next, learning with every single one. These days the tools seemed light as he carried them. Back then they felt like the weight of the past and the future on his shoulder.

'We should be able to get the shape of this today. I'll work with you.'

Alan's hands moved furiously. No, he wanted to do the job himself, to prove that he could. John could watch, help if he needed it, advise and instruct. But the boy wanted to do the work on his own.

'If that's what you want, then I'll let you,' John told him.

Alan sensed how it should all be. He could look and see the picture in his mind. He could feel the wood and understand immediately how it needed to be worked. Why one piece might be fine and another that looked the same completely wrong. Exactly as John could.

The boy was feeling his way into his true nature. How long before Alan went from being his pupil to his competitor? Was there enough work around Chesterfield for two carpenters? Never mind. Never mind. So much could happen before that. They might all be dead.

His hand slipped forward just as Alan was about to use the chisel.

'No,' he said. 'There's an easier way. Let me show you.' He took hold of the tool and demonstrated. That was good; at least the boy still had plenty to learn.

• • •

'In the last twelve months, John?' Walter frowned. They were sitting out in the garden behind the house. Katherine had been busy planting, and in the warm weather plenty of shoots were coming through. She kept her young sisters weeding, out with the hoe each day so the earth looked dark and rich. He knew nothing about plants, happy to leave it to her and eat the food she grew.

'Since the start of summer last year when Father Crispin arrived.'

In the long silence John took a sip of ale. The nights were still comfortable enough for sleeping. If this weather stayed, though, come high summer they'd all be sweating and turning uncomfortably in their beds. Those who remained alive, anyway. Another two cases of plague confirmed that day. A shoemaker on Soutergate and his wife. A cross had been painted on their door. Their three children, in there with them, hadn't been affected yet. Which would be better for the little ones, he wondered? To live on or to die? Live, he decided. Whatever happened, they could learn how to survive. And in life there was always hope.

'I can think of four,' Walter announced finally.

'Who are they?'

'Richard the Salter, William of Hull, Henry the Mason, and Hugh the Carter.'

'No one else?'

'No, John,' Walter told him. 'I'm sure.'

He trusted the lad; if he was certain, then it was right.

He'd seen all the men around, even spoken to William and Henry. Richard had moved here from somewhere in the west, a man who brought salt over from the mines in Cheshire and distributed it across the area. He'd bought an empty house out towards Brampton.

William had leased Martha's home on Knifesmithgate and moved in with his wife, three children and a servant. He was a merchant from the east coast, he claimed, and travelled often. If he ever said what he bought and sold, John had forgotten. He'd chosen to live in Chesterfield because it was more central, he claimed, easier to reach most of the places he visited. The man seemed polite enough: well-to-do but rarely even in the town, it seemed. Had he even been here when Crispin vanished?

Like John, Henry had worked on the church when it was being built. But he'd moved on once the job was complete. Henry had come back because he liked the place too much and had been sweet on a girl. They'd married and found an abandoned house that he'd rebuilt. Now he was scraping a living from small jobs around Chesterfield.

Hugh the Carter. Another man with a family. John had only exchanged a nod and a greeting with him. Hugh had a family, lived by West Bar, but that was all he knew.

'Tell me about Hugh. What do you know about him?' he asked Walter.

'He came here from Lincoln. That's what someone told me.'

'Lincoln?' He sat up straight. The city where Crispin had served after his ordination. The bishop's seat. That was interesting, and a point worth pursuing.

'Did you ever see him talk to Father Crispin?'

'No, John, I don't think so.' The lad blinked. 'Why?'

'I just wondered.' He smiled. 'Thank you, that's helpful.'

He had information. He had names and the start of a plan. Now he needed to talk to them all.

• • •

'Lincoln,' the coroner said, once told of Hugh the Carter.

'That's what I wondered,' John agreed.

'What do we know about him?'

'Nothing.'

De Harville looked at the monk. Robert seemed to be a small, fragile figure in the corner, wrapped in his habit, slowly withering away.

'Brother? Can you tell us anything?'

'Not really. I've seen him at service and in his cart. His wife is a very modest woman. I've noticed her in church and in the marketplace.'

'Find out about him, Carpenter,' the coroner ordered. 'Those others, too.'

• • •

The place to begin was the alehouse on Low Pavement. At dinnertime it was busy to overflowing as men took a rest from their work. He found Henry the Mason there, arms and hair covered in stone dust, supping from a mug of ale. Tiny scars from stone chips covered the back of his hands and holes the size of pinpricks dotted his hose.

'It looks like you've been working.' John sat on the bench across from him. 'Keeping busy?'

Henry laughed. 'These days I'm just grateful there's so much poor craftsmanship that needs repair. Between the churches and the grand houses I'm making enough to get by. How about you?'

'Steady.'

'I hear you've taken on a boy to help you.'

'He's a good lad, has the feel for it. How often do you find someone like that?'

Henry nodded; he understood how important it was. 'I'd consider an apprentice myself, but who knows what's going to happen?'

There was no need to say more. They both had families. They both felt the constant fear within. And they were both powerless.

'Did you know Father Crispin at all?'

'The priest?' Henry frowned. 'Why would I?'

'No reason. I'm trying to find out more about him.'

'That's right, I'd forgotten. You do some work for the coroner.'

'For my sins.' John smiled and drank deep.

'I never talked to Crispin. Never had cause. All I knew were his services on Sundays and I didn't understand a word of those.' He leaned forward. 'Who's the other one that was killed? No one's saying.'

'I don't know,' John answered honestly. 'It's nobody I've ever seen before. Have you noticed any strangers around?' He described the armed men who'd visited the priest's house and vanished again.

'No.' Henry shook his head. 'I'd best get myself home. These days she worries if I'm gone too long.'

That was something any man could understand. John drank up and returned to his own family.

• • •

In the morning, before he called for Alan, John visited Martha's old house. He was hoping for the chance to talk to William the Merchant. But he wasn't there.

'He's been gone these ten days, Master, and no word,' the man's wife told him, 'and I'm worried sick.'

He could see it on her face. She had deep smudges under her eyes. A few strands of lank hair peeked from her wimple and she seemed drawn, on the edge of exhaustion.

'When did he go, Mistress?'

'Two days before the priest was killed,' she answered. 'He was supposed to be back by now.' He could hear the children moving round up in the solar and the reproving voice of the servant. 'I'm scared for him.'

'I'm sure he'll be home and safe soon.' They sounded like empty words, but what else could he offer her?

• • •

By day's end the new door was hung. He'd shown Alan how to join and seal the boards, and the tricks involved in making sure it sat flush, then opened and closed freely. Small things, but all useful for the future. Finally he was satisfied, tousling the lad's hair.

For once, they cleaned the tools together. It felt like too long since he'd done it, letting the film of oil cover the metal, feeling it on his fingers before rubbing it away again. There was no pitting or rust on the metal. For years he'd looked after them like the treasures they were. He passed a chisel to Alan to sharpen on the whetstone. All these things had lasted him for so long. Handling them could bring memories of better times. Safer times. But now there was precious little safety for anyone. High-born or low, they all took their chances now. No doors could stop the pestilence.

CHAPTER SEVEN

John looked at his wife.

'None today,' she told him and he exhaled slowly. Men and women might be dying, but plague still hadn't taken a firm grip on Chesterfield. By now he would have expected the list of the dead to be long. But maybe this was how it would be with this visitation. Stalking and selecting its victims instead of going after them all, like a cat toying with a mouse.

He held her for a long time, her body so familiar in his arms, the smell of her so comforting.

'Juliana?'

'She spent the day in the garden.' Katherine smiled. 'I had to keep stopping her from trying to pull up my onions. As soon as I turned my back she'd be at it.'

'Where is she now?'

'With Martha.' Her face softened. 'We did the right thing, you know, bringing Martha to live here.'

He'd never doubted it. John had been the woman's lodger when he first came to town. She'd been kind, generous. A rare woman, she was family even before she settled in the room off the buttery.

'How is she?'

'No more spells. I've been keeping an eye on her.'

'Pray God they won't return.'

• • •

The day dawned cloudy, with just enough coolness to make him smile. A new job, replacing the floor in the solar of a house. It was tricky work, and removing the old boards needed more strength than Alan possessed at eight years of age.

Concentration, that was what it took. For a short while, at least, while he could forget about plague and murder and simply think of the job in front of him. He set Alan to smoothing the new boards so there would be no splinters to pierce bare feet. When he finished they were as smooth as skin.

In the end it took them almost three days. The coroner didn't come calling, there were no new cases of pestilence, and the bell only tolled twice. He'd arrive home with questions in his eyes, then stand in the garden and pour cold water over his flesh to wash off all the sawdust, happy to be alive.

William the Merchant hadn't returned yet. Both Richard the Salter and Hugh the Carter were away. Those two men had been here when Crispin died, though; he'd learnt that much. He'd see them once they were home.

• • •

On the fourth morning the coroner came. He wore a crisp linen shirt with a deep red surcote, boots glistening in the warm morning sun.

'God be with you, Carpenter.' There was no joy in his words; he was frowning.

'And with you, Master.'

'Come with me.' He began to walk away, not even waiting. John had to hurry to catch up.

'Where are we going?'

But the man didn't answer, simply continued with long strides, out of town and to the Tapton road. The marks

71

remained on the hillside where they'd dragged the body up from the riverbank. Why were they here, he wondered?

A poor soul passed them, baskets of this and that on his back to sell at the weekday market. He touched his forehead in a salute to the coroner and moved away silently.

'I have a name for the man we found here,' de Harville said, looking down the hill.

'Who was he? Someone from Chesterfield?'

'No. His name was Guy. He was the steward of a manor.'

'A steward?' John asked in disbelief. He wasn't like any that he'd ever met. His clothes were too rich and those hands had never seen any hard work on the land.

'That's what they told me.' De Harville shrugged. 'I don't believe it, but that hardly matters.'

'Where's he from? How did you find out?'

'A note that arrived last night. He lived on a manor near Conisbrough. The description fitted him perfectly. He vanished last week. His master believed something must have happened and sent messengers around to try and find word of him.'

It seemed like odd behaviour, to go to such lengths for a steward. But then, dead Guy obviously hadn't been any ordinary steward.

'What else did the note say? Any more than that?'

'No. But I talked to the man who delivered it. It seems that Guy had been a king's soldier before he left the royal service. He arrived as steward five years ago, although it's others who do everything on the manor.' He gave a wry smile. 'He wasn't well regarded by the men there.'

'Five years?' John said. 'That's when Crispin left the King's service and was ordained.'

'It's a curious coincidence, isn't it?' De Harville's tone was dry. 'I tried to discover more but the messenger didn't know.

I've arranged to return the body.' His face hardened. 'I thought I'd travel with it. The lord there might be able to shed some light on all this.'

John held his breath, expecting the coroner to demand that he come along. But the words didn't arrive. Instead he turned and began the walk back in to Chesterfield.

'Why?'

'*Why?*' De Harville's voice flared. 'Two corpses, Carpenter. One of them a priest. And here, where my writ from the King runs. We need to find out *who*. How much of a fool do you think I'll look if I can't sniff out the killer? It would be an ideal excuse to give the job to someone else.'

The anger was there, and hidden beneath it, the fear.

'Maybe you can find the key to the puzzle,' John said.

'Maybe so. I want you to think about this, Carpenter – why was Guy left here? It would have been simpler to murder him and leave the body close to the manor. This took planning. It was deliberate.'

But John had realised that long before, as soon as no one knew the corpse. Someone was trying to deliver a message of some kind.

'We still don't know enough. All we can do is guess.'

The coroner snorted. 'Any word on the carter and the salter? Or the merchant?'

'They hadn't come back yesterday; I asked.'

'I want you to talk to them as soon as they're in Chesterfield. You're certain the mason had nothing to do with it?'

'Henry worked on the church here. What would he be doing as an assassin?'

De Harville pinched his lips together and gave a short nod. All his suspects were slipping through his fingers like sand.

'When are you leaving, Master?'

'Within the hour. The coffin went at first light, but I'll catch up with them soon enough. If you discover anything, tell Brother Robert.'

But John had his own work to fill his time. He'd refused one job at the fulling mill down on the river. It was too close to where the plague had begun. The air was always damp there and the stench from the mill enough to make a man gag. Every day alive was a risk but he could do a little to help himself.

The owner of the mill had sighed. 'I can pay six pence a day, Master,' he said, the most generous offer he could afford to make, but John had shaken his head. It was tempting, but some things were more precious than money.

'Once the plague has passed,' he promised, and the man sighed once more before he reluctantly nodded his agreement.

• • •

The coroner returned on the Saturday. The market in the square had just finished and John was preparing to walk home. More people with items to sell this time. But there had been only a handful of plague cases during the week; folk would be thankful, and ready to go out, believing the danger was passing. Or perhaps they simply needed the money. The stalls weren't as busy as they had been in the spring, but the traders were smiling, full of laughter, describing everything they sold as a bargain.

John saw de Harville lead his horse along the High Street, looking dust-worn and weary.

The groom was taking the beast to the stable as he entered the yard. The coroner was removing his gloves, turning at the sound of boots on the cobbles.

'Well met, Carpenter. What news here?'

'Only two more with plague,' he replied, and the man nodded. 'What did you learn in Conisbrough?'

De Harville didn't answer immediately, just led the way into his hall, pouring himself a glass of wine from a jug.

'A thirsty ride.' He looked out of the window, watching the nurse playing with his son in the garden. 'But well worth the trip.'

'What did you find out about Guy?'

'Patience. He was a steward; that much is true. But it was only in name. The lord was away somewhere, but I was able to speak to the man who owns the neighbouring manor. Guy arrived there about five years ago. Yet he travelled a great deal and dressed more like a noble than a steward. The neighbour said he was only in Conisbrough a month or two out of the year.' He snorted in disbelief.

'Did he tell you how Guy came to be steward?'

The coroner shook his head. 'He didn't know, and thought it was better not to ask. It appears that Guy was very friendly with his lord. They'd sit up drinking together, more like equals.' He raised his eyebrows. 'Can you imagine that, Carpenter?'

'No,' John answered honestly. Society had its ranks and they faithfully kept their distance.

'Guy would practise with his sword when he was at the manor. Out there in the yard for an hour every day. And he owned a good horse. Tell me, Carpenter, does that sound like any steward you've ever known?'

'Not at all.' It sounded more like a soldier.

'But no armour,' de Harville continued. 'I asked. Sword and dagger, a good quilted jacket, jerkin, and a heavy cloak.'

There had been none of that when they found him. A stout leather jerkin and a well-padded coat might have kept out the needle.

'What else did you find, Master?'

'Precious little. Guy kept himself to himself. He didn't have a woman on the manor. He didn't seem bothered. He wasn't local, everyone knew that. He boasted that he'd lived in France and London before.'

'French?' John asked.

De Harville shook his head. 'English. What do you make of that, Carpenter?'

He didn't know. Guy was a soldier of some kind, that was obvious, and he'd arrived on a manor at the same time Crispin was ordained in Lincoln. Five years. More than coincidence. He strained his mind to think if anything important had happened then.

But there was nothing he could recall. Would he have even noticed, though? The things John considered important all happened closer to home. The work of kings and nobles meant nothing; they were as distant as the moon, with their own orbits and laws. Caught up in his own world, he might never have noticed something.

'What happened five years ago? What was so important?'

'Politics, killings, small battles. It could have been almost anything. I thought about that as I rode home. So much and so little.' He shrugged. 'Guy had been gone for over a week when we found his body. He could already have been down here.'

'He hadn't been dead that long,' John said. 'No more than the night before.'

'Then fashion me an answer, Carpenter. Find me a killer.'

• • •

'John?'

Martha hobbled out into the garden, leaning on her stick. She lowered herself slowly on to the bench and let out a tired sigh. Over dinner he'd told them about Guy. The girls kept whispering to each other, paying no attention. Katherine fussed with Juliana; the heat prickled the child and left her fractious and quick to cry.

'What is it? Is something wrong?'

She settled, stretched out her legs and smiled.

'I should sit out here more often. The warmth feels good on my bones. Where were you five years ago?'

'I was in York.' She knew that; he'd told her his tale often enough.

'Do you remember the things happening on the border with Scotland then?'

There were always skirmishes up there in the wild country. Raids from both sides. People died, cattle were stolen. It was how they lived, a world apart. He paid it no attention. They were secure in York, with its soldiers and thick walls; the place was well defended. No Scot would be foolhardy enough to attack it.

'No. Why, do you know something?'

The old woman shook her head. 'How would we ever know much down here? All we ever got was gossip from the travellers. But I recall some leader being killed around then. I don't know why, but it stuck in my mind.'

He felt the beating in his heart quicken. 'Do you remember when? Or who?'

'No. I couldn't even tell you who said it. Still, it must have been important for someone to mention it.'

'I'll ask de Harville. Maybe he could find out. Or Brother Robert.'

Martha gave her gentle smile and the wrinkled face lit up. 'He's the reason I came out here, John. You need to talk to the coroner about him. Robert's dying.'

'But—' he began, then stopped. The monk was ill; that was obvious. How old was he? How old was Martha, come to that? They were of an age. 'What do you want me to do?'

'Talk to de Harville. Persuade him to let Robert go back to the abbey. He's been away from it for too long. Send him back so he can die in peace.'

'I already tried. He wouldn't listen.'

She reached out, placing a tiny, bony hand over his wrist. 'Try again, John. Please, for me.'

'He said it was too dangerous to travel with plague all around.'

'Calke isn't that far. A carter would take him. I'd be happy to pay.'

She had money. How much, he didn't know, but she'd never struggled.

'I'll ask.'

'I'd be grateful.' She was silent for a moment, then said, 'There's something else.'

'What is it?'

'I went to see the lawyer yesterday.'

He knew who she meant. There was only one in Chesterfield; not enough business in the town to support more.

'Is there a problem? Can we help?'

'It's nothing like that. I decided to change my will.' He opened his mouth to speak but she held up a finger. 'Hear me out first. There's money for my children and grandchildren, not that I ever see any of them. But I've prayed on it. I'm leaving my house to you. To Katherine, too.'

'You can't.' At first he couldn't believe what he'd just heard.

'John,' she told him gently. 'It's my house. My property that my husband left to me. I can do what I want with it.'

'But...' he began.

'Hush. It's for all of you. The girls and Walter; Juliana, too.'

'I don't know what to say.' He couldn't even have imagined anything like this. A satchel of tools had seemed like a big enough gift when he'd inherited it from his father. This... it defied thought.

'Don't say anything,' she said. 'It's already settled.'

'You're not going to die for a long time yet.'

'I'll go when the Lord decides.' Her voice was steady. 'With the plague here, who knows when that will be? It helped me make up my mind.' She began to push herself up from the bench. He rose to help her.

'Thank you.' The words seemed too small and inadequate.

'You're my family,' she said.

• • •

Katherine cried, then went to Martha's room and sat with the old woman for a long time. She was in tears again when she came out, but this time they were different, a mix of joy and sorrow.

'She thinks she might die soon,' was all she would say. In the bed she held John very close.

CHAPTER EIGHT

It was a morning of drenching rain, arriving in heavy squalls, drops bouncing up from the road. They made a sullen parade to church, skirting the puddles, the long grass in the graveyard soaking boots and hose. The farmers might need it but it did little good elsewhere, John thought.

The curate from Clay Cross said mass, and a service for those who'd died since his last visit. He intoned their names, and everyone bowed their heads, remembering, praying that they wouldn't be next.

By the time he finished, all that remained in the air was a misting drizzle. The heat was beginning to rise, steam coming off the earth as if the ground was cooking. Katherine and the girls left, Walter prowled away somewhere, and Martha sat in the porch with the other goodwives, exchanging the gossip they didn't have time to tell before prayers began.

De Harville was squatting at the lych gate, talking to his son. The boy held his mother's hand tightly, the nurse fretting behind her. The coroner stood and ruffled the boy's hair, watching as the others moved away.

'Carpenter. I wanted to see you.'

'Master?'

'Have you had any new thoughts about Crispin and Guy?'

'Dame Martha believed there might have been an incident up on the Scots border around five years ago. She didn't know what it was, though.'

The coroner frowned. 'Walk home with me. Maybe Robert can recall it.'

De Harville had said the name. It was time to broach the topic again. 'You should let him go back to the abbey. He's not well. He could rest there.'

'He rests in good comfort at my house.' There was the first small flare of temper. 'He's well-fed, a better bed than he'd find in any monk's cell. And I told you before, not while there's plague around. He's a frail man.'

That was all the more reason to let him go. 'Have you asked him, Master?'

'Why would I need to do that? I've known him most of my life.'

'It would be a kindness.'

De Harville strode ahead, leaving bootprints in the mud. The door to the house hung open. He was already in the hall, pouring a goblet of wine. The monk sat in the corner, a cushion under his old bones.

'Five years ago,' the coroner said to Robert. 'Up on the border. Do you remember anything important?'

The brother gazed at him with rheumy eyes and remained quiet for a long time.

'Wasn't there something about a lord who was killed?' he said eventually.

The coroner paced the floor, drinking, staring out of the glazed window, thinking. Suddenly he turned.

'Yes. Yes, I can remember it now. But wasn't it only whispers? Something about an earl. The King had sent him to hammer down on the raiders. Let me see.' He walked more, thinking and talking. 'If I recall it properly, the story was that he'd ridden his horse down to a river to water it and he was surprised by a group of men. By the time they began to look for him, the killers had gone and all they found was his body.'

An earl. A very powerful man indeed.

'Crispin and Guy were Englishmen,' John said.

'Who better to kill an earl who's causing trouble at court and blame it on the Scots?' the coroner asked.

'But we don't know if any of this is true, do we?' It made for a good tale. For anything more…

'It would fit,' de Harville said, as if it was now fixed in his mind.

John looked over at Robert. The monk's face showed no expression. This was a flight of fancy, a stretch of the imagination with not a single shred of proof.

'What do you think, Brother?'

'I don't know, John.' His voice had all the weariness of age. 'I've learned that men can do more terrible things than I've ever dreamed about.'

'If it's true—' He paused. 'If it's true, it could be someone taking revenge.'

'Well done, Carpenter.'

He ignored the jibe. 'But why would they do it here?' If there'd even been an assassination, it had happened far to the north.

'Crispin was here,' the coroner answered. 'Guy wasn't far away. Two bodies killed the same way, left close to the same town. That sends a message.'

It certainly did that. A brutal one that seemed to ignore all the people who lived here, as if they didn't matter, and their lives weren't worth consideration.

And if de Harville's idea was true, looking into the deaths meant they were meddling with people who were too powerful and deadly for comfort.

'If you're right, Master, you know we'll never bring the killers to justice.'

'Perhaps we won't,' the coroner admitted, 'but at least we'll know the truth of it.'

It was the truth that could kill them. He wanted no part of it.

John turned to the monk again. 'Brother, you don't look well.'

'I'm tired,' Robert answered with a faint smile. 'But even when I sleep, these days I never feel much peace from it.'

'You should be back in the abbey.' He could feel the coroner's dark glance as he spoke.

'I'd like that.'

'There's plague everywhere,' de Harville said.

'What's the worst it can do, Master? Kill me?' Robert told him quietly.

'Then go. If that's all your loyalty means, leave.' He clattered the wine cup down on the table. Liquid spilled over and formed a small puddle on the wood. He stalked out of the room.

'Thank you, John.' The monk spoke into the silence. 'It's time.'

'Just say farewell to Dame Martha before you go.'

'I will. I promise.'

• • •

Monday morning brought a warm breeze out of the west, enough to flap at the linen of his old shirt. He set out for Cutthorpe with Alan at his side. Four miles in each direction, a strain for the lad, but he'd manage without complaint. That was his way. No new cases of plague in Chesterfield. Like everyone else, he wanted to believe it had passed, just brushed by them and moved on, but deep in his soul he knew it wasn't true. Life wouldn't be that kind.

They had to replace the rotted boards on a cow byre, to make it ready for the autumn. His heart sank when he saw the place. It was going to need far more work than he thought. One entire wall and half of another was gone. The thatch on the roof needed to be replaced, too, but that would be work for someone else.

'What do you think?' he asked Alan after they'd inspected the place. The boy's fingers moved quickly.

'You're probably right,' John agreed with a laugh. Better to tear the whole place down and start over. 'But I don't think they want to hear that.'

They spent half a day simply sizing up the job, taking measurements and estimating everything they'd need. Too many of the rotten boards simply couldn't be salvaged. After they'd eaten they began to tear out all the bad wood.

He stopped before twilight; better not to walk home in the darkness. Part of the byre was as stripped as a skeleton, only the bones of the frame remaining. In the morning they'd start to add new flesh.

By the time they reached the spire, he was exhausted. Glancing down, Alan was almost asleep on his feet, slogging along. He'd just escorted the boy home, thoughts of his own house on Saltergate in his head, when one of the bailiffs called his name.

'The coroner's been looking all over for you. Your wife said you were off somewhere at work.'

'What does he want?'

The man shrugged his broad shoulders. 'He doesn't tell me. But you know what he's like; I'd get over there to see him now if I were you.'

John sighed. All he desired was to be at home, to settle with his family for the night. Not more talk and ideas. No chasing murderers they'd never find.

'Any more cases today?'

The bailiff lowered his head. 'One. A little girl. You know Richard, the baker's helper?'

'I do.' Richard was a big, bluff man. Simple, but a happy, eager worker.

'His youngest.'

John crossed himself. May the good Lord save them all.

• • •

De Harville was working on manor accounts. He owned three of them now, all small; none would ever make him the rich man he wanted to be. Brother Robert sat on the bench, a quill in his twisted fingers, grimacing as he wrote.

'Carpenter. I'm sure you'll be pleased to know that Robert is going back to Calke Abbey in two days.'

'Thank you, Master.' He looked at the monk; the old man's eyes were smiling.

'I saw Hugh the Carter in town today. Have you talked to him?'

'I've been working. I'll speak to him in the morning.'

'What about William? The merchant. And the salter?'

'The last I heard, they were still on their travels.'

'Make sure you question them both. I want some answers.'

'Yes, Master.'

• • •

Hugh was out in his yard not long after first light, feeding the horse and inspecting its shoes. The cart stood off to one side, empty. The sides were beginning to pull away from the frame.

'God be with you,' John said.

'And you,' the carter answered warily. 'Can I help you, Master?'

'I was passing. I saw this—' he tapped the wood '—and wanted to tell you. The sides need tightening against the posts.'

'I know. I just returned yesterday. If I'm ever home for a few days, I'll rebuild it.'

'It's no more than a couple of hours' work.'

Hugh snorted. 'If you have the skill.'

'I do. I'm a carpenter.'

'Oh aye? How much to do it, then?'

'Three pence. Me and the lad who works with me. We can have it finished before dinner. I live in town. Ask anyone about my work.'

'Aye, I've seen you. I'm Hugh.' He extended his hand.

'John.' They shook. Three pennies.

He collected Alan and explained the work.

'The byre can wait a few hours. It's quick money, easy enough.'

• • •

Hugh stayed outside as they worked, sometimes watching, sometimes tending his horse.

'I hear you came from Lincoln,' John said, making it seem like idle conversation. 'It's a big place, from all they say.'

'Big enough. A castle and a cathedral. The whole place is so full of priests and soldiers there's no room for ordinary folk.'

'Our priest was from there, the one who was killed. Did you know him at all?'

The carter laughed. 'You're joking, aren't you? The likes of them aren't ever going to notice people like me. I'd never even heard of him until we moved here.'

John laughed. 'I used to live in York. It was the same up there, all the clergy go round with their noses high in the air.' He paused to work in a screw while Alan pushed the board tight. 'Were you here when Crispin died?'

'I was, and when they found the body.' He narrowed his eyes. 'That was you, wasn't it?'

'It was,' John admitted. 'What made you move to Chesterfield? Surely there'd be more work for you in Lincoln.'

'More work there, true enough, and too many people chasing it to be able to make a proper living. I'd been through here a few times and saw there was only one carter.' He shrugged. 'I weighed my chances and talked to my wife. So far it seems like a good decision. I've been busy enough since I arrived. If it wasn't for this plague everywhere I'd be doing very well now.'

'Doesn't it scare you?'

Hugh shrugged. 'God's will. It's not for me to understand. I just do what I can for my family and pray.'

'How far do you travel?'

'Wherever they want things delivered. I'm taking a cartload of peat from Hathersage to Calke Abbey tomorrow. Setting off to pick it up as soon you're done.'

'Another few minutes and we'll be done.'

Hugh was no assassin. He felt it in his bones. He was a straightforward man, a hard worker who was simply trying to survive, the same as everyone else. They talked a little more, then John tested all the joints for strength, nodding as he finished.

'That's as good as it'll ever be,' he said. 'It'll see you a few more years. And that seat won't bounce around any more.'

The carter nodded his thanks and counted out the money from his scrip. John passed one to Alan; the boy had earned it.

'Worth it if it holds together.'

'It will, I promise you that.'

• • •

As they walked away Alan's fingers moved with silent questions. Why did they do that instead of going out and working on the byre? Did John know him?

'No, I've never talked to him before. I needed to ask him a few questions.' He stopped and placed a hand on the boy's shoulder. 'You know I do some work for the coroner, don't you? It was about that. We'll go back out to Cutthorpe tomorrow; it's too late today. By the time we got there we'd have to turn around and come home.'

He watched as Alan ran off, satisfied. They'd have ample chance to deal with the byre in the morning. For a moment he thought about going straight home. Katherine would be surprised to see him so soon. Instead, duty won. He wandered across the empty market square and down the road towards Brampton.

Richard the Salter's house stood by itself, a squat, windowless stone building set behind it. Probably his warehouse. There was no sign of life in the yard but he knocked on the heavy door. No answer.

Never mind. He'd return and try again later. It meant that he had the afternoon to enjoy his family.

• • •

Juliana was sleeping when he returned. Dame Martha was giving the girls their lessons, making them write on their pieces of slate. At first he'd thought it was pointless – what need would a woman ever have of writing? But he'd come to see sense in it. She taught Walter too, when he was at home and had the time.

Knowledge gave freedom. If they could read and write, they could learn. He'd considered asking Martha to teach him, but he was too old; he'd survived well enough without it.

Instead he left them to their task, took Katherine by the hand and climbed quietly to the solar. Later, as they lay in bed, the soft breeze blowing from outside, he held her close, praying that moments like these would never end.

But these chances for indulgence were so rare. They weren't lords, able to rest on their money. There were always things to be done. Reluctantly, John dressed, taking pleasure in watching his wife. Then he was on his way to the salter's house again with a smile on his face.

This time the door was open to the stone building behind the house. A cart stood in the yard, drawn by an ox, two pack horses behind it.

He tapped on the wood, waiting until a heavy, sweating man emerged. He wiped his forehead with the back of his hand.

'If you're looking for work, you're too late. We've just unloaded the shipment.' Somewhere inside John could hear another man moving around.

'Thank you, but I have plenty of work. I'm John the Carpenter.'

'There's nothing for you here if you're touting for jobs.' He was stripped to his linen and hose, dark, damp patches under his arms. He had a bristly, brusque manner.

'Not that either, Master.' The words caught the salter's attention.

'What do you want, then?'

'You heard about the priest being murdered?'

'Priest?' Richard looked astonished, reaching out a hand and resting it against the door jamb. 'When?'

John gave him the details of both murders.

'Why?' The salter asked. 'Do you know?'

'Not yet. I'm working for the coroner on this. I've done it before.'

That brought a raised eyebrow, a question that went unasked.

'Did you know Father Crispin at all?' John asked.

The man pursed his mouth. 'I never spoke to the man. I know he came here a little before I did, but that's all.'

'Then I'll wish you good day, Master. And may God save us all from the plague.'

'I'd heard about that, right enough.' He crossed himself. 'The first case came just before I left. I took my wife and children over to Cheshire to keep them safe. How bad is it?'

Richard was old enough. He would remember the power of the first visitation.

'Not as bad as it was the first time. But it's lingering.'

'I'll pray for them. No plague in Cheshire yet, thanks be to God.'

• • •

'I'd swear on it,' John said. 'None of the three I've talked to had anything to do with the deaths.'

'What about the fourth?' de Harville asked sharply.

'William the Merchant. He's still not returned. I've spoken to the others, they're just trying to make a living.'

The coroner had been eating one of last autumn's wrinkled apples. He looked at it then threw it into a corner of the hall, down among the rushes.

'What now, Carpenter? We're back where we began. We don't have anyone for the crimes.'

'I know.'

John turned to leave. They could do nothing more, and he wouldn't be sorry to see the back of it. This was flirting too close to powerful men for his liking.

• • •

Brother Robert was at the house on Saltergate when he arrived home. The old man's face was heavily lined, his eyes lightly clouded, but somehow he looked more carefree, as if a heavy weight that he'd carried for too long had been lifted from his body.

Dame Martha sat beside him, her bony hand covering his.

'You're leaving tomorrow then, Brother.'

'Yes, John.' He smiled. 'And thank you again.'

'You ought to thank Martha. She's the one who pushed me to ask again. By the bye, I met the carter who'll be taking you there. His name's Hugh. A good man.'

The girls were sitting, obediently listening. Katherine played with Juliana. The child saw her father, beamed, and toddled towards him with the tentative, tip-toed walk of the very young. John bent, opened him arms, and scooped her up, making her squeal with delight.

'We'll miss you,' he said.

The monk nodded. 'I'll miss all of you.' He chuckled. 'It seems as if Chesterfield has been my life for too long. I'll even miss Coroner de Harville. I know he has his faults, but I've lived in his house for so many years now that I know his ways.' He gave a contented sigh. 'But I can't deny that it'll be good to go back to Calke.'

When he finally left, Martha insisted on walking back to the High Street with him. They'd be the last moments the two would ever spend together. She took hold of her stick and put her other arm through the monk's.

'They look like a pair of lovers,' Katherine said as she watched them amble slowly away.

'Maybe they would have been in another life.'

She sighed. 'Maybe.'

'We have what God gives us,' John said. 'Good and bad.'

'As long as you think I'm part of the good,' she said with a smile.

'None better, ever.'

• • •

They were out early to wave their farewells. Brother Robert was a small, shrunken figure on the seat next to Hugh. He had a tiny bundle on his lap, and the portable desk was stacked behind on top of the peat. Fifty or so had come to see him depart; the monk was well-liked and respected in Chesterfield. De Harville had gathered his family and servants at the gate.

Just before the corner of the street, Robert turned and lifted his hand once. Then the cart was out of sight. Katherine put her arms around Martha as the old woman began to sob.

'I know how much he needs this, but I'm sorry to see him go. I feel I've just said goodbye to my past.'

John was glad to shoulder his satchel of tools and leave. The sun was bright, warmth in the air as he collected Alan and they walked out to Cutthorpe. The byre was waiting for him. He examined it again, deciding it would need even more work than he'd estimated before. The owner was a fool for letting it go so long. If he'd done something a few years earlier, many of these boards would never have rotted.

He worked with the boy, starting the preparations. Cut and shape the boards, fit them as snugly as possible, then warm some pitch to seal the cracks between them. The work would take days, but that was fine. With each nightfall he'd have earned five more pennies.

By the time they stopped for dinner he realised he hadn't thought once about the murders. Good riddance to them. Instead, his mind had dwelt on the monk. He'd grown to feel real affection for the old man, his ways and his quiet wisdom.

He wished the man peace and hoped that the coroner's new clerk would be as thoughtful.

At day's end John examined his work. They'd made a fair start. Already some of the new boards were in place, flush and even. He could see the shape of it. The byre would look reasonable when they finished. Not new, because you could never find gold in a midden, but it would hold and last a while.

The walk back to Chesterfield felt wearying. His arms ached. Alan wasn't even trying to communicate; the boy looked almost asleep on his feet. The church spire rose in the distance, for so long just tantalisingly out of reach.

Then they were in the town. Alan seemed to find his strength again, small legs striding out as he neared home. John smiled. At that age, with his father dead, no relatives, there had been no home for him. No safety, no security. Nothing beyond work and survival. A time he wouldn't wish on anyone. Learning, always moving, discovering how to stay alive from one day to the next.

He'd just turned on to Saltergate when he saw the bailiff. The man was saying goodbye to Katherine and turning.

'Master,' he called. 'I've been looking for you.'

Behind him, John saw Katherine's face, mouth downturned.

'Then you can look a little longer. What is it?'

'The coroner wants you, Master. A body, just like the others.'

'If someone's dead, he can wait two more minutes.'

John left the satchel of tools in a corner of the hall, kissed his wife and daughter, then washed. The sting of cold water on his face roused him.

'John...'

He shook his head, letting water cascade around. 'If it's another of the same, we won't be able to do anything,' he told her. He didn't want to go, to end up mired deeper in this mess.

'You have a daughter now,' Katherine told him. 'You have responsibilities here.'

'I know.' He took hold of her hand. 'I'll be back as soon as I can.'

• • •

The bailiff was pacing in a tight circle outside the door.

'Where are we going?' John asked.

'Out near the lepers,' the man answered with distaste. The fear was natural. People kept their distance from the lazar hospital. No one knew about leprosy, how a man might catch it. All that was certain was that it became a lingering, horrible death sentence. The leper colony lay out beyond the River Hipper, set out and away from everything. Sometimes, when John passed, one of the inmates would be sitting by the gate, head covered in a cowl, ringing his bell and begging for alms.

Now, though, with the plague in Chesterfield starting by the river, most folk took care to avoid the area.

The bailiff hurried down Soutergate and across the bridge as if he'd been holding his breath the whole way. He only slowed once they'd passed the last houses. Fields stretched as far as the eye could see, only a thin strip of road running between them.

They turned along a track, moving towards a copse at the top of a rise. John could see the coroner's horse tethered to a tree, and the man himself, colourful in a green tunic and blue hose, leaning against a tree.

Down in the long, coarse grass of a clearing lay a body carefully wrapped in a shroud. Exactly the same as the other two.

CHAPTER NINE

'An inmate from the lazar house was out gathering wood,' de Harville said. His mouth twisted for a moment. 'He found the body. The priest in charge sent someone to find me.'

John knelt and cut through the thick fabric of the shroud. Slowly, he pulled it apart until he could see the face.

'This doesn't make sense,' he said as he rose. He was looking at the body of Richard the Salter.

'It would seem you were wrong about him.'

John sliced through the rest of the sheet, looking for blood, wounds, anything. Then he turned the corpse and saw the small hole from the nalbinding needle.

'I must have been. I only spoke to him yesterday.' He felt shaken. The other dead men were remote figures, even Father Crispin. This struck close to home. He'd met the man, talked to him. He could still hear Richard's gruff voice in his head. He'd felt so certain that the salter hadn't been involved in anything.

'Did anyone see a cart or a man out here, or hear anything? It must have happened during the night.'

'Ask at the leper colony if you like, Carpenter. They're the only ones close. I've raised the hue and cry, for all the good it will do.'

'We need to search Richard's house. I saw him unloading salt. I could smell it. He was definitely a merchant, there's no doubt about that.'

'And Crispin was a priest,' the coroner pointed out. 'But who was Richard before he began selling salt?'

A liar, it appeared. And a good one. He already knew there was nothing he could learn from this body. Instead, he walked over the grassy edge of the fields to the road and the lazar house beyond.

The walls cut the lepers off from the world, some small safety for those inside and out. By the gate a figure sat with a cup at its feet, shapeless in a worn habit, the cowl pulled low to hide the face. As John approached, the figure began to ring a bell.

'Alms, master, for the love of God.' The voice was a croak, sexless and gaunt. John dropped a coin into the cup. 'Thank you. May God give those you love life and peace.'

He'd pray for that.

'I need to see the priest here about the body that was found.'

'You're welcome to go in. Few want to, though.' The laugh sounded like a bark.

'I'll take my chances. What's your name?'

There was a wait before the answer. 'Alison, Master.'

'Then God be with you, Alison.'

John opened the gate and entered. It felt like a calm, restful place. Lepers tended rows of crops, bent over with their hoes. All of them covered from head to toe, their bodies somehow less than substantial, as if they were gradually transforming themselves into ghosts.

Only the priest had his head bare, his tonsure glinting in the sun. He came hurrying, a short man with clear, merry eyes.

'You came here a few years ago,' he said. 'I remember you.'

'Yes, Father.' He was right; it wasn't his first visit to this place in the coroner's service. 'I'm sure you can guess why I'm here again.'

'The body isn't plague, is it?' he asked worriedly.

'No.' He saw the worry begin to leave the man's face. 'It's murder.'

The priest crossed himself and whispered a prayer under his breath. 'Should I go there?'

'No need. They'll be taking his body away very soon. How was he found?'

'One of the lepers was searching for firewood. It's hard to find at this time of year, and they prefer to stay out of sight. He was in the wood and saw it. When he told me, I sent someone to town.'

Just as the coroner had said.

'Did anyone hear anything during the night? A cart, perhaps, maybe a horse?' The body might have been slung over the back of an animal.

'I can ask,' the priest said and paused. 'This seems an odd thing for a carpenter to be doing.'

'We can't always choose how we live our lives,' John answered with a rueful smile. 'If anyone heard or saw something I'll need to talk to them. It could be important.'

'If there's any word to send, I'll let you know. Go in peace, my son.'

• • •

The coroner was already inside the salter's house, marching through, picking things up and putting them down again.

'Anything from the lazar house, Carpenter?'

'Not yet, Master. There may be something if we have luck.' But only a small chance of that. He glanced around the hall.

A tapestry hung on the wall. Poor work, but a sign that the man had money to spend. A settle, a bench at the table.

'There's a servant. She's out in the kitchen.'

John walked through the buttery and into the garden. Herbs were growing, some other plants he didn't recognise. Like all houses, the kitchen was built away from the house for safety: if a fire broke out, the home would be spared.

She was just a girl, perhaps fifteen summers on her. He'd seen her in the marketplace; Walter seemed to know her. She was shaking, scared. Of course she was; death had touched her and men with authority were here. That would terrify anyone.

'What's your name, Mistress?'

'Cecilia, Master.' A quiet, nervous voice.

'Don't worry, no one believes you have anything to do with Richard's death.' He smiled at her. 'Truly. When did you see him last?'

'Yesterday evening before I went home. I fetched him supper. He wasn't here when I came this morning, but he's often gone.'

'Did he say he'd be away again?'

She shook her head. 'He only tells me if he's going on a journey. But he'd barely returned.'

'I know. I talked to him. When he's here, is he often out at night?'

'I don't know, Master.' She kept her eyes downcast. 'Once or twice he hasn't been here in the morning when I came to work.'

'What about friends?' John asked. 'Did Richard have many visitors?'

'Men,' she replied. 'They'd come to talk business with him.'

'Did you know any of them? Maybe two on horseback, richly dressed, with weapons, a month or so ago?'

'Not that I saw, Master.'

'The priest, Father Crispin. Did he ever come here?'

'Twice,' she answered. 'He didn't stay long, but the master told me I wasn't to disturb them.'

That was a connection. The salter had been definitely been lying when he said he didn't know Crispin. He thought for a moment.

'The other men who came. Were they local?'

'No, Master. I didn't know them.'

'Who else did Richard employ?' He saw her wince at the past tense.

'Just a boy to help sometimes in the warehouse.'

'Who travelled with him?'

'He met up with people, that's how he explained it to me,' she said. 'Safer in groups, he said, what with all the masterless men on the roads these days.'

That was true enough; the country was devilled with out-laws. 'He took his family on the last trip, didn't he?'

'Yes, Master. He thought they'd be safer over there with so much plague around.'

'Where in Cheshire were they going?' John asked.

'I don't know, Master,' the girl answered. 'I'm sorry. He didn't say and I never felt it was my place to ask.'

'Of course. Thank you.'

• • •

The sacks of salt in the warehouse gave the building a strange, clean smell, as if everything had been freshly washed. John poked in the corners and felt along the rafters. Nothing. Back in the house, he climbed up to the solar.

De Harville had forced the lock on Richard's chest and pulled out the contents. Clothes, good boots, a few rolls of vellum. A sword belt hung from a nail on the wall, the weapon still heavy in its scabbard. By itself that didn't mean much. The salter would have needed that on his journeys to keep himself safe. The leather on the hilt was worn; he must have owned it for many years. John drew it out. The blade shone, engraved with delicate scrollwork. The edge was exquisitely sharp. It was better than most men could afford. Maybe his business had done well. Or perhaps there was much more to the tale, layers hidden away in history.

'Where are his wife and children?' the coroner asked.

'In Cheshire, he said. Away from the plague.'

De Harville snorted. 'If plague's here, it's everywhere. I had a report of two more with it before I came out.'

'Who, Master?' John weighed the weapon in his hand.

'A weaver and his wife out along the Newbold Road.' He bent and dug out a pair of vellum scrolls from the chest. Slowly, he unrolled the first and began to read. 'Well, well,' he said finally.

'What does it say?'

'It thanks Richard of Chester for his service to the King and grants him a small pension.' He paused. 'And it's dated five years ago.' He left the proclamation fall. 'Another one who was in the King's service at that time. We've gone far beyond the point of coincidence, don't you think?'

'That sword could be a knight's weapon.'

'It might,' the coroner agreed, and picked up the other scroll. 'An indulgence to free him of his sins.' He read more closely. 'Not just bought from an ordinary pardoner, either. This is signed by the Bishop of Durham.' The coroner raised an eyebrow. 'That should give him less time in purgatory, God help him. His soul's going to need it now. And that's dated from five years ago, too.'

'Why would he need the Bishop's signature on it?' He'd seen the pardoners who travelled the roads and sold their indulgences. All false faith and cheap words.

'Because he knew important people and he'd done something very bad, Carpenter. Very bad indeed, and he wanted to be assured of his place in heaven.'

Three men killed in Chesterfield. Three men who'd all left the king's service around the same time. Two of them living in the town. Why here, he wondered? What brought them to this place? And what had they done? He shuddered. Someone walking over his grave. But not yet, he hoped. Not for a long time yet.

'What do we do, Master?'

'We do our job. We find out who murdered them.' De Harville's face was grim. 'Still, it makes me wonder. Did he really move his family because of plague, or was there another reason?'

'Safety?'

'It's possible. But until we can find out where they are, we won't know.'

'They never told the servant where they were going.'

The coroner sighed. 'What do you make of it all?'

'We can be certain the three deaths are connected,' John began. That was obvious, even to a blind man. 'Whoever's behind it all is close. He might have been here for a long time. He might be hiding out in the woods. But he's clever and he's trained. It probably relates to something that happened up on the Borders five years ago. And the killer likes to leave the bodies already shrouded.' He looked up. 'That's what we know.'

'And what do you think?'

'I don't,' John replied. 'We have bodies, all murdered the same way. Apart from that, the only things we have are rumours on the air. All I'd be doing was guessing.'

'Then guess for me, Carpenter.' The coroner stroked his chin.

'I think this is personal, not political,' John said after a moment. 'A relative of whoever was killed five years ago, perhaps. The dead men were involved, or whoever's behind this believes they were. Perhaps the winds have shifted in London and that's why all these things are happening now. A family that fell out of favour is back in the King's good graces again, so they feel they have the freedom to do this. It would explain why no one seems too eager for answers.'

De Harville nodded slowly. 'You might be right. But this happened here. I have my duty to solve it until I'm told otherwise.'

'Yes, Master.' What else could he say?

'Keep asking questions around the town.'

• • •

John walked back to the place where the body had been found. It had been taken away and all the long grass under the trees had been trampled down. The dirt on the path was too dry and packed to show any hoof prints.

He wandered, searching, lost in his own thoughts. There was nothing to see here, nothing he'd missed earlier. Simply a place where a body had been left. He moved deeper into the copse, half-looking but not really seeing anything. He thought he heard a noise and started to turn.

And then… blackness.

CHAPTER TEN

John struggled awake, opening his eyes. Nothing. The world was dark. He blinked. Still only blackness. Then he felt something against his eyelashes. A blindfold. He tried to move his arms but it was impossible. His wrists were bound. Ankles, too.

His head pounded. Someone must have hit him hard. He hadn't been aware, hadn't felt anyone around…

'He's back with us.' A deep voice, one he didn't know. 'Shall we just slit his throat now?'

'No.' Another man.

Something touched his neck. Something sharp, with just enough pressure to start a trickle of warm blood on his skin.

'I hope you're listening. I'm going to say this once, and it's the only warning you'll ever receive. Do you understand?'

John tried to nod and felt pain shoot through his skull. His mouth was dry. Fear ran through him.

'You'll have nothing more to do with this investigation,' the voice continued. 'I don't care what you tell that coroner of yours. Lie through your teeth if you have to. But if you keep on, you'll be one more dead man on the list.' Another prick against his throat, another few warm drops of blood on his flesh. 'And one more makes no difference to us. The only difference is we won't be paid a penny for you.'

'Yes,' John croaked.

'Consider yourself lucky. Killing you would be easy.'

He heard feet moving away through the grass and waited. But he didn't feel the beat of hooves on the ground or hear the whinnying of an animal. They were on foot.

His head hurt as if someone had taken a hammer and his skull was the anvil. John tried to move his wrists, but the bonds had been carefully tied; turning and twisting his arms only made the rope chafe hard against his skin. The same at his ankles.

Standing was impossible. He was here until someone found him. Sooner or later they were bound to come looking.

But he was alive. By the grace of God, that felt like a miracle enough. His heart was thumping. He felt as if could hear his blood roaring in his ears. His head was on fire.

He'd been taken by a pair who knew exactly what they were doing. They could have left him for dead as easy as breathing.

Then why didn't they? What stopped them? The voice had said it would make no difference.

Through the murk, his mind tried to make sense of it all.

They knew exactly who he was, what he did, who he was working for. Still, that wasn't too difficult to discover in Chesterfield. He didn't recognise either of the voices. He couldn't even place the accents. The only thing certain was that they weren't local.

So they must have an accomplice in the town, a man to pass them information. And somewhere a master who'd given the orders to kill and paid them well for the task.

As he worked it through, step by step, the shaking lessened and his breathing slowed. He felt safer now. They weren't coming back. This was his rough warning: leave it alone or die.

He wanted water; his tongue felt too big for his mouth.

Without warning, something pushed down on him, rolling him on to his belly. John tried to resist, to fight back, but he was helpless.

They'd returned after all. Decided it was safer to kill him. This was the end.

The weight vanished. He could move his arms. His legs. John shuffled away, one hand tugging the blindfold from his eyes.

A figure squatted close by, wearing a habit, the cowl too low to make out the face.

'Thank you.' It was all John could say. His voice was as dry as rust and his heart felt it might burst from fear. He could barely breathe. 'Did you see them?'

The figure raised an arm, pointing through the woods. The sleeve slipped back, Mottled, stippled flesh, the bones twisted, two of the fingers missing. One of the inmates from the lazar house.

'Did you see what they looked like?'

'No, Master.' This voice he remembered: she'd been begging for alms at the gate of the leper colony.

'Thank you again, Alison.'

The blood had dried on his throat. He rubbed his wrists where the rope had rubbed, then checked his body. His scrip was still there, his knife in its sheath; they'd been so confident that they hadn't even bothered to disarm him. Slowly, he stood. His knees buckled for a moment, and he believed he'd fall. Then he was upright, breathing hard.

'Let me help you,' the woman offered.

'I'll be fine.' He waved her away. 'Water?'

She pointed to the stream on the other side of the willows. He hobbled over, drank deep and washed his face. Better, John decided; he felt a little stronger. He'd been lucky; God had smiled on him. 'I asked the priest if anyone noticed anything last night. Did you see anyone?'

Deep in her cowl, Alison shook her head.

He still felt unsteady but that would pass. It was the shock. He held up a hand and saw how it shook. John took a few paces. He could walk well enough. And it was less than a mile to Chesterfield.

'Thank you,' he said once more.

• • •

'What?' De Harville's voice exploded in the room. 'Who were they?'

'I never saw them. When I came to I had a blindfold over my eyes. But I didn't know their voices at all.' He drank from a mug of ale the serving girl had brought. Outside the sun shone bright like a mockery.

'And what about the warning?'

He repeated it. He could hear the man's voice, every tone and hard inflection. Even now, safe in the coroner's house, it scared him.

'What should we do about it, do you think, Carpenter?' There was a sly edge to his words.

'Do?' John said in astonishment. 'I'm going to do what he said. Do you truly think we're going to find men like that, Master? They're assassins. They're soldiers. And they're working for someone.' Let the deaths go unpunished, he thought. All because someone did something far away. It wasn't his business. It certainly wasn't worth his life.

'I'll consider it.' It was a dismissal and he was glad of it. John watched from the corners of his eyes as he walked back to Saltergate. He'd washed again in the buttery at de Harville's house. The cuts looked like small pinpricks on his neck, nothing at all. Had that been the nalbinding needle, he wondered?

He had to tell his wife and he knew how she'd react.

. . .

She stood and walked out of the hall, climbed the steps to the solar without saying a word. He found her lying on the bed, turned towards the wall. He sat by her and took hold of her hand.

'They won't come after me again,' he said.

'Don't lie to me, husband. You know they will if you keep on with this.'

'I'm not going to do that. It's over.'

'How many times have you made that promise to me before and broken it?' Her eyes were red and her cheeks damp with tears. He brushed them away with a finger-tip. 'It's bad enough with death all around. I can't take you bringing it to our door. To us.' She took a breath. 'There were two fresh cases of plague today. Did you know that?'

'Yes,' he said quietly. 'The coroner told me.'

'The world's falling apart, John. I feel like I'm drowning in death. I need something firm. A rock.'

'I'm not going to die over these men. They weren't anything to me.'

He left her there. Dame Martha was waiting in the hall for him.

'Come into my room, John.'

She closed the door behind him.

'I heard the two of you,' Martha said. 'She loves you, you know that.'

'I love her, too,' he began, but she spoke over his words.

'And you're giving her pain doing this for de Harville. She's terrified, John. She's scared for your daughter, she's scared for all of us.'

'I told her, this is the end of it. I'm not going to be killed because some lordling wants his revenge.' He winced as pain shot through his head.

'Let me take a look at that,' Martha said. She pulled his hair away. 'You took a hard hit. Just as well you have a thick skull.' Her fingers felt gently around the lump. 'At least the skin's not broken. Just be careful, please.'

'I will. I know they could have killed me if they'd wanted.'

'Then praise God that they didn't, John.'

'I'm not going to give them any reason to try again.'

'Make sure you don't. You know Katherine: she'll believe deeds, not words.'

He nodded; the old woman was right. He'd made the same vows before and shattered them. This time he had the wounds. This time he had real fear.

A wave of exhaustion rose up through his body. He felt as if he could barely stand.

'I need my bed,' John said. 'It's been a long day.'

• • •

He woke with the dawn. His head throbbed and the flesh was tender where he'd been hit. But he'd survived. The fear remained, slowly receding. But he knew it would stay, a small, hard lump inside. And that was exactly what the men wanted, for him to do nothing. Well, they'd won.

Dressed, with a few mouthfuls of bread and a swig of ale for his stomach, he put the satchel on his shoulder and kissed Katherine goodbye. She looked into his eyes, then smiled. Good, he thought as he walked down Saltergate, hoping she'd seen the truth on his face. No more hunting killers. God knew, there was already enough death on this earth. Without thinking, he crossed himself.

The boy was full of questions as they strode out to Cutthorpe. The news of the attack had grown in the telling until it became a tale where he'd been confronted by five men and fought his way out. John laughed; the truth was always dull.

'The only thing we need to worry about now is finishing this cow byre. That's going to take all our concentration.'

More than that; it was going to require ingenuity, he realised as they worked. The steward has said exactly how much he was willing to pay. Not a penny more. But it was barely enough for the work that needed doing. He'd argued the case, showed the man how much was rotted, but the steward remained adamant. Now, as John discovered, it would be impossible to mend this building as it stood. Not for that money.

Better to tear it down and start over, that was what Alan had said. Maybe he was right… John tested the frame. One post would need replacing, but all the other beams were fine. If he made the byre smaller, though, they'd need less wood. He wouldn't reduce the size too much, perhaps a yard. If he did that, it would be stronger, and their wood might just cover everything.

He explained his idea to the boy, who listened and looked, judging the changes in his mind. After a moment's thought he signed that it could work. He offered a few ideas and John smiled. Two of those would help; the others were impossible fancies.

But now they had a place to start properly, and do more than patch the byre. It would take longer, but the result would be so much better.

CHRIS NICKSON

By the time they finished for the day John was sweating, stripped down to his hose and boots. He rubbed himself off with an old piece of linen before dressing again. They'd made real progress. And he'd steered his thoughts away from dead men and killers.

· · ·

The days passed and the byre took shape. Today they'd nail up the final boards and hang the door. John had loved the challenge of it. It became easy enough once they'd achieved a rhythm in the cutting and shaping. Now the building should be strong enough to outlast them all, especially with pitch in the cracks on the base of the boards where they met the ground. By tomorrow it would be complete.

He sighed in satisfaction as they cleaned the tools. He inspected the blades of the chisels and the saw, making sure there was no pitting. But the workmanship was still fine; after all these years they held up well. How long ago had his father bought them, John wondered? How much did he pay for something as fine as this? So many questions he would love to have been able to ask. But that chance had vanished long ago. Maybe when they met again in heaven.

He strolled back to town, Alan by his side. The boy had grown used to the walk. With each job his skills improved. Not speaking would be a problem, of course it would. He'd get by, though; the lad was quick and resourceful.

And the wood sang to him, the way it did to John. Soon it would be time to teach him the basics of carving. He might have the touch for it; John didn't. Maybe Alan would have the opportunity to work on fine churches, to really show what he could do. He glanced down at the top of the boy's head. Who knew where life might lead him?

He'd heard nothing more from the coroner. Good. Better to let those deaths disappear out of memory.

• • •

On Sunday they processed to church. The sky was a crisp, pale blue, curlews on the wing in the distance. Summer warmth was in the air, and just enough of a breeze to take the sting from the heat. Dame Martha, dressed in good sarcenet, paused to breathe deep, smiling as she took in the scents.

Only two other plague cases during the week, and both of those had been down by the river, close to the fulling mill and its foul air. Nothing in the last three days. For the first time in weeks John let himself believe that the worst might have passed, that they could really have escaped so lightly. He still glanced over his shoulder as he walked and kept his hand close to the hilt of his knife. But each morning the fear was a little less.

Katherine had her arm through his, the girls holding on to Juliana as she toddled slowly, raising her eyes to try to see the top of the spire. What was she thinking as she saw it, he wondered. How high did it seem to her? Did it reach all the way to heaven in her mind?

De Harville's wife stood in the churchyard after the service, looking frail and nervous. The servant was already on her way home, keeping tight hold of the boy's hand.

As John emerged, drinking in the air, she approached him cautiously and he realised he hadn't seen the coroner at the service.

'Master?' she asked. 'You're John the Carpenter, aren't you?'

'Yes, Mistress.' Surely she knew that by now. She'd seen him with her husband, he'd been to her house often enough. Her skin was so pale it almost shone, hair gathered close under a

111

wimple. But there were deep shadows under her eyes, as if she hadn't slept.

Katherine came up to them with Juliana in her arms. The little girl's face was red and blotchy from the heat inside the church.

'Mistress,' she said, and made a small curtsey.

'I hope you'll forgive me,' the coroner's wife said. 'I need to speak to your husband for a moment.'

'Of course.' Katherine reached out and squeezed his arm, then walked away, the girls trailing behind her.

'You have a full family, Master.'

He tried to read her face but all he could see was terror.

'Has something happened?'

She nodded and he saw a tear roll down her cheek.

'What is it, Mistress?'

'These deaths,' she began. Words failed her for a moment. He saw her building the courage to say more. 'My husband won't leave them be. He received a message yesterday. Someone claimed to have information. He wanted to meet.'

'Did the coroner go?'

'Yes.' The word came out in a short, sad breath. 'Before dusk. He hasn't come home.'

'Where were they meeting?' he asked. The skin prickled on his arms.

'He didn't tell me. But he rode there.'

By itself that didn't mean much; the man liked to ride almost everywhere.

'Do you still have the note?'

She shook her head. 'He put it in his scrip.' Her eyes cast down, she said: 'I'm scared. I have no right to ask, Master, but would you look for him? Please. I know he put faith in what you could do. Please, Master.'

How could he refuse her when she was so desperate? But where could he even begin?

'I'll try,' he answered.

'Thank you.' She began to walk away, still staring at the ground. After a few paces, she turned. 'Whatever you need. Money, a horse, just tell me and it's yours.'

• • •

For once Katherine didn't try to stop him.

'Go,' she urged. 'This time you have to.'

'I will.' But where could he go? Where could he look? He could take a fair guess what had happened. Was he going to find the man's corpse?

Walter was waiting at the door. 'Can I help, John?'

'Yes. Come on. Let's go and find him.'

The head of the bailiffs was in his office at the Guildhall by the market square. He listened carefully.

'Aye, I'll get them out and looking.'

'The places where we found the first two bodies.' John paused for a second. 'And try the salter's house, too.'

That meeting could have taken place anywhere. But John knew who'd sent the note: the two armed men who'd taken him by surprise and delivered their warning. The killers. It had to be the reason de Harville hadn't returned. Was the man that stupid? Or did he truly believe his small rank was a shield?

He began to walk out along Beetwell Street, where the houses jettied up, storey upon storey, then down Soutergate and across the bridge over the Hipper.

They'd want somewhere secluded. But there were so many choices outside Chesterfield. Somewhere the men knew, where they'd walked the land and knew where to hide. Nowhere was better than the place Richard the Salter's body had been discovered, where the men had taken him down. Quiet, out of sight of the road and any travellers.

'Where are we going, John?' Walter asked.

'Where I was attacked.' Even as he said the word he could feel the grip of panic in his throat. 'We need to be very quiet. Don't say a word unless you have to. And stay off the track. We'll approach from the far side of the copse.' He drew his knife, knowing that if he needed to use it he was already dead, fighting against men who killed for their living.

CHAPTER ELEVEN

He tried not to make a sound, watching the ground before each pace to be certain he wouldn't break a twig. His head throbbed and he could feel his heart thumping. Walter was somewhere to his right, moving as silently as a cat.

Here and there the long grass had been flattened. What did that mean? Did it signify anything at all? John stopped and listened, straining for the smallest noise. But there was nothing beyond the call of birds and the soft snuffling of creatures in the undergrowth.

Would they kill de Harville? The death of a King's Coroner would bring attention. Surely they'd want to avoid that? They'd let a carpenter live, but he was nothing. They'd murdered men who'd been far more important. Men who'd been allowed to walk away from their pasts. History had caught up with them.

He was close to the edge of the trees now, able to make out the clearing. He tried to swallow but his mouth was too dry. Crouching, he took a couple of paces until he was behind a tree trunk. The clearing was empty.

No, it wasn't. Light glinted on something. Metal, shining as the sun caught it.

John froze. It could be a trap, something to lure them in. A little time passed. No movement, no noise. Knife drawn, looking all around, he walked very quietly out into the open ground.

It was a sword. Next to it, a scabbard. De Harville's; he recognised the design in the worn leather. He'd never leave it behind. This was what – a hint? A warning? He picked them up and sheathed the weapon. Whoever put it here had to be long gone.

This was their way of saying they had the coroner. Still alive, too. The body would have been left here otherwise.

He heard a soft rustle and turned, knife at the ready. But it was only Walter, shaking his head. He held his slingshot in one hand, two or three stones in the other. His weapon, and he was good with it. Fast and accurate.

'They have de Harville.'

He couldn't be too far away, John reasoned. Everything in this revolved around Chesterfield for some reason. They'd stay close.

'We might as well go back,' he continued. 'There won't be anything else to find here.'

These men were too good, too clever to forget anything, to leave any clue.

It felt like a long walk back to the road. At the end of the track John stopped.

'You go on ahead,' he told the lad. 'I'm going to see if they know anything at the leper colony.'

'I can come with you, John.'

'Are you sure?' He raised an eyebrow.

'If you're not scared of them, I'm not, either.'

He laughed. Walter looked so serious, so intent. 'Come on then.'

The leper by the gate rattled a cup.

'Alms, Masters, for the love of God.'

Cowled and hidden, he couldn't tell if it was Alison. He gave a coin and received the blessing, then opened the gate.

The priest was in the small stone church that smelt of incense and tallow wax. The floor was beaten earth, the windows unglazed.

'I hadn't expected to see you again so soon, my son.'

'I didn't think I'd come back, Father. This is my wife's brother, Walter.' In a few sentences he explained what had happened. 'I need to know if any of the lepers saw anything.'

'Last night?' the priest said doubtfully. 'We close the gates at seven. No one goes in or out after that.'

'No one?' People would always find their ways if they wanted.

'No.' His voice was firm. 'It's one of our rules. I can ask, if you wish, but I don't think they can help.'

'Please do,' John said. 'It's important. The coroner's life might depend on it.'

'Wait here.'

It was almost half an hour before he returned. John examined the wood. Quick carvings, cheap work. But what should he expect in a place like this? Joints were loose and uneven. A doorway slightly askew. Another few years and this place would tumble to the ground.

'I'm sorry,' the priest said breathlessly. There was a hint of triumph in his voice.

'Thank you, Father.' He'd hoped for luck, but God hadn't been that generous.

A figure waited by the gate. Impossible to tell if it was man or woman until the creature spoke.

'I heard something last night, Master.'

Alison. He glanced at Walter; the boy didn't seem wary or fearful.

'What did you hear?'

'People riding. They went off the road, along the track to the clearing.'

'When was this?'

'Not too long after dark.'

'How many horses?'

'Three, I think,' she said after a small hesitation. 'Two came first, then another a few minutes later.'

So that was the meeting place, where they'd wanted the coroner to come. As he'd thought.

'Did you see them?'

'I didn't look, Master.'

'Did you hear them leave?'

'No, Master.'

But it was enough, a confirmation. He drew a coin from his scrip ready to give to her.

'Please, Master,' she said. Her misshapen hand appeared from the sleeve and he dropped the money into her palm.

'Thank you,' he said.

• • •

The head bailiff sat in his room at the Guildhall. He gazed up expectantly as John entered.

'Any sign?' the carpenter asked.

'Aye, Master. The coroner's horse was tethered by the spot on Tapton where we discovered the steward's body. And we found his cloak inside the house near Holywell where we found Crispin.'

John held up the sword and scabbard.

'This is from the clearing where they left the salter's body. He met them there. What have you done with the other things?'

'Took them to his house. Where do you want us to look now?'

Where? He was still thinking when Alfred and another of the bailiffs came in from the jakes, still tying their braies.

'Gather everyone here,' he said. 'I'll be back very soon. Bring anyone else who's willing to search.'

Outside, he turned to Walter. 'Go and tell Katherine what's happened. See if she or Dame Martha have any ideas for places to search.'

'Yes, John. Where are you going?'

He looked across the market square to the High Street. 'I'm going to talk to the coroner's wife.'

• • •

He placed the sword and scabbard on the table. The neatly folded cloak lay next to it. De Harville's horse was in the stable.

'Where is he?' The woman asked. 'Do you know?'

'No, Mistress. I wish I did.'

She seemed to be in complete control of herself, not allowing her face to betray any of her feelings. But inside, he knew her heart would be shrieking. Her fingertips traced the pattern on the leather scabbard.

'Is he alive?'

'Yes, I believe he is.' If they murdered the coroner then they carried even more power than he thought; they were untouchable.

'Can you find him?'

'I'm trying, Mistress. The bailiffs have been looking—'

She cut him off. 'I don't care about them. I need you. He's always said you have a gift for it.'

John reddened. 'With God's blessing we'll bring him home. But at the moment I don't know where else to search.'

She thought for a moment. 'He likes to ride on the far side of the Hipper, upstream.' She paused and cocked her head. 'Of course, he doesn't have a horse right now, does he?'

It seemed like a strange thing for her to say. But he simply replied: 'No, Mistress.'

'Bring him home to me,' she begged. 'Please.'

• • •

All six of the bailiffs were at the Guildhall. A dozen other men had gathered. He knew them all by sight, some to talk to in the marketplace or the alehouse. Walter waited at the back of the room.

'Two men have taken the coroner,' John began. He stared into hard faces, heard the murmuring and the shifting of feet. 'I need you to search in groups of three.'

'Will we find him alive?' someone called.

'I hope so,' John answered quietly. 'We should all pray for that.'

That was enough to quieten them. He gave out the tasks – by the Brampton road, out towards Newbold, others in the direction of Whittington, some following the track out to Bolsover. They'd meet back here at dusk.

Finally, the only one remaining was Walter.

'Come on,' John told him. 'We're crossing the river again.' To where the coroner liked to ride. It was as good a guess as any other. Maybe God would listen to some prayers for once.

• • •

Something had come along here. There was a thin track of dry earth as wide as a man's feet, but the grass on either side had been crushed down. In one spot where damp wallowed up he could make out the print of a horseshoe.

They pressed on. John kept the dagger in his hand, ready for the worst. Walter had his slingshot and pebbles.

A fallow field, empty, only dry earth that showed nothing to give them direction.

'Which way now, John?'

'Straight,' he decided. 'We'll follow the river and see what happens.' If he didn't spot any signs they'd go back and around the field. The riders had gone somewhere, they hadn't vanished off the face of the earth.

There it was. Tall grasses bent and trodden down. He picked up his pace, with Walter keeping step. No talking, eyes on the ground. The river curled around a point. He followed the track until he came to a clearing and stopped at the edge, raising his hand.

De Harville was there, tied firmly to a tree, eyes blindfolded, a piece of dirty linen stuffed into his mouth as a gag. Was this the luck he'd asked for, or did his wife see things? The coroner's head lolled. Jesu, was he alive?

John stood, watching, listening very closely. This might be a trap; the men could have their horses hobbled somewhere out of sight. They would be hidden and waiting. It was an ideal spot, and these were men with patience and experience.

'Slip back and around,' he whispered to Walter. 'A hundred yards or so.' He waited until the lad nodded. 'Then I want you to fire a couple of stones from the shot. Aim them towards the clearing. Hit some trees.'

Walter nodded again and vanished noiselessly into the undergrowth. John stayed still in the cover of a bush. Wait, he thought; another few minutes won't matter either way to the coroner.

Finally came the short crack of stone on wood. Once, twice, three times. He tensed, ready to spot any movement, but there was only a flutter of wings as startled birds rose from the branches. He stood a little longer, then edged along the outside of the clearing until he was behind de Harville.

He counted off the moments. Ten, twenty of them, and then he eased forward into the light, slicing through the ropes that fastened the coroner to the tree. The man collapsed in a heap. Dear God, let him still be alive. He worked the gag out of de Harville's mouth and heard him draw in a sharp breath. Good. John pulled off the blindfold.

The coroner opened his eyes then closed them again. He hadn't moved. But there was no sign of blood on his body. John let out a low whistle. Soon enough Walter was there.

'Help me with him. Let's sit him up, put his back against the tree.'

He fetched water from the river, rubbing it on the man's face to rouse him, letting a few drops sprinkle on his tongue. The man lapped at them eagerly.

'More,' John ordered, and Walter raced down to the bank.

No words, no questions yet. De Harville was alive but he was drained. There were bruises on his face and he winced as John felt his skull.

'Run back to town,' he told Walter. 'Tell whoever you can find. We're going to need a cart out here to take him home.'

• • •

Just the pair of them. The eternal burble of the river, the sound of birdsong high in the trees. The warmth of the sun. On any other day this might have seemed like perfect peace.

He waited, squatting on his heels, carefully watching the coroner's face. There was a thick knot at the back of his head, a match for John's. The man drowsed on. Better for him that way. A few times he began to stir, then settled once more. He didn't seem to be injured, but he'd been out here for a night; God alone knew what had happened to him. Rest was the best medicine now; the tale could wait.

De Harville came to just as John heard the faint rumble of cart wheels in the distance.

'What?' He blinked in surprise. His voice was thick and awkward in his mouth. 'Carpenter?'

'I'm here, Master.'

The coroner gazed around, blinking his eyes and trying to make sense of everything.

'Where are we?'

'By the river. Where we found you.'

The man started to shake his head, as if it might help him remember. His face creased with pain. The cart drew nearer and John saw Walter sitting next to Hugh of Lincoln.

'There were two men…' de Harville began uncertainly. He sat upright. 'My horse.'

'Safe at home, Master, and waiting for you. We'll get you back there.'

John helped the coroner stand. With assistance he pulled him into the back of the cart. They jostled and rolled as it bumped back along the track.

'I can't remember,' he said bleakly.

'You received a note to meet someone.'

'Yes.' The man smiled and reached for his scrip. 'I have it in here.'

But it was gone. All his money, every other item was still there, only the note was missing. They'd been careful, John thought. Men who attended to every detail.

'You must have met them where we found Richard the Salter's body.' He offered the prompt. De Harville smiled again as the image came into his head.

'Yes, I did. A big man. I was asking him what he knew. He told me to stop looking or he'd kill me. The next thing I knew I must have been in the clearing. But I couldn't see anything and I couldn't shout.' He raised a shaky hand to his mouth and traced its outline.

John recounted how they'd found him.

'God was smiling on us,' he finished. 'You might have been anywhere.'

'You always seem to have luck, don't you, Carpenter?' His voice was little more than a soft croak.

No more conversation today, John decided. By morning the coroner might have remembered more. It would all wait.

• • •

'And was he thankful?' Katherine asked as they sat at the table for supper.

'In his own way. We left him in his bed with a flagon of ale beside him. He'll feel better soon enough.'

'And will he stop looking?' she asked tartly.

'You know he won't,' Dame Martha said quietly. 'He's not made that way. People saw him come back in a cart. He's been humiliated and beaten. His honour won't stand for that.'

'Maybe it'll teach him a lesson.' Katherine reached for another ladleful of pottage. Sitting on her lap, Juliana's intent gaze moved from adult to adult as they spoke.

'Martha's right,' John said. 'The only thing it will do is make him more determined.'

'Then good luck to him. Just make sure you're not dragged back into it, husband.'

'I promise,' he told her.

CHAPTER TWELVE

He'd go and see the coroner later in the day, John decided. First he had work to do, money to earn. Back to Cutthorpe with Alan at his side. The leather satchel of tools banged against his hip as he walked.

A final day at the byre, heating and applying the last of the pitch. The whole job had taken longer than he expected. Too long, really. But the result was worthwhile. Cattle would be snug in there during the cold weather. And he knew he'd done a solid job.

He was cleaning up as the steward arrived. The man walked around the building, inside and out, no expression showing on his face.

'It's smaller than it was before,' he complained.

'I explained why,' John reminded him. 'You agreed.'

It looked as if he was ready to labour the point. Then he shrugged and smiled.

'You've done fair work, I'll grant you that. The pair of you,' he added, nodding at Alan. The boy beamed. 'I might have more for you in the autumn.'

'Send word, Master.'

'If we're any of us still alive.' He crossed himself.

The news had been bad that morning. Three more cases, all in one family, just as they were starting to believe the worst had passed. This plague played with their hearts as well as their lives, giving them hope then tugging it away.

'With God's blessing,' said John.

The steward counted out the money and walked back towards his house. Alan began to clean the tools, rubbing them over and over with the oily rag. Tomorrow a new job, something very different. But John was proud of what he'd created here. He'd taken a ruin and made it into something sturdy and worthwhile. With help. Alan's suggestion had made the difference.

For once, it seemed to take no time to reach Chesterfield. He escorted Alan to his door and counted out the pennies the boy was owed. He knew he should go home and wash off the dirt of the day. Instead he crossed the market place to the coroner's house.

The servant didn't want to let him in. It was de Harville's wife who insisted, leading him through to the hall.

'I never thanked you yesterday,' she said.

John shrugged; he never expected real gratitude from this family. 'How is he?'

'Cantankerous.' She allowed herself a fleeting smile. 'He's resting. He wanted to rise this morning but I made him stay in bed.'

Anyone who could exert her will over the coroner had true power, he thought wryly.

'No ill effects?'

'No,' she began. 'The night mares rode, but he seems better today. The wise woman gave him some poppy juice. She said it will help him sleep. I'm grateful to you for bringing my husband back, Master.'

'I found him, that's all. I looked where you suggested. A lucky guess.' He hesitated. 'Next time they'll kill him, Mistress. This was a warning. Persuade him to leave it go.'

'I've tried. He won't.' She shook her head sadly. 'I can command him in some things, but not that. If it's stuck in his head, he'll do it. Could you help him?'

'My wife insists I don't. I'm not as strong-headed as she is.'

'Thank God for sensible women.' She put a hand on his arm. 'You're a good man, John. Bless you.'

• • •

At home he sat in the garden with Katherine by his side. Juliana scrabbled in the dirt.

'Will he really pursue them?'

'I'm certain of it.' John didn't even need to consider his reply. 'He has to. It'll be a matter of pride for him now.'

'Don't do that,' she told Juliana gently, as the child tried to scoop dirt into her mouth, waiting until the girl showed a wide grin and obeyed. 'He'll want you to help. You know that.'

'He has the bailiffs for that. And he can write to the King. He holds the Crown's office.'

'He trusts you. You said his wife told you that.'

'And I repaid it.' He sipped at the ale, eyes following a butterfly on the wing from one flower to another. 'I found him. That's all. She asked if I'd help him find them and I said no. I'd told him these deaths weren't worth my life.'

'Maybe he'll wake in the morning and think the same.'

He gave a sad smile. 'You have more faith than I do. It might save him a lot of pain if he did. But you know what he's like, he's wilful. More than that, he's been humiliated.'

'Don't let him drag you along with him. Please, John.' She tightened her grip around his arm.

But he'd already made up his mind to keep clear of it all. These men were killers. Tangling with them again would be a death sentence. He'd been lucky once; fate would not be so kind a second time.

There'd been one more case of plague, an old man found dead in his home on the Unstone Road. No one had seen him for a few days. When someone called to visit it was too late; the black buboes under his arms and in his groin had burst, leaving the air heavy and stinking. At first none would touch him. Finally a woman came forward from Christian charity and wrapped him in a shroud for burial. He was already in the ground at the churchyard, under a thin covering of earth and lime in the long open grave.

• • •

'A boat?' John asked. 'Why do you want a boat?'

Alan's hands moved rapidly. To sail to the sea, of course. He had to laugh. The boy worked so hard, so often he appeared to be mature that it was easy to forget he was still a child, full of fancies and dreams.

'I've never built a boat. I wouldn't even know how to begin.' Steam the wood for the hull and curve it, he supposed, the way coopers did with barrels. 'Anyway, you need to save your money for tools.'

More swift movements of the boy's hands.

'No, they won't be the same as mine. These are old, you know that.' In time he'd need to replace them and lose the only link to his past. What would he become then? Someone weightless and drifting? Or would family and child give him a new history here?

They sweated all day long, starting to fashion a new table and bench for one of the wealthy houses on Knifesmithgate. It was delicate, exacting work, and the owner demanded carvings on each of the supports.

He left Alan to work on the frame, keeping a wary eye out as he sketched a rough design on the wood in charcoal. It would need someone better than him for a fine finish, but there was no one with that ability in Chesterfield. He'd done this work before, in York, but he knew how crude it appeared next to the masters'.

Gently, John ran his hands over the wood, feeling the way it spoke to him. Then he picked up the thin chisel and worked it in, moving it lightly along the grain, taking no more than a sliver at a time. When Alan stopped to eat, John continued. He had the feel of it now, not just in his head but in his hand, along his fingers. It was as if someone else was guiding him. The boy watched, eyes following every movement, assessing and judging it, working out how he might do it himself.

At day's end John knew he'd made a good start. He cleaned the tools, sharpening the chisels ready for the morning, while Alan ran his fingertips over the carved surfaces.

'How?' he asked with his fingers. 'How do you know what shapes to cut? How do you make them that way?'

'Practice,' he answered. 'The wood tells you what it wants to be. You have to listen. Select the right piece, let it speak to you, then do what it says.'

It made little sense, but it was the only way he could describe it. There was craft, but above all there was patience. The boy had the skill, he just needed to learn how to use it.

He was walking back across the market square, lost in his thoughts, when he was suddenly aware of hooves. Two sets of them. He turned his head towards the sound, one hand reaching for his knife, feeling the panic rise. Had they come back for him?

'Friend, not foe, Carpenter.' The coroner reined in the roan. Behind him, one of the bailiffs tugged on the reins of his own horse, a spavined, unhealthy nag. At least de Harville had someone with him now; he'd learned that much.

'You look well, Master.'

'No lasting damage done,' de Harville said, 'except to my pride.' He smiled ruefully. His sword hung in his scabbard, a dagger on the other side. He wore a quilted jerkin with a jacket of heavy leather on top, never mind that it was a warm day. Better to sweat and stay alive. The bailiff was fully armed, too.

'Sometimes that can be the worst injury.'

'Maybe so. My wife told me what you did. I hadn't thanked you.' He extended a hand and John took it, astonished. The two men shook.

'And what now, Master? Are you still going after them?'

'You ought to know me by now, Carpenter. What do you think?'

'That you'll hunt them.'

The man nodded. 'It's what I've been doing all day. But it's like chasing spirits. They've gone and there's nothing but air remaining.'

'Perhaps they're no longer in Chesterfield.'

'No,' the coroner replied. 'The salter was dead days before they took me. If their business was complete, why were they still here?'

Was there someone else, another man on the list still walking around town? If so, who could it be?

'If that's what you believe, you shouldn't be searching for them. Look for the man they're going to kill.'

'And who's that?' The coroner's lips curled in a smile.

'I've no idea, Master.'

De Harville smiled. 'You could help me look, Carpenter.'

'No. One warning was enough to keep me away.'

For a moment it looked as if de Harville was ready to say more. Anger flickered in his eyes and vanished again.

'As you wish.' He pulled on the horse's reins to turn the animal. 'As you wish.'

CHAPTER THIRTEEN

His hands ached from holding the chisel for so long. For work like this he really needed a proper set of carving tools. Curved and angled blades. But he didn't possess them, didn't even know where he'd find any. He'd have to manage with what he owned.

Pottage for his supper. Patiently, he fed Juliana spoonful after spoonful until the girl turned her head away. He wiped her mouth with a scrap of old linen and gave her a sip of well-watered ale from a cup.

His heart still swelled whenever he saw her. So lovely, so fragile. And on the other side of the table, Dame Martha. His oldest friend in Chesterfield. One at the start of life, the other close to its end.

His wife, her family. *His* family. How had he become so lucky? Pray God that the pestilence took none of them from him. No new cases that day, at least.

• • •

It was the dead of night when he heard the hammering on the door. At first he thought it was a dream, then it came again as he opened his eyes. He slipped down the stairs from the solar, knife in his hand, and drew back the latch.

One of the bailiffs. Unshaven, dirty, carrying his rusted sword in his hand.

'Can you come, Master? Please. The coroner asked for you.'

'What's happened?' As soon as he saw the man's face, John's head cleared of sleep. 'Who?'

'Alfred, Master.'

'Give me a moment.' He held the door wide. 'There's ale and a cup on the table.'

He could make out Katherine's shape in the darkness, sitting up in the bed. Walter and the girls slept on; it would take more than a little noise to rouse them.

'What is it?' she hissed.

'I don't know. One of the bailiffs.' He struggled into his hose, tying them at the waist, then slipping his tunic over his shirt, the leather jerkin on top.

'Be careful.'

'I will.' He kissed her tenderly.

• • •

Torches had been stuck into the earth. Flames burned bright, casting shadows and illuminating a figure on the ground. De Harville stood, wrapped in his riding cloak, three bailiffs close by.

'He's dead, Carpenter.'

They were on the north side of the churchyard, by the site of the weekday market. John knelt. There were wounds on Alfred's arms, one on the cheek, another on his body. From the blood pooled under him, that had been the killing blow.

He was still warm to the touch, as if he might be caught somewhere between the living and the dead. A sword lay near his right hand. In the flickering light John could see blood on the blade; Alfred had given a good fight.

'Has anyone begun asking in the houses by here?' He could see candles burning behind the shutters. People were curious; many would be terrified. 'They must have heard something.'

'Go,' the coroner ordered the men. 'Do what he says.'

He pulled out one of the brands, circling the corpse. If Alfred had wounded someone, there might be a trail of blood to show where he'd gone. But it was hopeless. Too dark now to pick anything out on the ground. They'd have to wait for morning.

John stood. De Harville was waiting. The light picked out the deep furrows in his face. One of the bailiffs remained, the biggest man, a hand on his sword hilt, constantly looking around for any danger.

'It could have been a drunk. He might have broken up a fight. I can't tell from this.'

'No. Alfred was a good swordsman.'

'Someone else was better,' John said emptily.

'It could have been someone who was well-trained.'

It was pointless even to imagine until they knew more. John looked down at the body. Alfred was no more than a handful of years older than himself. Big, powerful, but with a ready grin, willing to laugh at any joke. Married, he remembered, two children. Who'd look after them now?

There was nothing to be done here until it was light. Better to cover the body and send someone to tell his widow. But that was the coroner's job. He could hear men assembling by the church porch, the hue and cry. Not that they'd manage to find anything during the night. They'd blunder around, the way they always did, then claim four pence and ale for their searching.

'I'll come back at dawn,' John said. 'For an hour. Then I have work to do.'

For once, the coroner didn't put up an argument. He merely nodded as if the words had been a fleeting distraction from his thoughts.

• • •

He sat at the table with a mug of ale. His mind was awake; he'd never get back to sleep. It wasn't even worth trying for the short time he'd rest.

'John.' He hadn't heard Dame Martha approach. Her grey hair was hidden under a cap, feet bare on the rushes. 'What's happened?'

He told her and watched as she closed her eyes, mouth moving in a silent prayer.

'Poor, poor man. Do you know who did it?'

He shook his head. He didn't want to talk about it, didn't even want to think about it. Dawn would arrive soon enough.

'I wish you hadn't changed your will,' he said.

'Why?' She cocked her head.

'Because…' Because sometimes the responsibility of a family seemed to overwhelm him. He loved them all more than his own life, but how could he look after them? How could he protect them? He was just one man. To have more piled on top of that felt like a weight he couldn't bear. 'It's too much. It's too generous.'

She smiled under her cap, the lines on her face turning into deep creases. 'You don't think it was generous to offer me a home with you? To have Eleanor and Jeanette to teach and Juliana to love?'

'It just seemed the natural thing to do.' It was the only answer he could give. 'We all care for you. You're part of our family.'

'Then all I'm doing is leaving my house to my family.' There was nothing he could say except accept defeat graciously. Martha might be old but she could still gently outwit him. 'Promise me one thing, John.'

'What?' he asked cautiously.

'That you'll leave this business of the dead men alone. You don't know how scared Katherine is.'

But he did. The fear was there in her eyes and on her face every time she looked at him. He knew.

'All the gold in England couldn't tempt me back there,' he said, and she patted his hand. A mother's gesture. Somewhere off in the treetops an early magpie chattered busily.

'I miss Robert,' Martha said.

'You were the one who wanted him to go.' But he understood what she meant. He'd been the last piece of her childhood here, the one who'd known her back in those days when she was young, without cares or aches. With that severed she must feel lost. She needed him, Katherine, the children, more than ever. 'And you were right. Being at the abbey will bring him peace.'

'The coroner won't give up, will he?' she asked.

'No.'

She sighed. 'He was always a wilful man. This could get him killed.'

'He believes in justice,' John said.

'May God keep him safe.' She turned her gaze on him. 'And you, too.'

• • •

First light had arrived and the sun had risen when he returned to the churchyard. A bailiff guarded the body, a nervous young man who kept his sword drawn and peered around every few moments.

John drew back the sheet covering Alfred. There was no peace on his face, just the pain he must have felt before he died. Five wounds in all, two deep, then the one to his chest that took his life. He'd fought hard before it was over.

The blood had dried to a dark rust colour on his sword blade. From the amount, he must have done some damage. His murderer would need bandages, something to help him heal. Squatting, John tried to pick out blood on the dirt, a trail he might be able to follow.

This time he saw it, flecks here and there leading across the churchyard. He could follow it for a few yards, then nothing. John scoured the area. A pace, parting the grass, kneeling and staring. Finally he found it again, near the barren corner with the open grave for the plague victims. Heavier now, larger drops. But after the wall it vanished, and impossible to follow on the other side. The killer had escaped but he was badly hurt.

The coroner was sitting in the church porch, his guard close by.

'Well?' He raised his head as John entered.

'The murderer can't have gone too far. He was losing blood. What did the people living close by have to say?'

'It seems that Alfred must have seen someone when he was on his rounds. A mother was up tending her baby. She heard him give a challenge, then the sound of fighting.'

'Did she see anything?'

De Harville shook his head. 'Too scared to look.'

'Did anyone peer out of their shutters?'

'Most of them slept through it, Carpenter.'

'Whoever he was, he's lost blood. He's badly wounded. From the look of it he'll need some help. He must have somewhere quite close.'

'Then perhaps we'll find him.' The coroner had a glint of hope in his eyes. 'I could use your help.'

'I've already given it, Master. As much as I can offer. Bringing him to justice is for the hue and cry.' He glanced at the guard. 'And the bailiffs.'

• • •

An hour later he was carving a rose for the table while Alan secured the planks for the top. John sat on his heels and assessed the work he'd done. Country carving, he decided. Rough, fair, but no better than that. No style and precious little skill. It would have no place in a church or a grand house in a city. A true craftsman would have dismissed it as worthless. For here, though, it might suffice, especially after polishing.

Show me, Alan signed with his fingers.

'You need someone better than me to teach this.'

It's beautiful, the boy insisted.

John laughed. 'Come on with your flattery, then. Pass me that other piece of wood. Don't expect much, though.'

• • •

The job was close enough to have dinner in their homes. A break from work that required so much concentration.

He'd barely started eating the bean and bacon pottage when a fist began knocking on the door. Wearily he walked across and opened it. The captain of the bailiffs. His face was bruised but he was smiling.

'Coroner de Harville wants you to come to the jail.'

'I'm eating, then I have more work to do.'

'It's important. That's what he says, Master.' He grinned. 'We found the churl who killed Alfred. In a bad way but he still put up a fight.'

'Good. Why does he want me there?'

'It's not my business to question him, Master. Or yours,' he added as a warning.

John sighed. 'I'll be there soon if it's so important.'

• • •

It was the middle of the day but torches hung on the wall of the jail. The cell lay underground, dank and dark, only a small barred window for daylight. The man lay where he'd been tossed on the straw. One arm looked useless, dried blood caked around a deep cut. He cradled it with his other hand. Blood had dried around his mouth; even injured, he hadn't come easily.

De Harville stood over the man, a look of contempt on his face.

'Does he look familiar, Carpenter?'

'No.' He was a stranger, a big man with a dark, heavy beard. His clothes were patched with dirt, but the surcote looked to be good quality, and the leather of his boots still had a rich glow under the dust. 'Where did you find him?'

'He was hiding in the reeds on the far side of the river. He wasn't happy to see the bailiffs when they discovered him.'

'Is he one of the men who took you?' John asked.

'I was blindfolded. The same as you, Carpenter. I'd need to hear his voice, but he doesn't want to speak.' He kicked the prisoner in the belly. No words, just a grunt. 'Do you think we can make him talk?'

They could. They would. But he didn't want to be here to watch it happen. De Harville would stay. It would help rid him of the humiliation of being taken captive.

'I'm certain you can.' He turned and climbed the stairs back to daylight.

• • •

Throughout the afternoon he couldn't push the man's face from his mind. He knew the coroner needed information. And that the man he was questioning was trained to take pain and punishment. But he had no desire to witness that battle.

His skills seemed to desert him as he tried to carve. Each move felt awkward and wrong. Better to leave it and do something else. Alan looked at him questioningly. John smiled and shook his head. Instead he helped with the joints, making sure all the edges were clean and smooth as they fitted together.

The boy did excellent work. When John checked it, he found it hard to believe the lad was only eight years old. There were men making their living as carpenters who weren't as skilful or as thorough. Yes, he still had plenty to learn, but he'd do that quickly enough. He grinned and tousled Alan's hair.

Tomorrow he'd return to the carving, once his mind was clear again. It would never satisfy a critical eye but it might pass.

'Come on,' he said finally. 'Let's clean the tools. There's nothing more we can do today.'

• • •

'What did the bailiff want?' Katherine asked. She was supervising the girls as they span wool. It wasn't necessary; they knew full well how to do the job.

'They found the man who probably killed Alfred.'

She crossed herself at the name of the dead man.

'Did you see him?'

'Yes. They intended to make him talk. I left.'

She reached across and took his hand, squeezing it tight. 'Do you think they'll succeed?'

'I imagine so,' he answered. He didn't want to think about it. 'I'll go and wake Martha.'

The old woman had started to sleep through the afternoon. She claimed that the summer heat wearied her but he saw through the words. It was age. Bit by bit she was preparing to leave the world.

At first she didn't want to stir and he felt the panic rise in his throat. Then, slowly, she opened her eyes.

'Was I resting long?'

'An hour,' he told her. A lie, of course; it was closer to two. But what did that matter to her?

Without her cap, he could see how thin and wispy her hair had become. It barely covered her skull. But there was still warmth in her smile and a fierce intelligence inside.

'Why did they come for you at dinner? What's happened?'

He told her, seeing her listen intently.

'What will happen to him?'

'I don't know.' Another lie. If he talked, the man would likely die. If he didn't, they'd kill him as they tried to make him speak. Either way he'd become one more corpse for the graveyard.

He helped her sit up. She weighed next to nothing, like a bird in his hands. How much longer would they have her with them, he wondered? Pray God a while yet.

'Any more cases of plague today?' she asked. He didn't know. With everything else happening, he'd never even asked.

No new cases, Katherine assured him with relief; word would have passed around town on the wind. Before bed, she nursed Juliana, holding the child against her breast as they talked. His mother must have done that for him, John thought. Sometimes he believed he could see her face in his mind. But the image would only stay still for a moment, not even long enough to take in all her features. A tender smile, he felt that, and warm dark eyes. But he could never make out the shape of her chin or the colour of her hair. Then, as quickly as it came, it would dissolve like shredding mist, leaving an ache, an awful loss, in the pit of his stomach.

His father, though: he remembered the rough, callused hand that held him so tenderly. The way the man had such patience as he taught him to work wood after seeing that his son had the gift of it. The miles they walked together, hand in hand, going to jobs around Leeds. The village was far smaller than Chesterfield, not enough work in the place to keep a carpenter busy. Sometimes they'd spend half a day walking to a job, work until dark, and then his father would hoist John on to his shoulder for the slow tramp home, and the boy would fall asleep to the reassuring slap of the old leather satchel against his father's hip.

'You're miles away,' Katherine said.

'Just remembering things,' he answered, and started to tell her. But the words grew tangled with his feelings and he faltered.

'They're looking down at you from heaven,' she assured him. 'They're together and they can watch over you. They've done a good job so far, haven't they?' She grinned. 'You have me, you have Juliana.'

He nodded. His throat felt tight, he didn't want to speak out loud. Please God, let it all last, he thought. Let me live long enough to see my daughter grow. Spare us, spare us all. From plague and from men.

• • •

He knew the knock on the door would come, but he didn't know when. He was about to blow out the tallow candle in the solar and settle down to his sleep. The flame guttered and spat, and then he heard it.

'John,' Katherine said. The word was a warning.

'I have to see who's there,' he told her, although he already knew. It was either a bailiff or the coroner.

De Harville stood there, his hood raised against the soft rain that was falling. His face looked gaunt, as if it had been chiselled from stone, not made of flesh.

'Come in, Master, please.'

Always show Christian hospitality. That was what the Church taught.

'Ale?' he asked when they were seated at the table, but the man shook his head.

'He's dead, Carpenter.'

But Alfred's killer was bound to die sooner rather than later; the bailiffs would make sure of revenge for murdering one of their own.

'How did it happen?'

'He tried to escape.' De Harville raised an eyebrow. 'I was there, Carpenter, I saw it. He shouldn't have had any strength left, not after all we'd done.' He shook his head in disbelief. 'But he did. He charged at my men. They didn't have any choice.'

'You have justice for Alfred, then. What did he tell you?'

'Not enough.' Wearily, the coroner ran a hand through his fair hair until it stood on end, as pointed as a cock's comb. 'Nowhere near enough.'

'What did he say?' John kept his voice low. There was no reason to keep the whole house awake.

'His name was Matthew. Fairly well-born – you could hear it in his voice. Schooled in war; he made sure we knew that, and his companions would come for us unless we let him go.'

De Harville snorted. 'Defiant until he died, I'll grant him that. But what did it buy him beyond an early grave?'

'Why was he here? Who was he working for? Did you discover that?'

'No. It didn't matter what we did, he wouldn't tell us. He stood the pain well. He wouldn't break.'

'So you don't know anything more.' It all seemed like a waste.

'A little. Two of them came. He was one of those who took me. Took you, too. And we did force him to admit they know someone here.'

'Who?'

The coroner gave a dark, sad smile. 'You think I didn't try to find out? He refused to say. He died without betraying anyone.'

Maybe Matthew took what little honour he possessed to the grave, but for what? He had met death unshriven, no state of grace. Damned. If he thought that a fair bargain, then he'd deserve what he found.

'You know a little more, at least. But what good does it do you, Master?'

'It tells me how many to look for,' de Harville replied. 'And that I need to be suspicious of everyone in Chesterfield.' He clenched his fists. 'If I could find out who they have here, I could discover some truth.'

'Did Matthew say why they killed Father Crispin and the others?'

'A debt. That was all he'd say. A debt of blood.'

It had proved to be a debt greater than his own life. That was a strong obligation.

'I need your help to find the man in town who's helping them, Carpenter.'

John shook his head. 'I can't, Master. I've made my vow.'

'He has.' They turned at the voice. Katherine, standing at the top of the stairs that led to the solar. She'd pulled a dress over her shift. Her hair flowed free and dark on to her shoulders. 'He made his vow to me.'

'And I made my own vow, Mistress,' the coroner said. 'To find these men. I gave my oath to the King.'

'No one here wants to stop you from that, sir. God and the saints know we all wish you well in it. But my husband is a carpenter, and I love him for that.' There was no tremor in her voice, only strength, belief. Love, he thought. She was fighting for what she needed. 'You use him, Master.' From the corner of his eyes, John saw the coroner open his mouth to speak, but she continued. 'He's done as you asked in the past. He came out to find you when your wife begged. He's been a good servant to you. Like Brother Robert.'

She let that hang like an accusation.

'Is that what you believe, Carpenter?'

'It is.'

'I see.' De Harville stood slowly and gave a small bow to Katherine. 'Forgive me for disturbing your night, Mistress. And Master Carpenter, I wish you well.'

The latch clicked into place behind him and John locked the door.

'Is that the end of it?' Katherine asked quietly. 'Are we free of him?'

'I don't know. Let's hope so. You were very eloquent.'

'I spoke my mind. Nothing more.' She wrapped her arms around her body as if she was cold. 'I've never liked him, ever since I was a girl. He's always been so arrogant. No one's ever stood up to him.'

'You did.'

'Because I love you.'

145

In bed he held her close. For a few minutes she kept shivering, small shudders rippling through her body. Finally she calmed and fell asleep. He lay awake longer, wondering what would happen now.

CHAPTER FOURTEEN

The day dawned dry and clear, with a bright sun to burn the dampness from the ground. Walking across the market square to collect Alan, he felt lighter, happier, a weight gone from his life. And it had. Thanks to his wife, he'd made a true break from the coroner's service.

He carved with pleasure and for once, with some faint skill. Once he'd completed the rough design, he stopped to show the boy how to apply polish to the wood, let it dry and then sand it down smooth again. Why? Alan asked.

'Because we want to give it a beautiful surface,' he answered. 'A hard surface that will last. That's what they're paying for. Besides,' John added with a wink, 'if the table looks good, they might not notice how badly I carve.'

At day's end he felt happy and fulfilled. They'd done a fine day's work. And tomorrow more of the same.

Walking home he noticed Gilbert the shoemaker hurrying along.

'Good morrow, God's blessing.'

'Nothing good about it.' The man paused, looking around as if people might be searching for him. 'My neighbour has the plague now.' He scurried away.

All his exhilaration vanished. It was almost full summer now, and still the plague would neither bloom nor vanish. It nipped at the edges of them, taking people here and there.

Katherine's mouth fell as he told her, and Dame Martha crossed herself.

'Edric lives next door to him,' the old woman said. 'With his wife and five children.'

'But his youngest is only a baby,' Katherine said as she shook her head.

Only June and already the large graves overflowed with the dead. The first, in the empty corner of the churchyard, had been filled in and another, even bigger, dug close by. However much they prayed, whatever they did, everyone in town knew what might happen and made their preparations. The grave-diggers would stay busy this year.

• • •

The days continued. John worked, and on Saturday he went to the weekly market. Now it was almost as busy as it had been before the pestilence came. Folk wanted this and that and the merchants needed to make their money to survive. The plague was here, the guest that refused to depart; by now, people were willing to take their chances.

John bought his good iron nails from the smith from Apperknowle. Katherine walked with Martha, stopping to admire fabrics as John waited, neck craning around for familiar faces. He saw the coroner in the crowd with his wife, his son walking behind, holding on to the nurse's hand.

The man didn't look towards him and John decided to keep his distance. De Harville was still alive. If he'd caught the other killer, then the gossip would have passed around like a wild fire.

Leave it be, he told himself. It's not your business any more. Another smith was offering tools for sale and a chisel caught his eye. It had a beautiful edge to the blade, the handle smooth and easy to grasp. He talked the man down from the price he was asking and counted out his money. From there to the leather worker with his stall in a different part of the market square. The man had a neat leather satchel; he'd noticed it a few weeks before. Plain, simple, but it looked right in a way he couldn't put into words. John hefted it on to his shoulder and knew; the balance was ideal. He paid, put the chisel in the satchel and went to find his wife.

But it was Dame Martha who spoke first.

'I thought you loved your old bag.'

'I do.' He grinned. 'But Alan's going to need something for his tools, isn't he?' He produced the chisel and slid it back down into the leather. 'And something to start. He'll have to buy the rest himself.'

Martha raised an eyebrow. 'That's very generous, John.'

It didn't seem that way to him. It was no more than a small push along the path that would make the boy his living. An encouragement.

• • •

He could see his way to the end of the carving. From a distance people might believe it was a rose. The closer they drew, the crudity of it would be obvious. But Alan thought them the loveliest things he'd ever seen. He traced them with his fingertips and stopped his own work to watch as John put the final touches to the flower.

His fingers moved. Could he really learn to do that? How long did it take to master?

'You can learn it,' John assured him. 'I did. You can probably be better than me.'

But it's beautiful, the boy insisted. All John could do was laugh. He unwrapped the sack he'd carried with him.

'Here, this is for you.'

Alan's eyes widened. He couldn't believe what he saw. For me? he signed.

'Yes. There's something inside.'

The boy lifted the flap and drew out the chisel. He held it tenderly and drew a small finger along the hard metal. Do you mean it, he asked?

'Yes. It's yours.'

Alan thanked him over and over, until John stopped him.

'We still have plenty to do here. Take some wood home and you can practise carving.'

For the rest of the day they worked well. Whenever they took a break to drink, Alan reached out to stroke the leather of his satchel, as if he couldn't quite believe it was real.

They'd done a good job, but there could be no rushing the polishing of a table. Layer after layer of it, allowed to dry and then rubbed down before another coat was added, the same for the legs and the carvings. By day's end he felt satisfied with all they'd done, though it wasn't over yet.

Alan oiled the tools, including his own chisel, and walked home proudly with his own satchel over his shoulder.

'Master,' his mother said, as the boy explained it to her with his signs, 'you shouldn't have done that.'

'He's going to need it, and many more tools.'

'But,' the woman began, 'you're teaching him. You pay him. We can't thank you enough for that.'

'I'm glad to have him, and I make sure he earns his money.' The boy looked up and smiled. 'Use it to buy what he needs. He knows about tools.' It began to rain and he raised the thick hood on his tunic. 'Tomorrow,' he said, lifted a hand and began to stride out for home. With luck he'd reach the house before he was soaked.

He was dashing across the market square when he heard someone call his name. John glanced around. Nobody was there. Strange. He must have imagined it, he decided, and started to run on. Then it was there again. It seemed to come from one of the small gennels across from the Shambles.

He could ignore it or he could investigate. But he knew himself too well; it wasn't in his nature to act as if nothing had happened. He needed to know. Cautiously, he drew his knife.

'Who's there?' he called. But there was only silence. The street was empty as everyone took shelter from the heavy shower. The day was still warm but he felt the prickles of fear crawling up his spine. Go, he thought, walk away. Forget you ever heard anything.

Instead he took a pace forward into the passage and called out again. He tightened his grip on the handle of the blade.

It was gloomy here, full of shadows where a man could hide. He stopped and listened, straining for the merest sound. A few yards away he caught the faint rasp of breath.

'Who are you?'

Still there was no reply. He swallowed hard, feeling the dryness in his mouth. John let a few moments pass, then began to back away. Whatever was here, he wanted no part of it.

'Wait.' The voice was harsh, a rasp. A man, he thought, and no one he'd ever heard before.

'Show yourself,' John said, but there was no movement. 'What do you want?'

'To help you.' It sounded as though the man found it hard to catch his breath.

'Then let me see you like an honest man.'

'I'll stay here.' A grating chuckle. 'Don't come any closer,' he warned as John took a pace. 'I'm armed and I can kill you.'

The easy, throwaway manner of the words were chilling.

'I'll ask once more,' John said. 'What do you want?'

'Don't you want to catch a murderer? He killed the priest, the steward, and the salter. Him and his friend, they could have killed you, too, and that coroner you work for.' A pause so long he wondered if there would be more. 'Don't you want him?'

'It's not my business now.'

'It's always a man's business when someone threatens his life. It's like a noose around his neck. It needs to be cut so you can breathe again.'

The man wanted to tell it all. Let him; John could listen and pass word to de Harville.

'Who are you?'

'Someone who thinks it's time for the blood to stop flowing. No,' he warned, 'I told you, not a pace forward unless you want it to be your last. You want a man called Roland. But when you find him, you'd better make sure he's dead. That's the only justice you'll ever get.'

'Why is he doing this?'

'He has his orders. That's all I'm saying. Turn now, and go.' He waited a moment. 'I said go!'

Out in the street the rain came tumbling down. The encounter seemed like a strange dream, but the knife was in his fist and he could still hear the rough, scratchy voice in his head.

The coroner was in his hall, dictating to a young monk.

'Come to your senses and decided to help me, Carpenter?' De Harville smirked.

'No, Master. I've made my vow and I'm keeping to it. But I've something you might want to hear.'

He recounted the conversation word for word, as if it was burned on his memory. By the time he finished the coroner was sitting up straight.

'That's all? How's that supposed to help me?'

'I'm telling you what he said, Master.' John glanced over at the monk. He was barely more than a novice, with smooth, pale skin. But his face was pale and frightened as he sat with his quill poised above the vellum. 'Don't write this down,' the coroner snapped, and the monk's face reddened in embarrassment.

'I'm John the Carpenter.'

'He's Brother Edmund. Fresh from the abbey. He writes a good hand and he'll learn in time. Now, Carpenter, who was the man who said all this to you?'

'I don't know. I've never heard his voice before, I'm sure of that. He stayed in the shadows so I couldn't see him at all, but he spoke like someone who could kill without it troubling him too much. He said there had been enough bloodshed.'

'Was he local?'

'He was no one I knew.' How many people lived in Chesterfield? Surely he'd heard every one of them speak in his time here? But this man had a voice that sat in his mind, one he'd know again in an instant. And Roland. The man had said to search for Roland. There was no one of that name here, not that he remembered.

'You've told me now, Carpenter. You've done your duty.' He said the word with a sneer, as if duty wasn't enough.

'Then I wish you well of the day and godspeed, Master.'

The rain had drifted to a misting drizzle, barely enough to dampen his face as he walked back to Saltergate. In the house everything felt alive and joyful. The girls were playing, done with their spinning and their lessons. They were trying to teach Juliana to say 'Mama.' She made sounds, some that resembled words. Something that could have been mama. It would come in time, then the phrases and sentences and questions would all tumble out, one after another. One more miracle in this world. And another: no cases of plague that day.

After supper he took Walter aside, out into the garden. He could hear the laughter and the women's voices from inside.

'You know all the people in town, don't you?'

The boy looked surprised. 'Some of them, I suppose,' he answered.

'Is there a man called Roland?'

'There are two of them, John,' Walter replied after a little thought. 'Why do you want to know?'

'It's just something I heard,' he lied. 'Nothing important. Can you tell me about them?'

'There's a Roland in the Shambles. He's an old man.' Old could mean anything to someone so young. 'And there's another one who lives on the Brampton Road. I've never spoken to him.'

'The second one – what does he look like?'

'He's big. He has dark hair. And a scar on his face.' With a fingertip he traced a line down his cheek. 'Right there.'

'Do you know much about him?'

'Has he done something, John?'

'No.' He smiled. 'It's a name that came up. I was curious.'

'I think it must be about three years since he came here.' Walter looked back into his memory. 'Somewhere close to that time. Folk say he can have a temper on him.'

'Does he have a family?'

Walter frowned. 'I've never heard of one.'

'Thank you.' He knew enough now. Here for three years. Long before Crispin. Before the salter. Since he lived away from town, not so many in Chesterfield would know him. And a scar… there were many ways to get those, but battle was certainly one. It was food for thought.

'Are you brooding, husband?'

Katherine came out into the garden. He was standing, thinking. The earth was dark from the rain and drops had gathered on the shoots and young plants. It was full night now but the moon was up, throwing out its light.

'Not really.' He put his arm around her shoulders and told her about his strange encounter. Her body stiffened a little as she listened. 'I went and told the coroner. It's up to him now.'

'I heard you. You were asking Walter about someone called Roland.'

'I was curious. I'm not going to do anything about it.'

'De Harville can find out for himself. The bailiffs are sure to know the man.'

'Yes,' he replied gladly.

• • •

More time polishing the wood, working the rag into all the crannies of the carving. After that, all they could do was sit and wait for it to dry.

Show me how to carve, Alan signed. He'd carried his satchel proudly to the job and now he reached inside for the chisel. John laughed. Why not? They had nothing better to do.

'All right. Bring me those two small blocks of wood over there. First, though, you need to know what you're carving.' The boy nodded eagerly. 'You start by making a design, like this.' He drew the outline of a flower with a piece of charcoal. 'You try it.'

Alan might have had a feeling for wood that ran deep in his bones, but he couldn't draw. He looked at what he'd done and compared it to John's, then his mouth set in frustration. Perhaps he was too young. Or it could be that he had no talent for it. No matter.

'Go ahead and use what I've done,' John said. 'You need to scoop out between these lines so they look like petals.' He demonstrated, then handed over the wood. 'Take things very slowly and carefully. Carving needs patience.'

An hour later the boy had finished. It was a first attempt, crude and awkward. But had his own work been any better when he was young? He'd been lucky, a carver in York had shown him and helped him.

'That's very good,' he said and Alan beamed at the praise, although doubt still shone in his eyes. 'I mean it. You've made a start. Now we have to carve the back of the petals. Make sure your edge is very sharp.'

He'd completed three of them by the time the polish had dried. One final coat, John decided, and tomorrow they'd attach the legs to the table. Then it would be done, and on to the next job. There was little chance to grow bored in this work. Always something different, always another problem to solve.

'Take that home and work on it,' John suggested. 'Give it to your mother when you've finished. She'll love that.'

CHAPTER FIFTEEN

A fair morning, just a few clouds drifting high in the sky turning a brilliant pink in the early sun. John stood in the garden with a piece of bread and a mug of ale. The air was still cool, hardly a breath of wind stirring.

He'd slept fitfully, troubled by something. But only now could he see what it was. He needed to tell the coroner about Roland living out towards Brampton. Yes, Katherine was right, the bailiffs should know the man. Yet he felt the responsibility like a weight around his neck.

By the time he gathered his satchel of tools he knew what he had to do. Men were up and around on the way to their labours, the forge or the field. He turned into the yard by de Harville's house. The man was already up and around, supervising as the groom saddled his roan.

'You've checked his hooves? Last time there was a stone.' He turned at the sound of John's feet. 'God's grace, Carpenter. I hadn't expected to see you here again.' A haughty look.

'I have more information for you, Master.' He passed on what Walter had said about Roland.

'I've never seen the man. I'll have the bailiffs bring him to me later.' With that, he looked at the groom, who laced his hands together. The coroner put one foot in them and pushed himself up into the saddle. A small tug on the horse's reins and he was gone.

So much for good deeds, John thought as he walked to collect Alan. The boy was waiting, eager to go. Together they inspected the table, the surface shining, feeling like the finest silk. It was ready.

The carvings on the feet looked crude and awkward to his eyes, but the boy loved them. He brought out his own effort; he'd worked on it before sleeping.

The shape was there, very rough and uneven. But it was a start and Alan was proud of it, so John praised it carefully. There would be other chances for him to practise if he wanted.

'Let's put this table together,' he said.

Everything had to be perfect, and handled gently. Alan wanted to help, but this demanded delicacy. If anything went wrong, any mistakes, John only wanted to blame himself. The boy could hand him screws and trim the wooden plugs.

The work took three hours, measuring then measuring again, testing and finally drilling the holes for the screws. Eventually, though, it was done and he gave the table a final wipe with his rag to remove the last of the sawdust. Clean up, sweep, and then he could invite the master and mistress of the house to inspect it.

They approved. The man kept running his fingertips over the surface in amazement while the woman admired the carvings. They paid willingly for the work, with two extra pennies as thanks. Then it was time to clean the tools they'd used.

Only half the day had passed but there was no sense in beginning anything new. Tomorrow would be soon enough for that.

He ambled through the last of the weekday market. Traders were packing away their wares and counting their money, hoping it was enough. Two chickens packed in a wooden cage stared at him.

It was rare for him to come here; usually he was busy working during the day. This was a place for the goodwives to strike their bargains and gossip together. But few of them remained, gone home to their chores and their dinner.

A few yards away, inside the church, the sickly sweet smell of incense seemed to cling to the stone. He crossed himself, then knelt and prayed, offering up his thoughts for those who'd died of the plague so far.

He'd heard no word of more victims as he wandered through town. That was a blessing, although he knew it couldn't continue. The pestilence wasn't done with them yet. Like a cat playing with a trapped mouse, it gave them hope then wounded again. More would perish, and no one knew if their name was on that list.

Only home was a constant comfort, he thought as he walked through the door. The empty pottage bowls were still on the table. Dame Martha was sitting on the bench and talking earnestly while Katherine listened. Juliana was stacking her blocks under the supervision of the girls. The only person missing was Walter and he was rarely here these days. He had a life that was all his own, always off working or with his friends.

His wife smiled to see him.

'The food's still warm if you're hungry. We've only just eaten.'

He realised his belly felt empty and nodded.

'This is a short day for you, John,' Martha said.

'We finished the job. A few hours break seemed like a good idea. What were you talking about?'

For a moment she looked down at the table, then raised her head again.

'The house on Knifesmithgate. The one that will be yours.'

He frowned, confused. 'What about it?'

'You remember that William the Merchant has leased it?'

'Of course.' One of those who'd come to Chesterfield in the last year. The man had gone off on business before the plague arrived, and they still awaited his return.

'His wife came to see me today. She had word from the north. Her husband is dead.'

'Dead? What happened?' For a moment he wondered if William had been murdered.

'An accident', she said. 'His horse stumbled and he fell. He broke his neck.'

Without thinking, John crossed himself.

'What is she going to do?'

'Go and live with her parents. They have a small manor near Locksley.'

'Then what will she do about your house?' he asked.

'That's what we were discussing. I thought we could move there.' She waved a hand. 'You know it's bigger than this place. And you made sure it was in good repair.'

That was true. There would be more room for them all; a larger garden, a grander solar for sleeping.

'What do you think?' he asked Katherine.

'I like the idea,' she said as she returned with a full bowl and a wooden spoon. 'What do you say, husband?'

'Do I have a say?' John said with a grin. 'It sounds as if you've already arranged it all. But yes,' he looked around the table, 'we'll be happy there.'

• • •

'What is it?' John asked as he looked at the shape that Alan had carved in the lump of wood. A bear, the boy signed. I've heard about bears in stories.

It was… something. He'd seen the chained bears in York, huge beasts with fur and claws and sad, pitiful eyes. He doubted Alan had ever laid eyes on one. This was a child's imagination, just a general shape of curves and lumps.

'It's good,' he said with a smile and a nod. 'You like carving, don't you?'

Alan's head moved up and down quickly. But the boy liked everything to do with wood. This was just another fancy; it would pass soon enough and he'd come back to the rest of the work.

'Today we work on the Guildhall,' John said, and Alan's eyes widened in astonishment. 'Nothing that important. It's just more of the work we're used to doing.'

Standing at the west of the market square, it was a half-timbered building. Two storeys with a glazed window upstairs, small mullions joined with lead. That was where they'd be working, with the clerk forced to move his desk so they had room. The sill under the window had rotted and needed to be replaced.

It was going to be a difficult job, John had known that as soon as he saw it. The only way to do it was remove the entire window and frame, then rebuild everything. When he first looked at the job, he suggested replacing all the wood in the frame, but the town leaders weren't willing to go that far: it was too expensive. On their heads be it, he thought as he took out the glassed windows and leaned them carefully against the wall.

He explained each step to Alan as he worked; the boy was too small to help him with this. But he was skilled enough to start cutting and shaping the new sill. A breeze blew through the gap, easing the heat of the day, but he was still sweating as he began to dismantle the frame.

Dinnertime, and there was progress. But he was hungry and thirsty. Alan's work was taking form, but they'd leave the details until the sill was in place.

'Come on,' John said, 'let's go to the pie shop on Low Pavement.'

It was a treat for the lad, something hot in his belly. Working men stood outside, dusty, hair damp and matted from their labours. He saw Henry the Mason, still covered in dust.

'God's peace to you,' John said as he passed Alan a coin and sent him in to buy two of the pies. The scent of spiced meat and hot pastry filled the air.

'How's that lad?'

'Talented and a good worker.' They laughed; both knew the two often didn't go together. 'How's your business?'

'Fair.' The smile faded from his face. 'Have you heard the news?'

'What?'

'Four down with the plague today. Two different families, neighbours on Beetwell Street.'

Poor souls. The mood had soured; they ate with occasional glimmers of talk, then dispersed. A few doors down he bought a mug of ale for himself, another of small beer for the boy.

Will the plague ever end? Alan asked with his fingers. How could he answer a question like that? God made the decisions, but often it seemed as if he'd turned his back on the world and left them to whatever might happen.

During the afternoon John removed the shutters and eased out one side of the window frame. It took time; this had been built well. If the lintel was equally firm there'd be no need to remove it, he thought. He was teasing the wood away from the wall when he heard men talking as they passed below.

The voice chilled him. It was the one who'd lured him into the passage, the one who'd told him about Roland and threatened to kill him.

John leaned out. There was little to see beyond a pair of figures dressed in green jerkins and hose. He couldn't see either face.

'Keep working,' he told Alan. 'I'll be back soon.'

He hurried down the stairs and out into the street. The men were thirty yards ahead, paying no attention to anything else. John kept his distance, trying to be invisible, walking with his head down and his shoulders hunched.

This was the man. There could be no mistaking that rasp. Yet here he was, strolling around Chesterfield as if he had nothing to fear, as if he owned the town. It would help the coroner to know who the man might be, where he was going.

Their path took them by the churchyard wall. Walter was there, talking to a girl whose face looked familiar. It took a moment to place her: the servant from the salter's house. John raised a finger to his lips and moved past them. In an instant Walter was beside him.

'What are you doing, John?'

'Do you know those men ahead of us?'

The lad shook his head.

'One of them, he told me about Roland. I'd like to know who he is.'

They were on the Unstone Road, leaving town. There were few travellers on the road. To follow would be too obvious, too open.

'Do you want me to see where they go?'

'How?'

Walter smiled as if the answer was obvious.

'I can go through the woods.' He gestured to the trees that grew on either side of the road.

'Be careful,' he warned. 'Don't let them see you.'

'Don't worry, John.'

He slipped into the undergrowth. In no more than a few heartbeats he was out of sight and silent.

Jesu, but it was stupid. In his head he knew that. It was vain. He should have simply let the man go; it wasn't his business any more. But his heart spoke different words. This wasn't any kind of involvement, he told himself. Nothing more than seeing and hearing and then passing all that to the coroner.

Thoughtfully, John returned to the Guildhall. Alan gave him a questioning look.

'Business,' he explained. 'Someone I wanted to see.' It was truth of a sort, enough to satisfy the boy.

He continued working, but his heart wasn't in it any more. He was willing time to pass, so he could sit in the garden on Saltergate with Walter and hear where the men had gone. But that would happen, that would happen, he told himself. Patience.

He tried to let other thoughts fill his mind. Moving to Martha's old house. It wasn't far, no more than a few yards, but it would still be a big job. Katherine and her family had accumulated so much. So many chests full of this and that. What about the furniture? What about the garden his wife had planted? The thoughts occupied him as his hands moved without thinking. The tools felt so familiar, so natural, that they might have been part of his flesh.

Another hour and the remaining side of the frame was out. The fit was very tight; he'd been forced to use a chisel and work slowly, painstakingly. But the lintel held in place well; that was one job less.

There was time enough to make sure the new sill was the right size. One or two small adjustments, but Alan had done his work well. They'd need to make more tomorrow as everything was put in place, but that was fine. It was part of carpentry.

'You can't just leave a hole in the wall like that,' the clerk complained.

'It's what we have to do, Master,' John told him. 'Weigh down your documents, although there'll be no rain tonight.'

'What if someone climbs through the window?'

'You have the bailiffs below. No one would be that stupid.' He winked at Alan. Clumsily, the boy winked back.

• • •

Finally, he was home. The women were eagerly discussing all the details of the move. That was fine. He'd let them work it out and just lend his strong back to the cause. They'd have their way no matter what he suggested.

Walter hadn't returned yet. Every few minutes John looked to the door. Finally, just before supper, he arrived, grinning and happy. The family ate, all the talk of the new house and what might go where and what they'd do with this one.

It seemed to drag on and on, until finally the girls collected the plates. John refilled his mug of ale. With a look at Walter, he walked into the garden. Almost dusk, and still balmy, the June air warm against his skin. This was the beauty of summer, the evenings that seemed to spin out forever, as if daylight didn't want to leave.

Then the lad was next to him. Every day he was a little taller, John thought. When would he stop?

'Did you have any luck?'

'Yes, John. They never knew I was there.'

He'd had moments of worry that Walter might be discovered. But even if they'd seen him, he knew how fast the boy could run. After all, that was part of delivering important messages around town. They couldn't have caught him.

'Where did they go?'

'Just beyond Unstone. There's a house along a track to the right of the road. Before Dronfield.'

He'd passed it several times; he could picture it in his mind. A squat, solid building of dark stone on enough of a rise to look down on the road as it went by.

'Thank you. You've done very well.' He brought a coin from his scrip but Walter shook his head.

'I don't need to be paid for that,' he said seriously, sounding so mature and considered. Then his face split into a child's grin. 'I enjoyed it.'

'I'm grateful.'

'I'll do more if you wanted, John.' There was a hopeful look in his eye.

'Did you get a look at the men?'

'No. They were always in front of me.'

That wasn't important. It was enough to know where they'd gone. In the morning he'd tell the coroner. From there the man could follow the trail himself.

'You look satisfied, husband.'

Lost in his thoughts, he'd never heard Walter leave or Katherine appear at his side.

'I am.' He put an arm around her shoulder. 'Tell me, what do you want to do with this house once we leave?'

'Nothing until next spring.' Her answer surprised him. The year was only half-done. 'I thought we could clean it properly, put on new limewash. There are shutters that need to be mended, small things.'

He knew. All the jobs he'd put off as he earned a living.

'And what about after that?' He'd taken her gentle reproach for what it was.

'Lease it to someone,' she replied without hesitation. 'Then we'll have rent money every quarter day.'

It made sense. Chesterfield had been good to him. But there would be slack times in his trade. To have the assurance of money coming in would be a blessing.

He was quiet for a long time, then said, 'What about the pestilence?' No one had mentioned it over supper. All the chatter had been plans and happiness.

'We've already said everything we can, over and over.' She had the weight of sorrow in her voice. 'All we can do is trust to God.'

And hope He listened, John thought.

• • •

'For someone who wants nothing to do with me you've become a regular visitor here.' De Harville's voice curled with the relish of triumph. 'Or perhaps wood is too boring for you?'

He turned his head towards the corner where Brother Edmund appeared to be sleeping. His chin rested on his chest.

'God save us from lazy monks,' de Harville muttered. 'Even in his dotage, Robert could usually manage to stay awake.' He kicked the table and Edmund's head jerked up as he blinked his eyes. 'Now, what do you want, Carpenter?'

He recounted the tale and the way Walter had followed the men, seeing the coroner grow more interested with each word.

'You're absolutely certain this was the man who told you about Roland?'

'I am. There was no mistaking that voice, Master.'

'It seems I'd better visit this house and make sure I come back with some truth.' He smirked. 'You've brought me more since you stopped working for me than when I was paying you.'

'May it help you, Master.'

• • •

'What are we doing today?' Alan signed with his fingers.

'You might not want to come with me,' John told him. With the table complete, there were other jobs waiting, enough to keep them busy past harvest. But Dame Martha had told him about a man who lived on his own in a small cottage. Once he'd been tall and broad, but life had whittled him down. He was old now, she said, older than her. He'd lost all three of his sons in the Great Pestilence, his wife and daughter a few years later. Now he was alone and withered. His house was tumbling down and he no longer had the strength or the money to do anything.

He understood what she was asking when she told him, and today he'd do what he could. He had wood left from other jobs. He had his skill and his tools.

'Today is Christian charity,' he said to the boy. 'No payment, but good for the soul. But if you don't want to come, I understand.' How could an eight-year-old child realise what a good deed meant?

'If you're working, I'll come with you.' Alan's fingers moved quickly. He hadn't even needed to think before answering.

• • •

The house needed more than they could manage in a single day. Still, he thought as he gazed around the small single room, they could make a good start. Tom, the old man, sat in the corner, hardly aware they were in his home, far away in his own lost world. If he'd once been a strong, powerful man, now he was a husk of that.

This was a chance to trust some of the work to the boy. Alan had learned a lot; this would give him the opportunity to prove himself.

'The shutters on the windows need tightening. Can you start with those?' Immediately Alan was at work.

The door hinges were old; the screws all needed to be replaced. But the frame was sound; that was good. The roof beam sagged with age; there was nothing he could do about that. It would last until Tom was dead. At least they could make sure he'd spend a warm winter.

Each job seemed to reveal another. John swept the old, rotting rushes from the house. Better a bare floor than something that nursed rats and God alone knew what else. One of the goodwives could bring Tom something sweet-smelling.

By dinner he was sweating, stripped down to his hose and a soaked linen shirt. There were old cobwebs in his hair and dirt caked in his fingernails. Alan worked more slowly, taking his time to make sure everything was just right. The boy had a look of fierce concentration on his face. He'd kept going without a break.

'Come on,' John said. 'We both need to eat.' He put his tools into the satchel and slung it on his shoulder. Another lesson his father had taught him: the tools went wherever he went.

Alan seemed overwhelmed by the group around the table: the girls, Dame Martha, Katherine and Juliana. The boy ate quickly, with his head down, staying close to the only one here who could understand what his fingers said. The girls kept talking to him, puzzled when he didn't answer. John tried to explain that he couldn't speak, but their only response was to wonder why not. They couldn't understand that he'd been born that way.

Alan seemed relieved to leave, to be back doing something he understood and loved. He worked hard all through the afternoon, moving steadily along the tasks John had set. Still Old Tom said not a word. Sometimes he'd raise his head and stare at them without recognition. Then it would fall again and he'd drift off to his dreams of the past.

As they cleaned their tools, John knew he'd barely touched the surface of the work that was needed here. The real kindness would be tearing the house down and building something new. Still, they'd managed to take care of the worst. It was a start, but no more than that. He'd helped a little.

Are we going back there tomorrow? Alan asked as they walked home.

He knew that the boy liked working without supervision, to be allowed to do a thorough job on his own. It made him feel he'd achieved something.

'No. We have money to earn. But we'll return in time and do more.'

• • •

Perhaps he should have felt the warmth of charity in his blood. But as he opened the door to his house on Saltergate, the only sense was frustration. Tom's house needed a week of work, maybe more than that, and he had a living to make; he couldn't spare all that time. The man had probably never even known they were there.

He strode past the screen and into his hall, stopping short when he saw Brother Edmund on the settle, cradling a cup of ale as he talked to Katherine and Martha. From the back came the sound of the girls playing in the garden, then Juliana's happy screech.

'Brother,' he said in surprise. 'Welcome.'

The monk looked flustered, his young face colouring as if he'd been discovered doing something wrong. He stood quickly.

'Master. The coroner asked me to come and find you. Your wife and the good dame said you'd be home soon.'

'Sit,' John insisted. 'What does de Harville want?'

'He wants to see you. He went out to that house.'

'I'll be there soon. First I need to wash.' He held up a hand to show the dirt and sawdust. 'We'll walk back together.'

• • •

'How do you like Chesterfield?' John asked as they strode out. He felt refreshed by the cold water. If his skin didn't shine, then at least he was cleaner and cooler.

'It seems very big,' Edmund replied doubtfully. 'I keep losing my way. And there's the church with that spire.'

He laughed. 'This is a small place, Brother. I lived in York, if you want large. They have churches on almost every corner there.'

Edmund's eyes widened, as if he couldn't imagine such a place. He was the second son of a small landowner, he said, destined for the church from the moment he was born. But he was content with his life, he told John with a smile.

'I'll become used to the coroner's ways.' He sounded less sure of that.

'Did you talk to Brother Robert before you left the abbey?'

'Yes. He gave me advice. He's a gentle old soul, isn't he?'

'Yes. People here liked him. But I'm sure they'll feel that way about you in time.'

'I'm only here for a year. The abbot assured me.'

John raised his eyebrows. 'Have you told de Harville?'

'No,' Edmund said, and a hint of mischief crossed his face. 'Do you think I should?'

'Perhaps not.'

• • •

'Master. You wanted to see me?'

'That's right.' The coroner speared a piece of cold meat from a plate and ate it as he paced around the room. His hunting dog sat, watching him carefully, ready to pounce on any fallen scraps. 'I went to that house and took two of the bailiffs.' He snapped his fingers. 'I thought you might like to see what we found.'

The door opened and the man was pushed in, almost stumbling. His wrists were firmly bound with rope and his face covered in bruises and cuts. He'd been questioned and beaten to make him answer.

The figure had dark, curly hair, a patched tunic that was smeared now with dirt and blood. His hose were ripped at the knee and the soles of his boots were coming away from the uppers. Not a knight. Definitely not a rich man.

One of his eyes was swollen shut, but the other held a defiant glare. He was the type who'd always look as if he needed a shave, the dark stubble on his cheeks ready to sprout into a beard within hours.

'Do you know him, Carpenter?'

'No. I've never seen him before.'

'His name's Malcolm. He didn't want to come with us. The bailiffs had to persuade him.' He stared at the man. 'Speak.'

Malcolm let out a blast of curses until one of the bailiffs slapped the back of his head. John didn't know the man and he certainly didn't know the voice. He'd heard the accent before, though, when he lived in York.

'Familiar, Carpenter?'

'No. But he's from the border country. Up towards Scotland.'

'Is he now?' The coroner threw down the rest of his meat and the dog jumped on it, tearing it apart in his jaws. 'Where this might have all started five years ago.' He stroked his chin and looked at Malcolm again. 'What do you know about that?'

But the man stood with his back straight and his head high, saying nothing.

'Take him away and find out,' de Harville ordered. The bailiffs pushed him out of the room. 'Jesu, he sounds more like an animal than a man. But I suppose it's all you can expect up there.' He turned. 'You did well to spot that. How did you know?'

'I've met others from the area.'

'Maybe we'll get to the bottom of this after all.' His eyes shone. 'You keep the vow to your wife and I don't have to pay you. A good bargain, isn't it, Carpenter?'

John smiled. 'I wish you joy, Master.'

• • •

It kept his promise. Or did it? He'd been happy to let it all go, so glad to see the back of it and feel safe again. He could still feel the prick of the knife against his neck in the clearing and smell the sour breath of the man who held it. But he'd had no sense of being followed or watched since then.

He would have walked away from every part of it. But it kept returning to him. The man in the shadows on the lane. And hearing that voice again, he needed to know its owner and what it meant.

'John.' There was sadness in Katherine's voice. There were out in the kitchen, a distance from the house. She was kneading dough for tomorrow's bread, ready to leave it over-night to rise. 'Brother Edmund told us what happened. Why did you have to bring Walter into things?'

'He was safe, I made sure of that.' Even if they'd spotted him, the lad could lose them in the woods and outrun them.

Her fists were bunched, resting in the bowl. 'Why did you even need to know?' she asked

How could he explain it? That understanding seemed like the only way out of the spider's web that was all around him? It would never make sense to her; he wasn't sure it did to him.

'I'm trying to keep us all safe.'

She stopped, hands still deep in the dough, and gave him a sharp look.

'How?'

'As long as the killer is out there, we're in danger. All of us.'

'But—'

'I know what they said.' He placed his hands lightly on her shoulders. 'And I know he hasn't returned. As long as he's out there, though, we can never feel secure. I can't do anything about the plague. And I won't go up against these men, who-ever they are. I'm not going back on that. No risks. But small things…'

She breathed in and out a few times and started to push down, slamming the bread against the wooden board.

'Fine.' No anger, just acceptance. 'As long as it's nothing more than that.'

He kissed the back of her neck. Her skin was sweaty and he tasted salt.

'It won't be.'

CHAPTER SIXTEEN

A new day and the summer sun shimmered in the sky. The road was dry and dust rose with every footstep. They were walking out along the Sheffield Road. Not too far, barely a mile. The fields were divided into their strips, so many green now and fertile. A few, dotted around, were brown and fallow, resting for a year.

Alan had been full of questions and suggestions. Where were they going? What work were they going to do? Would there be more jobs like working for the old man yesterday?

'I don't even know if there's a name for where we're going,' John answered; he'd never heard one, anyway. 'The steward on the manor has some work for us. And yes, we'll do more charity work in time, I promise. Not often, though. We have to earn money, remember?' He smiled. Boys, always wanting to know everything.

The work was on the manor house, preparing it for a visit of the owner.

'He'll be here in a fortnight,' the steward said as he fussed around them. 'If everything's not right he could dismiss me.'

It wasn't a large house, not much bigger than any others around. Enough room for a family and perhaps one servant.

'When was he last on the manor?' John asked.

'Two years,' the steward answered, distracted as a small shape moved under the old rushes on the floor. 'He spends most of his time elsewhere.'

'How many manors does he own?'

'Six. He'll be staying here until they cut the grass in the fields.'

Late July, John thought. He'd be in the house for a few weeks.

'Leave it with us, Master. We'll have it fine for him.' The wood, at least. As to the rest, that was beyond his skills. He could see mortar crumbling between the stones on the walls; that would need a mason.

John walked around the outside, Alan at his side. In his head he made a list of the tasks: tighten the door on the kitchen building and a new shutter for the window. Trim the back door to the house where it stuck against the step. Fresh skirting in one of the bedrooms. Tighten all the shutters and replace two floorboards in the solar. It wasn't so much.

'What did you see?' he asked the boy. By now Alan should be able to spot things that were needed. He had noticed every task. It was enough work to keep them busy for a few days.

Once he began it was like falling into a dream, a reminder that he was born to do this job. Time passed without him even knowing as he became absorbed in his tasks. When Alan tapped him on the shoulder to check something he'd completed it came as a sudden awakening, cold water on his head.

'That's very good,' he said at the way the boy had replaced the skirting board. A fine fit, flush and smooth, all well-finished.

Come evening, they'd made a solid start on it all. As they walked back, the spire grew taller with every footstep and he felt happy, still brushing the sawdust off his clothes.

• • •

'Friend Malcolm still doesn't want to talk,' the coroner said. 'And when he does I can't understand his heathen tongue.'

A message had been waiting when John arrived home: de Harville wanted to see him. He'd let it linger until he'd eaten his supper, famished after a long day of work. Only then did he slip his good tunic over his linen and walk to the High Street. The man didn't own him; he could wait. He wanted time with his family. After the recent shower of plague, today had brought no more, and another of those who'd come down with it had survived – one more miracle to be celebrated, if not understood.

He could hear a child wailing up in the solar as the nurse persuaded the coroner's son reluctantly to bed. After a moment the crying and shouting ended abruptly.

'Do you understand how he speaks, Carpenter?'

'Not very well.' In York he'd talked with one or two who had that accent, but even then he'd had difficulty following the words. And that had been long ago.

'I'd like you to try.' De Harville paused. 'I'd be grateful.' He smiled. 'I'd pay for your time, of course.'

This was new. Greasing him with kindness and the offer instead of demands and orders. He considered the idea.

'I'll give him a few minutes. He's in the jail?'

'One of the bailiffs will be waiting.'

Better a bailiff than the jailer. That old sot had been unwilling to do anything more than necessary.

• • •

The brand in the sconce flickered patches of light around the cell, the flame jumping and shifting. Malcolm's wrists were in chains. There was enough room for small movements but the chain was bolted to the floor. Even so, the bailiff remained in the room, silent in the doorway with a hand on his sword hilt.

John handed the prisoner a mug of ale and let him wet his throat.

'Your name's Malcolm?'

'Aye.' The voice was dry as gravel.

'Where are you from?'

'Otterburn.'

'I don't know it,' John admitted.

'It's only a small place. North of Newcastle.' There was a glint of humour in his eye. 'You know *that* area, do you?'

He needed a few moments to make out the words and understand them.

'I've never been but I knew men from there when I was in York. What are you doing down here? It's a long way from home.'

'Trying to make a living. I've a family back there if the Lord's been kind enough to spare them.'

'What's your trade?'

'This and that.' He shrugged. 'Whatever needs doing, I can turn my hand to it. Not afraid of hard work.' He held up his hands. Under the dirt his palms were heavily callused.

'The men who came to see you. There were two of them.'

'Met him in the alehouse. He can understand what I say, like, so we started talking. Wanted to offer us a job.'

'Doing what?' John asked.

'He didn't say.'

That wasn't true and they both knew it. But he'd leave it be for now.

'How long have you been down here?'

'A little while now. Why?'

'I just wondered.'

A little while could cover a wide span of time. Anything from a year to a few weeks.

'This man had spent time up where you're from?'

'Aye, that's what he told us, like. He seemed quite canny.'

'What did he do up there?'

'I never asked.' Another lie. He'd want to know; anyone would, it was only natural.

'What do you know about nalbinding?'

'I've never heard the word. What is it?' But his answer came too quickly. Another lie.

'What do you know about something that happened in the borders five years ago? The way I heard things, a lord was killed.'

Malcolm raised his head enough to look into John's face. 'Plenty of men die up there. Honest men keep their heads down, stay quiet and try to stay alive. It's one good reason to leave.'

'And were you an honest man?'

That brought a fleeting smile. 'What do you think, like?'

'I think there's more you haven't said than you've spoken.'

'Happen there is. But I'll give you an answer. I'm a man who's been honest and not. Like everyone else on this earth.'

With that he sat back, leaned his head against the stone wall of the jail and closed his eyes. There'd be nothing more out of his mouth tonight.

John climbed the stairs into the long evening light. After the cell it seemed as bright as midday.

'Could you really understand that barking?' the bailiff asked.

'Some of it. You might as well tell the coroner that Malcolm doesn't want to say much.'

• • •

Back to work on the manor house. It seemed too small for any lord, but that wasn't for him to judge. With Alan at his side they worked through the day, stopping only to eat their dinner in the shade of a broad oak.

Nobody had whispered of more plague as he walked through Chesterfield that morning. All those it had taken were dead and in the ground, their bodies slaked with lime and dirt. No one had an explanation for why two had survived. They weren't especially godly folk. Just lucky to be spared.

If they continued to work like this until November he'd have money to tide the family through the darker days of winter, John thought. With the garden Katherine had planted, they wouldn't starve. Life felt blessed. And if the pestilence really dealt them no more than a passing blow this year, then God was watching over Chesterfield.

As they cleaned the tools, sharpening saw and chisels with a whetstone, he felt contentment. Bit by bit they were improving the place. It might never impress anyone who possessed real wealth and power, but the house would please the owner of the manor when he arrived.

The steward came to inspect the work they'd done. John pointed out all the tasks they'd completed.

'Where is the lord travelling from?'

'He didn't say. He has manors dotted all around England. The last I heard, he was on the land he owns north of Durham.'

Durham. That wasn't far from the border country where all these deaths seemed to have their root.

'What brings him here?'

'Touring what he owns.' The steward gave a fretful smile, as if he might have something to hide. 'It'll cost plenty to see he's comfortable while he's here. Then he'll complain because the manor didn't bring in more this year.'

And how much had been vanishing into the steward's scrip each season, he wondered?

'Since the Great Pestilence it's been hard enough to find tenants,' the man continued. 'Everyone wants to be his own master now. More people want to rent land now than give service. Times change.' There was sadness behind his eyes, as if he missed those older, harsher days.

Wearily, they walked back to town. Alan had worked as hard as any man. Left to his own devices there had been no playing or idling.

No signing, no talk. The boy was tired and well he should be.

• • •

That night John dreamed of Juliana as a woman, fully grown, on the way to her marriage. All her family was around her, even Dame Martha, older still and frail as a wisp. It was a sign, he felt as he woke and remembered the image in his mind. They'd survive.

• • •

Saturday and the mood was merry in the market square. Traders thronged the place the way they had before the plague visited. Still no fresh cases and hope began to show again in everyone's eyes. John walked with Katherine, Juliana toddling between them as she clutched their hands, overawed by the number of people and the display of colour. Silk the colour of blood, a bright blue ribbon that fascinated his daughter so much that he had to buy it for her, seeing her delight as Katherine braided it into the girl's hair. It was an extravagance, he knew that. But the joy that shone on her face made it worth every penny.

He bought more nails from the Apperknowle smith, a large parcel of them to weigh down his satchel. They were ready to leave when the word sped around: a girl had come down with the pestilence.

In minutes the customers had fled, as if a tide had washed them all away. The vendors were hurriedly packing up their goods and leaving.

The victim was a shoemaker's daughter living near the bottom of Soutergate, close to the bridge over the River Hipper. The plague had returned to the place where it began to tease and taunt them.

Katherine took Juliana home while John watched the dismantling of the market with fascination. De Harville strode through the people; they parted to let him pass.

'A good day turned bad, Carpenter.'

'You can't blame them, Master.'

'I don't,' the coroner said, defeat on his face. 'They fear for their families, the same as the rest of us. But the plague strikes where it will.'

'Is Malcolm still a prisoner?' What more was there to say about the pestilence? Nothing they didn't already know, nothing they hadn't heard a hundred times before.

'He is, and he can rot there until he talks.'

'Did you find a nalbinding needle in his house?'

'No. I searched it myself. There was nothing to tie him to the killings.'

'No one else has died,' John said. 'Maybe they've had all the revenge they wanted.'

'That tale hasn't ended yet,' the coroner said. 'I can feel that in my bones.' He sighed. 'Tell me, Carpenter, do you think an offering might help stop the plague here?'

'An offering?' He didn't understand. 'What do you mean, Master?'

'I was thinking of a bench in the church for the choir.'

He'd seen them before in York. Some were grand, carved affairs; the choir stall in the Minster was intricate and breathtaking in its beauty. Others were plain, honest in their simplicity.

'Do you honestly believe it might save us?'

'I'd like to believe something,' de Harville answered with a wry laugh. 'Isn't that enough?'

'I'm no priest, Master. I couldn't say.'

'More's the pity. We need a new one.' He sighed. 'Someone to look after our dead.'

'Who suggested Father Crispin for the living here and in Castleton?' John said thoughtfully. 'Do you remember?'

'They're both the Bishop of Lincoln's gift to give,' the coroner replied. 'What do you mean?'

'Someone must have suggested to the bishop that Crispin should be given the posts.'

'I see.' De Harville nodded. 'And that man would know Crispin's real story. I don't know who was responsible, but I can send a letter. Whether we'll receive a truthful answer is another matter.' He pushed himself away from the wall. 'Take care of yourself, Carpenter. I'll tell you when I want that bench.'

• • •

Sunday and the church was full. Outside it was a still day, not even the smallest breath of wind. Inside, the air seemed stifling. One goodwife had to be taken out to sit in the porch as the heat overcame her. People prayed for the plague victims, but even more for themselves and their families, that the disease would keep clear of them.

The churchyard felt clean and clear as they emerged. Juliana was hot to his touch and she pulled unhappily on their hands. Walter was chattering to a girl who looked up at him adoringly. John nudged his wife. She followed his gaze and smiled.

Soon the boy might well be courting, whether he realised it yet or not.

As he looked, a bailiff came running, searching around for the coroner then whispering in his ear. De Harville's mouth became a thin frown. He spoke quickly to his wife and strode off with the bailiff towards the jail.

Malcolm. It had to be. Either the man had decided to speak or he was dead.

'John,' Katherine said.

'I'm sorry.' He'd missed whatever she'd told him.

'We need to take Juliana home and bathe her with cold water.'

'Yes.' He felt the tug of a small arm. 'Come on. You'll feel better very soon.'

After they'd soothed the girl he dunked his own head in the basin and came up with his hair dripping, making her laugh. But it cleared his thoughts and refreshed him as the coolness trickled down his back.

'We could take a walk later,' he suggested.

'What about Martha?' Katherine asked. 'She can't walk far.'

'Ask her when she returns from church.'

Dinner was a welter of talk. Dame Martha brought her gossip from the gaggle of goodwives. Eleanor and Jeanette teased Walter about talking so long to a girl and Juliana decided it was a good time to wail. John drew his daughter on to his lap, slowly quietening her until her eyes closed and she began to doze.

'You and Katherine go for your walk,' Martha said at the end of the meal. 'The girls and I can look after Juliana.'

He looked at his wife. For a moment she was undecided, then gave a nod.

'Thank you.' She looked at her sisters. 'You can clear every-thing. And make sure you behave for Dame Martha.'

• • •

They kept to the shaded paths, where things felt cooler, with the light soft and dappled on the ground as it came through the leaves. He took hold of her hand and led her along the track. It was rare for them to be alone these days. With family, a daughter so young, his work… time was always precious, swallowed up by this and that.

John knew where he was going. The walking seemed aim-less, but he had a goal: to see the house where Malcolm lived. Not close, not inside. Simply from a distance, to fix it again in his mind.

The bracken felt soft when they sat and rested their backs against a tree. Somewhere close he could hear the gentle burble of a stream. Birds sang, but even they sounded lazy on this summer afternoon. He'd caught a glimpse of the building, nothing more, but that was enough to satisfy his curiosity.

'Have you done what you needed, husband?' Her voice was quietly teasing.

'What do you mean?'

'I'm not a fool.' She smiled. 'You brought me this way for a reason, I can tell. And you turned fast enough after we saw that house.'

He had to laugh. She was quick and observant, far too clever for him. He explained it all to her, adding, 'But it's also lovely here, with you, on our own.' He reached and took her hand.

'I think I'd like to stay here forever. Just let the world go by.' Katherine sighed. 'But we can't, can we?'

'No. We can rest a few minutes longer, though.'

They didn't speak, just let the sounds of the wood fill them. Cares, worries, fears all fell away for a short while. His head jerked up at the sound of footsteps on the road and he squinted for a view of the traveller.

Even from this distance he could pick out the scar on the man's face. His hood was pushed back, showing thick, ragged hair. Thin hose and a pair of boots that kicked up dust with every step. The man had a heavy staff as tall as himself, useful in a fight.

Roland. There was no one else it could be.

For a moment, John wanted to follow. But he knew better. Let him go; none of it concerned him now. Katherine drowsed on, her eyes closed, a peaceful smile on her face. He watched until the man was a speck in the distance and closed his eyes again. But the calm he'd enjoyed wouldn't return.

'Come on,' he said, standing and brushing off his hose. 'We should go home.'

They drifted back through the woods. She stopped to admire flowers caught in pools of sunlight. Finally they were back on Saltergate and her hand on the latch.

'I have an errand to run,' he told her. Before her frown could begin, he said, 'Only a few minutes. I promise.'

• • •

'How long ago was this?' the coroner asked.

'An hour, perhaps.'

'I suppose I should be grateful for the small fact of you telling me.' De Harville's mouth twisted in anger. 'He could be anywhere now. You should have followed him or tried to stop him, Carpenter.'

'No, Master.' It didn't need more explanation than that. He saw young Brother Edmund's gaze move between the two of them, the Adam's apple bobbing in his thin throat.

'What's done is done.' The coroner sighed. 'It means the man is still around Chesterfield. That's something to know. I'll have the bailiffs double their efforts.'

And that was his dismissal. He walked home, kicking a pebble along the street and watching it bounce. He'd done what he could. He'd kept his promise to Katherine and also kept faith with the coroner. That seemed an honest balance.

Nothing had gone wrong in the house while they walked. The building was still standing, everyone happy. Katherine gave him a curious look as he walked into the hall but she asked no questions and he didn't say where he'd been. She'd know, anyway; where else could have gone?

CHAPTER SEVENTEEN

He worked steadily with Alan at his side. Two more days should see them done on the manor house, but he wondered more about the lord who seemed happy to live in little more luxury than his tenants. Still, he was being paid for his work. Anything beyond that was their business. Perhaps the manor in Durham meant nothing.

The old order he'd known when he was a young boy had turned upside down. Even now, fifteen years after the Great Pestilence, there still weren't enough men to work the land properly. He'd seen fields left to go wild, animals unherded.

Where men once gave service to their lord, now they gave money; the steward was right. People settled elsewhere for the chance to make a better living. The ties that once bound had all been severed. It seemed to him that the new way was better, that people had some choice, and for the first time, some opportunity. He was lucky, he had a trade. Most, though, had nothing.

Some had bought small plots of land, enough to serve them and their families and sell produce in the markets; he knew one of two of them just outside Chesterfield. That could never have happened before. If the plague was God's punishment on mankind, the way so many insisted, perhaps it was for the system the rich had created. Those were heretical thoughts, treasonable, and he knew it. He'd never speak them to anyone, not even his own family. But still they remained in his head.

You've been quiet, Alan signed as they ate their dinner.

'Just thinking,' John answered. 'Don't worry, nothing to do with you.'

It was enough to satisfy.

Evening was slowly arriving as they put the tools in the satchels and began to walk home. Suddenly Alan had questions.

What tool should I buy next, his fingers asked.

'A hammer.' It was an obvious answer. By now the boy should know that. Perhaps he wanted to be certain. John studied the hand as it moved, then said, 'Yes, I'll come with you to choose it, if you like.'

He understood the reason. It was all too easy to take advantage of a child. With him there, no one would try to overcharge.

At least there had been no more plague victims since Saturday. He could see the small hope on the faces as he walked.

• • •

During supper Walter looked troubled. He stayed quiet and as soon as the meal was done, he went out into the garden. Katherine raised an eyebrow but John had already noticed. He followed the lad.

'Is something wrong?'

Walter paced up and down – three steps and turn, three steps and turn – biting his lip.

'The coroner stopped me today, John.'

'De Harville?' he asked in astonishment. 'What did he want?' Whatever it was, this wouldn't be welcome news.

'He said he wanted me to watch for Roland, the one with a scar on his face.'

'The man we discussed.'

'And if I saw him, I was to follow him and report on where he went.'

'I see.' It was one thing if he asked for the lad's assistance. He cared for Walter. For the coroner to do it was quite different. 'What did you tell him?'

'That I wanted to talk to you. He laughed and asked if I wasn't old enough to make my own decisions.'

John snorted. That sounded like the man, right enough. Pass on the danger.

'What do you think I should do, John?' Walter continued. 'He says he knows I can do it safely.'

He looked at the lad. As tall as a man, and growing quickly into his body. He was on the cusp, leaving one thing but not yet become another. De Harville knew how easy it was to flatter someone or to make them doubt themselves. He used all that with no thought to what might happen.

'Do you really want my advice?' He sat on the bench.

'Yes, John. I do.'

'Don't do it.'

'Why?' His face clouded; he didn't understand. 'You've worked for him and I've worked with you. Is that different?'

'Yes, it is. He isn't your family.' John wondered how he could explain it. 'Did he offer to pay you?'

'No.'

'Then he wants your help but he doesn't value it. Or you.'

'But shouldn't we arrest people who've killed, and hang them?'

'Of course we should. First we need to try them to be sure they're guilty.'

'Yes, but...' the lad's words faded.

Walter wanted some excitement in his life. He was young, his blood ran hot; all that was natural. He had a natural cleverness in many things. But the coroner was going against a very dangerous man.

'It's your decision to make,' he said finally. 'You asked me what I think and I told you. And I'm certain your sister would say the same thing. She doesn't trust him.'

It was all too easy to read Walter's face, the mix of disappointment and relief at not having to make the decision himself. The lad trusted him; with luck, he'd listen.

Finally, Walter nodded. 'I'm not going to do it.'

• • •

'It seems your family is snubbing me, Carpenter.'

He'd heard the hooves as he crossed the market square. The job at the manor was complete, the worried steward satisfied and smiling. John had walked with Alan to his house. Now he simply wanted to be home. Today had been hotter than before, and angry clouds were gathering in the hills to the west; the air was so close that he was soaked with sweat.

'Good day to you, Master.'

'Your wife's brother has said he doesn't want to work for me.'

The rowels of the coroner's spurs shone in the light. He was dressed in green and blue again and armed with a sword. The bailiff who was his shadow and guard sat awkwardly on another horse.

'That's his choice.'

'But you and your wife told him not to do it.'

John looked up at the man. 'I advised him. Roland is dangerous. Walter can make up his own mind. If he doesn't want to help you, that's his business.'

'And bringing men who murder to justice is everyone's business. It's the law, remember that. It's why we have juries and the hue and cry.'

'Haven't Walter and I have served you in the past?' He could feel his anger rising and the barbed edge in his voice. Better to control it, he thought; he'd never win an argument against this man.

'You have,' de Harville acknowledged reluctantly. 'Both of you. But it's your obligation to help whenever I need it.'

'Obligation, Master?'

'Yes.'

'I've fulfilled that. I was tied and almost killed, or have you forgotten that? When your wife asked me to find you after you'd been taken, I did that.' He knew he was almost shouting but he didn't care. The fury had boiled over. 'I've done more to help you than ten other men in this town. Walter's done his duty before, too, and you know it. No, Master. Find someone else.'

The coroner glared, then pulled on the reins to turn his horse and let it walk slowly away. Behind him, the bailiff grinned and winked before following.

An end to things? No, he thought. Some things never ended. De Harville would never give up so easily.

• • •

'The girl threw the hand after them and barred the door so they couldn't return,' Dame Martha finished the story with a flourish. 'At least, that's the way it was told to me.'

It sounded unlikely, sad and horrible. But no one would allow the truth to intrude on a good tale. The girls scrambled up, kissed her and left the room, giggling. They didn't believe it either, but they loved her stories.

Martha returned to sorting through her things and packing them into chests.

'Ready for moving back to your old house?'

She nodded. 'William's widow came to see me today. They'll be gone in a fortnight.' She picked up a dress of deep blue silk. 'It's odd. The older I grow, the less I want. I remember when I loved the idea of a new gown. Now I just wonder when I'd ever wear it.' She smiled. 'Silly old woman, I know.'

'Not so old.'

'Get away with you, John. You'd better go and help your wife. There's plenty she'll need to pack.'

Katherine had the girls working, arranging things in the kitchen so they'd be ready to go. She ran a hand across her forehead. The wimple sat a little askew, a few strands of hair escaping.

'There's so much to do. A lifetime of things. Ours, our mother's…'

'Take it all,' he told her. 'The new house has plenty of room.'

'Why? There's so much we don't need.'

'There are memories.'

'Those are in our hearts, John.' She looked at him tenderly. 'We carry them wherever we go.'

She was right, of course. The important things stayed inside, never lost. She shooed him away to let her work. Safer to go, to pour a cup of ale and sit in the garden. He'd need to hire a carter for the move. Hugh would do well if he was available. At least he knew the cart was solid, John thought with a smile.

He had calmed down. The coroner could make his blood boil and set his humours out of balance at times. All this talk of obligation. It flowed both ways, not that the man would ever think of that. He took all he could and gave nothing in return.

• • •

The days passed. He worked, Alan at his side. Small jobs that took no more than a few hours. But they were there and they paid money. Easy work; the boy could probably have managed most of it on his own.

He was ready for another good challenge. The byre out at Cutthorpe had offered that, but he was ready for more. Something that made him think hard and taxed his skills. He knew he shouldn't complain; he had work to keep him busy and already others wanted his services. But between that and the rush of cleaning and packing at home he needed something to test himself, to remind himself of what he could truly do.

One more case of the pestilence that day, the victim already moving quickly towards death. The one who'd lately recovered, though, was well enough to walk around the town. People kept their distance in a mix of awe and fear. Why had God spared him? Was there something special? Did he still have the disease? Could he pass it on? How long before that faded, John wondered? How much time before all the tears and the scars were just faint memories?

He'd given little more thought to the coroner and the man who killed with the nalbinding needle, happy to let it all fade. Let de Harville go after Roland, if that was what he desired.

John saw the coroner around the town, but always from a distance. The man would ignore him if they met, he felt certain; that was his choice. It didn't matter at all. And so his days continued. Each evening he came back to a house that looked a little more barren, as their things were packed away into chests for the move.

He arranged with Hugh to move their goods. And he prayed that nothing would happen before that. Martha had never experienced another episode of vanishing from the world for a few moments. Still, he and Katherine watched her carefully.

After the scare the Saturday before, fewer people attended this week's market. There were still enough to keep it busy, though. He walked down with Walter, only to see the lad quickly vanish as soon as he saw the girl he knew. Growing, John thought, and good luck to him.

In their livery, three of the bailiffs patrolled the crowd, eyes searching, hands on their weapons as people kept clear of them. They obviously hadn't found Roland yet, he decided. He spotted de Harville, twenty yards away and standing out in a blood red jerkin and yellow hose, displayed like the peacock he desired to be. None of his business, John told himself. None of his business.

He bought more nails and exchanged some gossip with the smith from Apperknowle, learning that the owner of the inn out there needed work on her house. A man he'd never met before stopped and asked how much it might cost to make a new set of shutters. A woman who lived out towards Holywell needed a latch for her door.

This was how most of his work came. People simply stopped him, at the market like this or on the street. By now people knew him, and word had passed that he did a good, honest job. But a reputation was a fragile flower. The smallest breath of doubt could ruin it.

From the corner of his eye he could see Walter and the girl walking away together. No sense in waiting for the lad. In most things he had his own life to live now. He bought the butter and eggs that Katherine wanted, balancing the packages as he slid between people and made his way home.

The girls were spinning, their lessons done. Their slates sat on the table, covered in letters and numbers, shapes he didn't understand. Dame Martha sat there, a small scrap of vellum in front of her.

'Something interesting?' he asked.

She raised her head. The old woman was smiling broadly even as the tears flowed down her cheeks.

'A note from Brother Robert. He begged the parchment and sent it with a carter who was coming to Chesterfield.'

'How is he?' John sat and looked at the scratchings in dark ink. He missed the monk. He'd been the only one who could keep the coroner in any kind of check.

'He's happy to be there at last. They haven't given him any duties. He helps where he wants.'

'I'm pleased for him. He's earned it ten times over.'

'I miss him, you know.'

He put his hand gently on top of hers. Her fingers were gnarled with age.

'Obviously he misses you, too. But he's happy. And we hope you are, too.'

'I am.'

'You could write back to him?'

Martha shook her head. 'I wouldn't know what to say.'

'There's plenty to tell him. What about the move? How things are in the town. He lived here long enough to be a part of things, of course he'd want to know. But if you do, send him our greetings.'

She pursed her lips. 'Maybe I will.'

• • •

The coroner and his family didn't appear for Sunday service. At first John paid it no mind. He was watching the choir and looking to see where a bench for them might fit, scarcely paying attention to the prayers.

But as people came out from the stuffy, thick air to breathe deeply in the light, rumours were already flying. They'd come down with the plague and were keeping it quiet; he'd taken his wife and son away so they'd be safe from the disease.

'Do you think any of it's true?' Katherine asked. She let Juliana go and watched the girl toddle a few steps, turn and laugh.

'No. If it was the sickness then we'd all have heard. You can't keep that quiet. Not here.' He glanced around, from the tall spire on the church across the spread of houses. In a place like this it was hard to keep many secrets. Not impossible; he'd learned that. But not when it came to illness.

'I wonder what it is?' Curiosity glinted in her eye for a moment, then she chased after Juliana, scooping her up and twirling her around.

Doubtless de Harville had his reasons. They'd come out in time. He waited for Martha as she gossiped with two of the other old goodwives. Soon, perhaps, they'd have their own priest again. The curate who came from Clay Cross did his best, but Chesterfield needed someone who lived here. Someone who would become part of the town, not like Father Crispin.

As he thought of the man his mind drifted to Roland, to Malcolm, and all the others dead and alive who were part of that tale. He pushed them away again. There were brighter things to consider on a beautiful Sunday. Perhaps he and Walter could walk up towards Brampton and try to catch a fish or two for supper. He'd cut poles for them the summer before and fashioned hooks from two old, bent nails.

• • •

In the end they caught one each. Small things, not even enough to feed everyone. But a lazy afternoon of sitting on the riverbank and enjoying the sun and shade was reward in itself. He and Walter barely spoke; they didn't need to, they just enjoyed being there, taking in the songs of the birds, the snuffle of animals in the undergrowth, A kingfisher dazzled for a moment with the subtle colours of its wings as it flashed by. Thirty yards upstream a heron swooped and made off with its catch.

. . .

There was a high, full moon riding in the sky and lighting up the land. John sat in the garden with a mug of ale. Everyone else in the house was asleep but rest wasn't ready to take him yet.

There was a gentle warmth to the night. He watched the play of shade as thin clouds crossed the sky. All the stars up there, too many for a hundred men to count in a lifetime, each as small as pins. What strings held them? He didn't know and he'd never asked anyone. They'd been there all his life and the generations before. They'd still be there for Juliana and the children she had.

Learned men might understand about stars and the moon and the sun. Let them; for him it was enough that they hung with light and warmth and magic. God placed them there, a priest told him once, back at the beginning of the world. That made enough sense to satisfy.

Tomorrow he'd begin work on another job, a settle for a shoemaker on Soutergate. The man had set his heart on one for years, saving his money until he could afford it. He'd even sketched out how he wanted it to look, using a stick in the dirt.

'Can you make that, Master?' he asked John.

He could. It was simple enough work. He'd already ordered stout oak; it was sitting in the plot behind the shoemaker's shop. Two days to bring a lifetime of joy to a man and be paid for the pleasure. That seemed a fair bargain.

• • •

He'd been sitting for almost an hour when the noise roused him. Someone hammering on the door loud enough to wake the whole street. He rushed through the house and opened the latch.

One of the bailiffs stood there, red-faced and breathless with an agony of worry in his eyes.

'Quick as you can, Master. The coroner needs you.'

'Needs me? Is someone dead?'

The man shook his head. 'He'll tell you, Master. Best he does it himself.'

Then he was gone.

CHAPTER EIGHTEEN

The knocking had woken Katherine. She stood at the top of the stairs to the solar, rubbing her eyes.

'What is it?' she asked sleepily.

'Something to do with de Harville,' John replied. 'That's all I know.' He pulled on his tunic, the leather jerkin on top of it.

'Please, John, leave it all.'

'I'm just going to see what it is. It seemed urgent.' He thought about the bailiff's expression. 'Desperate.'

The streets were empty. His footsteps echoed and he walked quickly. The houses were all dark until he reached the High Street. Light chinked through the shutters in the coroner's home. The door to the stable was open, a candle flickering inside.

The servant showed him through to the hall. De Harville's wife sat on the bench under the window with her head in her hands. At the table Brother Edmund wore a sorrowful expression. The coroner paced from one side of the room to another wearing a face like death.

'You wanted me, Master.'

The man halted and turned. He looked ten years older.

'My son's been taken.'

'Taken?' For a moment he didn't understand. Taken where? How?

'This evening he was in the garden with his nurse. She came back into the house for something. When she returned he wasn't there.'

He'd been in that garden. It was surrounded by a high wall. It would be impossible for any young boy to climb over. John heard the coroner's wife moan softly.

'You weren't in church today…'

'I wasn't well.' He dismissed it. 'We've searched everywhere. You know who's done it, don't you, Carpenter?'

'Maybe—'

'I said we've searched everywhere,' the coroner snapped. 'Someone was watching. They saw the opportunity and they took him. Roland.'

'Then tell the town,' John said. 'Wake them. Everyone would go looking for a young boy.'

'No.' The answer was firm. 'The bailiffs are already out.'

'You know the news will be all over by morning, Master.'

'My son has been taken as revenge,' the coroner continued. 'I know it. So do you.'

The woman was crying now, small sobs that racked her body. De Harville looked at her helplessly. He bit his lips and breathed hard.

'We can't do anything in the middle of the night.'

De Harville stared at him. 'I want you to lead the search, Carpenter.'

'Me? You have the bailiffs.'

'You,' he repeated. 'You have the skill for it.' For once there was humility in his voice. Pleading. 'I need you, Carpenter.'

'Please, Master,' de Harville's wife begged. She sounded as if her mind was stretched so tight it might snap.

'Yes,' he agreed. How could he refuse this? If someone snatched Juliana he'd have moved heaven itself to find her. He wouldn't stop until she was in his arms. Jesu, the boy must be terrified. 'As soon as it's light.'

'Thank you.' De Harville nodded. 'You'll have whatever you need. A sword, a horse, men. It will be at your command.'

John shook his head. 'Let me work by myself.' He didn't know how to wield a sword, especially not against an expert; he could barely ride, and men would simply get in his way.

Another few hours before sunrise. He needed to try and rest, to be fresh and alert so he could think clearly. But for the coroner and his wife, it would be hour after hour of fear and pain.

'I'll be back at first light,' he said. 'I promise.'

• • •

'What was it?' Katherine asked. She curled against him and he felt the comforting warmth of her body. He'd already stood for a moment and watched his daughter sleep, his heart filled with gratitude.

As soon as he told her, she was awake.

'You have to help. His wife…'

'I said I would. But there's nothing I can do until it's day.' He put an arm around her shoulders and gently pulled her down next to him.

His eyes closed but he couldn't sleep. His mind darted from one thought to the next. Where could the boy be? Where should he search first? There was so much land around Chesterfield. Someone might be holding the boy inside the town itself.

Before dawn he slid out of bed and dressed, washed himself and cleaned his teeth with a willow twig in the buttery and walked to the coroner's house. The candles were still burning, de Harville and a weary Brother Edmund sitting in the hall.

'Are you ready, Carpenter?'

Off to the east he could see the first band of light above the horizon. A little while longer and he'd be able to start. He could see the faint prayer of hope in the coroner's eyes and wondered what would be there by the end of the day.

'I'll do the best I can, Master.'

'I'm relying on you. Where do you want the bailiffs to look?'

Anywhere, he wanted to say. He had no sense of where to begin.

'The other side of the Hipper. Where I found you. Have them comb every field and all the woods.'

It was as good a place as any for them to begin.

'Where will you be, in case I need you?'

'Looking between here and Unstone.' He had no idea what made him say it. But Crispin's body had been found close to there and Malcolm's house was out that way.

'Then God be with you.'

John had barely passed the church when he heard someone running. Walter, with eagerness and worry on his face.

'Katherine told me. Are you going to search?' he asked. 'Can I help you?'

He wanted to say no, but another pair of good eyes might help. And working for the coroner now was a good deed, not serving the whim of a man's pride.

'Yes, of course.'

They each took one side of the road, beating into the bushes, looking at all the empty buildings they passed. Nothing. No hint that anyone had been in them.

The boy could be dead. They were words he would never say to de Harville. Not to any father. There was no need; the thought would already be there, hovering like a dark shadow at the back of the man's mind.

He saw Walter in the distance; the lad shook his head.

It went slowly, and with each pace his spirits sank a little lower. The abductor could have the boy miles away by now if he desired. Dead, alive, here, gone: it was impossible to know. Only to pray and have the feeling, the pale sense that they might be close.

He talked to every traveller he saw and stopped at all the homes. No one knew anything. By noon they hadn't found a single thing. John's belly rumbled; he hadn't broken his fast yet. They had no food, just some water from a stream as they sat under the shade of a tree.

'What do we do now, John?' Walter asked.

'I wish I knew.' They'd gone as far as Unstone, been through every room in the house where Malcolm lived. If the bailiffs had found the boy, a rider would have come to tell him. 'We'll head over towards Cutthorpe,' he decided. No reason to believe the boy might be there but at least he felt they were doing something.

But it was fruitless. They stayed out until the light began to fade, then walked back to Chesterfield. His feet ached and his head hurt. He needed sleep. First, though, he had to see the coroner.

'You go home,' he told Walter. 'I'll be there soon.'

The hall was silent, just de Harville seated in his chair. He turned enough to see the emptiness on John's face, and his expression slumped.

'The bailiffs...?'

'They didn't find anything. I sent them to look in the area around the leper colony but there was nothing. I went out towards Whittington.' He shook his head in despair.

'We've done all we can today, Master. We can't see any more out there.' Easy enough for him to say when it wasn't his child.

'I know.' The coroner gave a tight nod. 'People from the town have been out, too, God praise them. I feel so helpless.'

'How's your wife?'

'The wise woman gave me something to help her rest.'

'We'll start again at dawn.'

• • •

Katherine and Dame Martha had questions, one after another, and he tried to answer as he gulped down a bowl of pottage. What could he tell them that the gossips hadn't already put about? The boy had been taken. The coroner believed he knew who'd done it. But he still needed to be found. For now, that was the sum of the story.

He kissed his wife and climbed the steps to the solar. Rest was what he needed. He ached, tired to his bones. First, though, he took time to gaze down at Juliana, sleeping so innocently in her own small bed. Seeing her was enough to make him realise he'd continue with the search until they found the boy, alive or dead.

• • •

Katherine shook him awake. John stirred and rolled on to his back.

'It's almost light,' she whispered. He could see the small change in colour through the tiny gaps in the shutters. He was ready to rise. He dressed and shook Walter. There was time to eat, a little bread and cheese, enough to keep him going during the day.

A small crowd had gathered outside de Harville's stable, almost twenty men willing to hunt for the boy. Inside the house, the coroner looked as though he hadn't slept. He wore yesterday's clothes, had deep circles under his eyes and his skin was the colour of ash. A scrap of vellum lay on the table by his hand.

'I've had a note,' he said. His voice was bleak. 'The servant found it when she opened the door this morning. It was weighted down by a stone.'

'What does it say, Master?'

The man didn't need to look. It was in his memory as surely as if someone had burned it there.

'"You'll never find me. You know that. The only way to see your son alive again is to release Malcolm. When I see him, your boy will be free."'

'What are you going to do?'

'Tell me, Carpenter, and tell me honestly: what chance do you think you have?'

They both knew, but de Harville needed to hear the words.

'Beyond luck and God's good grace, none at all.'

'Then I have no choice.' The coroner sighed. He suddenly looked like an old, broken man. 'Thank you, Carpenter.'

'What are you going to do, Master?'

'What he demands. What choice do I have?'

'There are people outside willing to look.'

'No.' De Harville shook his head very slowly. 'He's won. He's put two lives on a scale and I know which means more to me.'

Outside, he addressed them all. Thanked them for their efforts and devotion. But it had all been solved, the man said, as John saw men turn to look at each other questioningly. His son would be free later.

He knew how much it must have cost for the coroner to admit he'd lost. Yet at the same time he couldn't help but admire the man. He'd come out and told them all.

With mutterings and odd backward glances the crowd dispersed. He waited until they were alone, then asked, 'How do you know he'll keep his side of the bargain?'

'I don't,' the coroner answered bleakly. 'The only thing I can do is trust him.'

John understood; faith was all the man possessed now. Better to let him cling to it than say more.

'Did he say how he wants it done?'

'Nothing more than I read to you, Carpenter.' He glanced up at the sky. Full daylight now but the sun was still low in the east and the night coolness still touched the air.

'He'll be watching somewhere.'

'Let him,' the coroner snapped. 'He has my son.'

A son, someone to continue the line. God's true gift to any family.

'Maybe afterwards you can find him and make him pay.'

'I'm not going to think of that.' He took a deep breath and straightened his back. 'I'm going to the jail, to see Malcolm released. You might as well come with me.'

The man was still in chains, looking more battered and bruised than before, skin swollen around his eyes and mouth. His skin was covered in dirt and blood, so he looked more animal than human.

'On your feet,' the coroner told him, and Malcolm struggled to rise. A bailiff unlocked his bonds. Malcolm cackled.

'What now? Going to take me out and kill me?'

'You're free to go,' de Harville said. 'Up the stairs and out of the door. No one will stop you.'

Malcolm stared suspiciously.

'Why?' He took a pace or two, unsteady on his legs. John moved forward to take his arm but the man brushed him away. 'Why?' he asked again.

'Go.' The coroner stared at him. 'Before I change my mind.'

Malcolm spat, looked around and then began to walk.

'Now we wait.'

• • •

There was nothing more he could do. The silence was oppressive, a prison in itself. Finally the coroner led the way back to the street. Malcolm was nowhere to be seen.

De Harville had his bailiffs around him. Roland would either keep his promise and show he was a man with some small honour, or they'd find the boy's body. Whichever way the dice rolled, John had no desire to be there for it.

• • •

A day of work, although his thoughts refused to stay on the job. Try as he might, he couldn't concentrate. Twice Alan had to point out small things he'd missed; the pupil correcting the master.

At least they were working in Chesterfield. When they finished for the day he took the boy home then walked quickly across the market square to de Harville's house.

Silence in the hall. Brother Edmund stared at nothing and the coroner was lost in his thoughts. Both turned sharply as John entered, their faces desperate for news, for anything.

'No word?'

'Nothing, Carpenter.' He picked up a wine goblet, swirled it around slowly, then drank. His voice was empty, lost.

'Maybe you'll hear soon, Master,' John said, but the man just shook his head.

'I threw the bones and I lost.'

What could he say? There was nothing he could offer, no more hope.

. . .

'Nothing at all?' Dame Martha asked.

'No.'

'For once I feel sorry for him,' she said.

'And his wife,' Katherine added. 'It must be worse for her.'

'True,' the old woman agreed with a sad nod. 'May God give strength to them both.'

'The boy,' John said. 'We don't even know if he's alive. We might never find out.'

. . .

Darkness had fallen when he heard the voices outside. One or two at first, then more. John opened his door and stepped on to Saltergate. Two men passed, laughing.

'What is it?'

'God be praised, the coroner has his son back.' They moved on, smiling and cheering.

He told his wife then slipped into his coat.

'Where are you going?'

'I want to find out what happened.'

. . .

He pushed through the small crowd gathered outside de Harville's house and into the yard. An anxious bailiff stood guard; John nodded and passed unquestioned.

The mood had changed in the hall. The coroner was smiling; even the young monk looked merry, a mug of ale in his hand.

'Drink, Carpenter,' de Harville insisted, pressing a mug into his hand. 'We have something to celebrate.'

'Is he safe? Unhurt?'

'No injuries, God be praised.' The man's eyes shone, his smile broad and relieved.

'Where was he?'

'Sitting by a tree on the Tapton Road. A boy delivered a message two hours ago to say we'd find him there.'

'From Roland?'

The coroner nodded. 'Who else? We questioned the messenger, he described the scar right enough. He kept his bargain.'

'What does your son say?'

'My wife and the nurse are coddling him.' For a moment the joy left his face. 'He's too young to be able to tell us properly. You know that, Carpenter.'

It was true; the lad wouldn't have the words to describe it all. Not old enough to even understand much of what had happened, probably. But the fear and the terror would remain with him.

'What now, Master?'

'Now I give thanks that my son is back with us. The bench I mentioned for the choir, have you thought about it?'

'I've considered it.'

'Can you make one?'

'If you wish, Master.'

'Yes.' He said the word slowly, starting to pace around the room. 'Yes, that would be good. My thanks to God for delivering my son.' He drained the goblet. 'Draw what you think and let me see it.'

'I will.' It wasn't what he'd come to hear, but it was work and only a fool would refuse that. 'What are you going to do about Roland?'

The coroner poured more wine and slammed down the jug. 'Nothing. Let him win. The bishop doesn't care, the Crown doesn't care. If justice doesn't matter to them, why should it to me? Maybe you were right when you made your choice.'

'Perhaps.' He raised the mug. 'Great good joy to you and your family, Master.'

. . .

'As simple as that? Just released him?' Katherine asked in astonishment. 'And the boy's not hurt at all?'

'That's what the coroner says,' he replied.

'God's smiled on them,' Dame Martha said.

'I didn't think Roland would honour his bargain,' John said. They were sitting at the table, the candle guttering. 'But he's won. De Harville is going to let it lie.'

'A pity it took this long to make him see sense.' Katherine shook her head. 'If he hadn't been so stubborn...'

He knew what she meant, and understood that her words included him. But she was right. It was time to let it go.

CHAPTER NINETEEN

Over?

He'd believed it, but he was less certain the next morning as he crossed the square to collect Alan. The coroner rode out of his gate, spurring the roan, three of the bailiffs on horseback behind him, all of them armed with swords. De Harville wore a hard, determined expression. Wherever he was going, he believed it was important and dangerous.

But it wasn't his business. Wood waited for him, and he lost himself in it for the day. Nothing to tax his skills, but today he found real pleasure in the exactness of measuring and cutting. Alan worked alongside him, slower, still not sure of himself. That would come in time. Practice makes perfect, an old man had told him once. None of them would ever be perfect in this world, but they might always keep improving.

As they walked home he heard the news: the coroner and his men had gone after a nest of outlaws hiding out towards Baslow who'd been robbing travellers on the roads. Four dead, including one of de Harville's men, and more wounded. Another three now in the jail, awaiting transport to Derby to stand trial.

That wasn't the man's job. A coroner brought justice to the dead, not the living. But he could understand. The man needed to do something, to prove to himself that he wasn't impotent. And maybe he'd hoped to find Roland there and exact his revenge.

If so, he was disappointed; there was no mention of him. He'd be far away by now. Or if he was still around Chesterfield it meant he had business to finish, and that could be worse.

None of it was his concern. The coroner's son was home unharmed; that was the important thing. He'd done what he could to help, but he'd have done as much for anyone's missing child.

At home the chests were piling up higher in each room. There was just enough still out for daily life. Katherine and Dame Martha had made their preparations well. Come the day to move it should go swiftly, although he wondered how long his back might take to recover.

He sat in the garden with a mug of ale, watching Juliana crawling on a small patch of grass, concentrating as she moved twigs around in a game that made sense only to her. Katherine was busy in the kitchen, the door propped open to catch the faint breeze. As she worked he could hear her humming a merry tune.

Linen was spread over the bushes to dry after a washing, stark white against the bright, lively green; Katherine had been down to the river today to clean their clothes.

With a stick, John began to draw a few rough ideas for a choir bench in the dust. The first was too plain, the second one better. He scratched them out and thought, then started to sketch again. Juliana toddled over, watching, then tried to make her own marks on top until he had to lift her on to his lap.

Finally he had it. Simple enough, but with some elegance. A plain bench, the sides rising in a curved design, and a plank at the back so the choir could rest their backs. Polished and glowing, it would look impressive and elegant, yet easy enough to make. Tomorrow he'd draw it for de Harville. If he approved and they reached a price, he and Alan would have even more work ahead.

• • •

'Is that it, Carpenter?'

The sketch was crude but it gave the idea of the thing. John had begged a scrap of parchment and the quill from Brother Edmund and scratched out a picture of the bench.

'It is, Master. It will fit well in the church.'

'And can you make it?' he asked doubtfully.

'I can.'

The coroner stared at it a little longer then nodded. 'Four pence a day and your ale as you work on it. But I want the best wood, good oak.'

'Five pence and ale.'

'Four is what I've paid you before,' the man countered sharply.

'And this is my trade. It's my skill.'

Eventually de Harville gave in. With a bad grace, as ever, but they sealed the bargain.

'I want it done soon. Not just to give thanks; it might help us with the plague. Did you hear, Carpenter? Another one this morning.'

'Who?' The news hadn't reached him.

'Rufus the Shoemaker.'

Someone else who lived close to the bottom of Soutergate, down by the river. John crossed himself.

'May God help him.'

'May He help us all. Tell me when you're starting to fashion this bench. I've a mind to see it progress.'

'Yes, Master.' He didn't like it; he always preferred to work without someone glancing over his shoulder and offering suggestions and criticism. But de Harville was paying the bill; he had the right.

If they hurried through the next two jobs they could begin work on the bench in a few days. There were other things, but no rush on them. And this excited him. Something that would be on display in the church day after day, work that would be judged by the whole town. It needed to be as good as he could make it.

He explained it all to Alan as they walked to their next task. This one was simple, building a small wooden shed behind a kitchen. The building itself would form the back wall. He dug the holes for the posts as Alan measured and cut the wood. By dinner the frame was all in place. Gravel at the bottom of each hole to allow the water to drain, then the earth packed tight around the wood, checking each of the posts stood straight and true. A little water, then tamp the dirt even tighter.

'Now it needs time to dry,' he told Alan. 'Then it will stay solid when we nail on the boards.' He showed what he meant and the boy grinned as he understood.

Nothing more they could do here today, other than hope there was no rain. Instead they walked across town to a house that overlooked the weekday market. The roof beam was beginning to sag.

'How would you do it?' he asked Alan.

The boy stared up at the wood, then walked around. His small feet tested the floor under them, locating the joists. What it needed was a new beam, his hands said. That was the proper solution.

'That's good,' John agreed. 'But we can't do that, they won't pay for it. We need to put in something upright to shore it up.'

Alan looked doubtful, and well he might. Eight years old and he already naturally understood more of construction than the man who owned this house.

'It's not up to us.' John shrugged. 'I told him about the pressure it would cause but he insisted. We'll use two beams, a little distance apart. That will help to spread the load. A broader pad of wood under each post will help, too.'

The measuring and cutting needed to be exact, but the trick was putting the wood precisely in place. Inch by inch with gentle pushing and hammering to make the posts completely straight, then securing each one to the roof beam to give yet more strength.

It was close to dusk when they finished. His arms and shoulders ached. All he wanted was to wash off the dust and dirt of the attic and sleep. Some supper in his belly, a scrub in cold water out in the garden and he was ready to rest.

Next day, the shed. First checking the sturdiness of the framework, then nailing planks to the posts, starting at the bottom, each one overlapping the one below to help keep out water and weather. Alan measured and cut, then John worked quickly and eagerly, teased by the prospect of the bench ahead. The sides were complete by the time the light began to fade. Two more days of work here and then they could move to the church.

First thing that morning he'd ordered the wood, taking Alan with him as he selected it. Trunks of matured oak, straight and true, cut two years before. The boards would be waiting in the churchyard. He was eager to shape them, to make the bench he saw in his mind.

• • •

The evening brought a short shower of rain, leaving the earth smelling dark and sweet. He kept the shutters open to draw in the fresh air and settled down in bed. The family was all asleep, the doors locked. The only thing he couldn't keep out was the pestilence. There'd been another during the afternoon, a child of three. What god claimed an innocent like that? No matter how much John thought, he couldn't see the justice or love in it.

It seemed he'd barely closed his eyes when the banging on the door woke him. Quietly he slid out of bed, holding the knife against his thigh. John drew back the bolts quietly. He'd expected a bailiff but it was the coroner himself, eyes glistening in the light of a full moon.

'I've had word of where Roland is.' He ran his tongue around his lips. 'I thought you might want to be there at the kill, Carpenter.'

'No.' He never wanted to see Roland or hear his name again. He'd learned his lesson well enough. 'You said you wouldn't pursue it, Master.'

'I kept that vow,' de Harville said. 'I haven't searched for him. The information came to me. He and Malcolm are camped out by Holymoorside. I've assembled the bailiffs, we're going to catch them in the darkness. Come and join us, you can have your revenge.'

'No,' John repeated.

'Why not? Do you think that men like that should be allowed to live?'

'You kill them and another pair will spring up in their place. Then another and another. There will always be men like those two. You can't rid the world of their type.'

'I only want to rid the world of these, Carpenter. Let someone else take care of the others.' He licked his lips.

'Then I pray that God keeps you safe, Master.'

'As you wish, Carpenter. You can see them when we bring them back, bound and ready to die.'

Did the man believe it would be easy? The bailiffs might be young and strong and eager, but they'd be pressed hard against two seasoned fighters with good weapons who'd always be ready for a surprise attack.

• • •

He slept in fits and starts, no more than a few minutes at a time, it seemed. There was the first sense of morning on the horizon when he woke fully and dressed. The town was still silent, but that would change soon enough as men set out for their work.

No lights at the jail, no commotion at the coroner's house as he passed. The few faces he saw had no news and for a moment he wondered if he'd dreamt de Harville's visit. But it was real enough, he remembered every detail. No matter; he'd learn more later. Word would pass soon enough.

He worked steadily through the morning. At dinner he treated Alan to a pie from the cookshop. Not from generosity; he wanted to hear the gossip. By now they all seemed to know about the raid. Three of the bailiffs seriously wounded; one was unlikely to survive. And no one captured.

Jesu, but the coroner was a fool. Now he looked it, too, and that would hurt him deeply. Two men defeating a force and escaping, all to satisfy a man's pride.

John stayed silent, listening to the accounts. Each a little different, every one a bit more exaggerated. Alan ate, then began to sign his questions.

'No, I didn't go,' John told him. 'I value my skin more than that.'

Another question.

'What will de Harville do now? I don't know, but it probably won't be the sensible thing.' He ruffled the boy's hair. 'Come on, let's go back to work. We still have plenty to do.'

• • •

One of the wounded bailiffs died during the night. No more cases of plague.

The only task remaining on the shed was to make and hang the door. He let Alan do much of the work to see how much he'd learned. It took time. The boy was careful, knowing it was a test. But it was one he passed easily. By the shank of the afternoon, when all the heat seemed to gather close to the ground, the job was complete. The shed still needed a roof, but that was work for a tiler. John accepted his payment and gave Alan his share. The boy's hand curled proudly around the coins and he slipped them into his scrip.

'You have ample for a hammer now,' John said. 'On Saturday we'll go to the market and buy one, shall we?'

Alan nodded his agreement eagerly. He had money to buy more than a hammer, his fingers said. He'd been saving his pay.

'A hammer will do for now,' John told him. 'Good tools aren't cheap, but they can last you a lifetime.' And pray God he'd have a long enough life to use them. 'Tomorrow we begin at the church. Are you ready?'

The boy nodded. He would do his best.

• • •

On the way home he spotted de Harville in the distance. But the man was striding briskly away from him. No sense in calling out; John had made it clear the night before that he wanted no part in this business. To say anything would simply salt the wound. But he wondered what would happen next. Would Roland and Malcolm let things be, or would they want retribution?

• • •

He rose before dawn, as excited as a child about the new job. Alan had to rush to be ready when John arrived early. Together they walked through town, only a few minutes across to the church.

Was it true about the spire, Alan signed. He craned his head back to stare upwards.

'It is. It's held on by its own weight.'

The boy blinked, trying to understand. John knew; it seemed impossible, but he'd seen it with his own eyes. John looked around. No one was watching. A few farmers were setting up at the weekday market on the other side of the church.

'Come on, I'll show you.'

They walked through the nave, genuflecting to the altar. Then John opened a small wooden door and they started up a spiral staircase made of stone. Up, up, up. He'd made this walk often when he first arrived in Chesterfield and worked on the church. It felt like another lifetime, though, as if a different man had done all that.

The windlass they'd used for hauling up timber was still in place, crowding out the chamber. There was the heavy beam that had broken his arm. Still the faint stain on the floor where he'd discovered a body. A room filled with bad memories.

'Look up now,' he said. 'You can see.'

Alan walked slowly around the room gazing up at the inside of the spire. A latticework of beams supported it as it rose, the careful jumble taking the strain. At the base, though, it was exactly as he'd said. Only the spire's own heavy weight stopped it from crashing down.

How, Alan wondered. But John had no answer. It had been explained to him but it still seemed more miracle than anything else. Finally the boy was sated. Eyes filled with wonder, they made their way back down the stairs.

By the door, John halted and held up his hand. Voices in the church and he knew one of them. Malcolm. But what was he doing here, in the middle of Chesterfield where anyone might spot him?

He pressed himself against the wall, motioning Alan to do the same. And he listened.

'It's a good idea,' Malcolm said. 'With no priest, no one will search his house.'

As best he could judge, the men were in the vestry.

'Safe enough if we only go out at night and don't have a fire. At least it's summer.' He didn't know the speaker. Was it Roland? He couldn't imagine who else it might be.

'I don't see why we've come in here,' Malcolm said softly. 'It's dangerous. Anyone could come in.'

'They won't. I told you, I need to search for something. It wasn't in Crispin's house. It's about the only thing that can damn us.'

'It was still a shock seeing him as a priest.' A short, quiet laugh. 'He almost looked the part.'

'He was always a bloodthirsty bastard. Shocked him when that needle pierced his skin.' A frustrated sigh. 'It's not here. We'd better go.'

'I wish I could have reached that coroner,' Malcolm said as they left. 'I owe him for what he did to me in jail.'

Only when he heard the soft click of the latch did John move.

'Go out to the porch and start looking over the wood,' he ordered Alan. 'I'll be there very soon.'

I can come with you, the boy signed.

'No. Do as I tell you.'

He needed to see for himself, to inspect the vestry. He was scared, although he knew they'd gone. But fear was good. It kept a man alert and alive. He moved silently into the room.

They'd been careful; everything looked in place. What had they been looking for? What could damn them? Whatever it was, they hadn't found it. Was that the reason they'd stayed in Chesterfield?

He should tell de Harville what he'd heard. That was his duty. But if he did the man would blunder off immediately. He would never take any counsel on it. Better to pass word later, so the coroner would wait until night when Malcolm and his companion were sleeping. A better chance of not dying.

The wood was waiting for him, but he found that his eagerness had palled. Hearing them had ruined it, at least for now. But it was work he'd wanted, something he'd designed himself. Time to begin.

He took the parchment from his scrip and unrolled it.

'This is what we're making,' he explained to Alan. 'It's simple enough. One board to sit on, another for their backs. Those bigger pieces are the sides. We'll put joints through to keep it secure, and another board right at the bottom, where it meets the floor, so it's stable. Cut and glue everything well and it should last a hundred years.' He brought out a ball of twine. 'We're going to start by measuring and we need to be certain it's exact. Do you remember what I taught you?'

Alan grinned and his fingers moved rapidly. Measure twice, cut once.

'Today we'll measure three times, just to be sure.'

• • •

It was the coroner's offering of thanks, but the execution of it was John's prayer. He wanted it to be exact, as beautiful as he could make it. He worked slowly, everything certain and checked as he sketched out his design in charcoal on one of the end pieces, then stood back, looked and made some small changes.

'What do you think?' he asked, and the boy pointed to two small areas. 'Well spotted.' He altered them and thought. 'Yes. That's it.' He knew the wood would look right in that shape; he simply sensed it. 'Finish measuring and marking the boards while I cut this.'

A rough cut only. Most of the shaping would come with the chisel, not the saw. That was fine. As he worked and the sawdust flew into the air he could already feel the wood talking, ready for this. After each step he stood back and looked, picturing it as it would be when he was finished. By evening he'd even begun the more demanding task of executing the curls and curves that he'd drawn.

It was a fair start. He was determined not to hurry this job. It would be on display to all for years to come, God willing, a real testament to his craft. It might even bring more work if people admired it.

No more victims of the pestilence today, no one dead.

Come the morning he would set to again with fierce concentration as he wielded the chisel. Alan knew enough not to suggest that he do some of the work. Instead he cut and smoothed the boards that would make the seat and the back.

• • •

'They were in the church?' De Harville almost shouted the words. 'Why didn't you come and tell me straight away?'

'What would you have done, Master?' He stood his ground. This man would not cow him any longer. It was evening, a wax candle illuminating the table in the coroner's hall.

'Taken the bailiffs to the priest's house and cut them down.'

There was no mention of capture this time, only death.

'And you'd have found them both awake and alert. They'll be sleeping soundly tonight, thinking they've been clever. Isn't that a better time? You have a key to the place, you can take them by surprise.'

The coroner acknowledged it with a curt nod. 'And you, Carpenter, are you coming with us?'

'No, Master. I've told you before.'

'Yes, your wife has made a coward out of you.'

Let the man think whatever he chose; John wasn't going to be baited. Fighting men could battle for their beliefs. He'd keep his distance.

'You said they were looking for something?' de Harville asked.

'Yes. But they hadn't found it in the house and it wasn't in the vestry. Something to damn them.'

'What is it? Have you thought? Where can it be?'

'I don't know.' He hadn't even spared a moment to consider it. 'I came to tell you, that's all.' He turned to leave.

'Wait,' the coroner ordered. 'I could use you tonight. Not to fight,' he added hastily. 'To watch and make sure they can't slip away. That brother of your wife's, too.'

'No, Master.' With a quick glance at Brother Edmund's worried face, he closed the door behind himself.

• • •

'Thank you,' Katherine said when he told them all. 'I feel better with you out of all that. And Walter, too.' She looked down the table at her brother; his head was bent as he ate with his spoon.

'She's right,' Dame Martha agreed. 'This is nothing to risk the lives of ordinary folk. If it all started with a lord, then let lord's men take care of it.'

'I made my vow,' he said, 'and I'll keep it.'

But he still listened closely for noises in the darkness and wondered what was going on. Whatever happened tonight, he'd helped set it in motion. And something was certain to occur. De Harville would never let it lie, and the bailiffs would be eager for their revenge. By the time he removed his hose and put his arm around Katherine in bed he'd heard nothing.

It came later, deep into the night, a time when honest men should be sleeping. Metal against metal, a shout, a scream. Instantly he was sitting upright and reaching for the knife at the side of the bed.

But it was distant. Someone else's fight. He might not sleep again before daylight, but he'd stay safe behind these walls and keep the doors locked and barred tight. In the faint light he could make out the heads of his family. Silently, he crept out of bed and stood over Juliana, standing silently until he could make out her soft breathing.

Martha was sitting at the table. There was a rushlight in front of her but the flame wasn't burning.

'You heard it, too?' she asked.

'Yes.' He poured ale from the jug and settled next to her. 'There'll be some sorrow in the morning.'

'Then be grateful we don't have to worry about you.'

'I am.' He didn't want to dwell on it, all the blood and death. And he didn't mention all the times he glanced over his shoulder, fearful that Roland might be behind him. 'Are you ready to move back into your old house?'

She gave a small, tinkling laugh. 'You know, I never expected to set foot in it again. It will seem strange, I'm sure. After all, the place will have a new mistress.'

'We'll always defer to you.'

'John, I hope you won't. It was mine for so long and now it's yours. I want you to make your own mark on it.'

'We all will,' he told her. Before he could say more there were footsteps outside and a fist hammering against the door.

'You'd be safer in your room,' John said. He waited until she was out of sight, then drew his knife. 'Who's there?'

'Bailiff,' a voice answered in a croak. 'For the love of Jesu, open up, Master.'

He lifted the bar and turned the key. The man almost tumbled in. There was blood on his jerkin, more on his face.

'Sit,' John ordered and put his ale into the man's hand. He struck a flint and the rushlight flared.

'What is it?' Katherine called. She was at the head of the stairs, hurriedly dressed.

'A wounded bailiff,' John answered. He turned to the man. 'How bad are you?'

'Better than some,' the man replied grimly. Quickly enough the women were working with water and cloths. The girls stood by the solar and stared until they were sent away. Walter came down, fully clothed, a dagger stuck in his belt.

'Did you take them?' John asked.

'We took them by surprise, for all the good it did.' He winced sharply as one of his wounds was bathed. 'But the pair of them fought like devils, Master, and that's no lie. I think one of them might be dead, but I'm not sure. The other escaped, I'm certain of that.'

'What about the coroner?'

He shook his head. 'I don't know. We were fighting just to stay alive.'

Martha brought a small jar of salve and rubbed some on the deep cuts. The man's face eased and he slowly drew breath.

'I ran, Master, and I'll admit it. It was that or die, and I have a family.'

'Rest here a while.' He saw Martha nod; the man would be well. John picked up his jerkin. 'I need to go and see how many are hurt.'

CHAPTER TWENTY

Men sat, dazed, as others wandered with burning torches that spread a few feet of light. John looked around for de Harville.

Inside, the priest's house looked like devastation. Table were overturned, the prie-dieu smashed. Broken dishes littered the floor of the buttery. The back door hung open, the garden behind it a deep black mystery.

John took one of the brands and went out. At the far corner he could pick out two shapes and moved cautiously towards them, knife ready in his other hand. Malcolm, one hand clutching his belly, trying to push everything back inside. But too late; his life was over. And next to him, sword still in his hand and a look of triumph on his face, de Harville.

John reached his fingertips to the man's neck. A faint beat there, enough that he might survive.

'Back here,' he called out. 'The coroner's wounded.'

He squatted by the man, tearing away at his collar, holding the flame high to try and inspect the wounds. He'd barely finished when two men appeared with a hurdle and eased de Harville on to it.

'Take him home,' John ordered. 'How many others?'

'Three dead, Master. One doesn't even look like he has a mark on him,' one of the men replied, wiping sweat away from his face. 'Another hurt so bad he'll likely join them.'

'We need to raise the hue and cry. Pass the word.'

He watched them carry de Harville away. There was nothing more he could do for the man. It was in God's hands now.

It was impossible to track Roland in the darkness. But if they didn't try, he'd have the chance to escape. Men started to gather, wondering what to do next.

'How many people can we assemble?' he asked one of the bailiffs. The man had a small cut on his face, another on his sword hand.

'Maybe forty by daylight, Master.'

'Go to all the houses. Rouse them so they're ready to go as soon as we can see. Does anyone have a dog that can track?'

'Old Edward has one he uses for hunting.'

'We'll need that. Have everyone meet by the church porch.'

He stalked off, seeing Walter standing in front of the priest's house.

'Come with me.' He led the way home.

The wounded bailiff was dozing. His arms were a pillow for his head as he rested.

'How bad is it?' Katherine asked.

'Three dead. Four if you include Malcolm. De Harville's wounded. With God's mercy he might live.' He filled a mug with ale and drank it down; his throat was parched. 'I'm going over to his house. The hue and cry's setting out at dawn.'

She nodded. Katherine understood he had to be a part of this; it was his duty as a townsman.

'Be careful, John,' Martha told him.

'I will.' He glanced down at the bailiff. 'How is he?'

'Exhausted,' Katherine said. 'But he'll heal. His wounds aren't bad. We've dressed them. As soon as he wakes I'll send him home.'

'I want to come with you,' Walter said.

John looked at his wife. Slowly, sadly, she nodded. Her brother was old enough now; she couldn't refuse him.

'Fine. Be in the church porch at first light.'

• • •

Candles were burning in the coroner's house. His wife came down from the solar.

'We're waiting for the wise woman,' she said. Her face betrayed no emotion, none of the fear that must be churning inside. 'Brother Edmund is praying over him.'

'How badly is he hurt?' John asked. 'I couldn't see out there.'

'Three wounds,' she replied. 'One of them is deep.'

'I'll pray for him, too. Mistress, if it helps, he killed Malcolm.'

'That won't seem like any consolation if I lose my husband.'

'I know.'

'And how many dead now, Master?' There was ice in her voice.

'Too many.'

'Do we even know what it's all for?'

'No. Perhaps lords revenging themselves on each other.'

'We end up caught in business that's none of our concern. You men and your pride.' She turned and climbed the stairs back to the solar.

• • •

The dead were laid out in the church. Candles burned around them. Men were muttering quietly, crossing themselves again and again.

Suddenly John remembered something. He found the head bailiff.

'Someone said one of your men was dead and he didn't look like he'd been touched.'

'Aye, Master. Roger here.' He pointed. John knelt and rolled the corpse on to his belly. There it was, a wound that pierced the padding on his jerkin, a small bloom of blood around the hole. Killed by the nalbinding needle. Roland was becoming almost as deadly as the pestilence.

• • •

At dawn there were thirty men ready and eager for the hunt. He'd see how they all felt after a few fruitless hours. One had a large hound that snuffled around, awaiting an order from its master. Before they met, John had been in the priest's house, searching for something of Roland's for the animal to smell. He found two small packs. Rummaging through them he discovered a shirt too small to belong to Malcolm. Now he held it in front of the animal.

'We'll need to start where the man was,' the owner explained.

The garden of the priest's house. In the light he could see the trampled grass and the dark patches where blood had soaked into the dirt.

'Go,' the man ordered his dog. It circled around for so long that John started to believe it was hopeless. Then it seemed to catch some scent and moved quickly, scrambling over the low wall and into the woods beyond as the hue and cry hurried to follow.

The dog seemed to lose the scent again, circling once more until it found a trail, then going more quickly, running through the undergrowth.

John stayed to the side, constantly glancing around. Whoever Roland might really be, he was a resourceful, fierce man. Certainly not an enemy to be taken lightly. And he was two hours ahead of them. That could carry a man a long way if he was running and desperate.

They continued for a mile, until they reached a stream a yard wide. The animal lost the scent. Nothing on the other side. Roland must have walked through the water and come out somewhere else. They tried both banks, upstream and down, for half a mile, but the dog couldn't find any trace.

The men gathered around him. Like it or not, he was their leader here and they wanted instructions. He tried to think, to guess, knowing all eyes were on him.

'Search all around,' John told them. 'Away from the banks on both sides. Keep your eyes open. We need a track to follow. And stay alert. He's dangerous.'

He looked, hearing the others moving around and talking loudly. If he had any sense, Roland would be far away by now. And if he'd stayed close, the noise they were making would give him ample warning to stay clear of them.

An urgent shout made him turn. It came again and he began to run, clearing the stream with a leap. Deep in the trees someone had found a trail, the grass bent, a line that moved around through the woods.

'We need the dog here,' John said. 'See if he can pick up the scent.' A wait until the owner arrived, and then as the dog sniffed at the earth. But that was all it did. Whatever had made the track, it wasn't Roland.

They stayed out until dinner. Sometimes he caught sight of Walter in the distance, working as hard as anyone else. But none of them managed to pick up on Roland's trail.

They must have looked a mile upstream and another down from where the dog had lost his scent. John returned to the spot as if it might tell him something. Instead, the lulling burble of the water sounded like a mockery. He sat on a fallen tree and thought. If he was Roland, where would he have gone. Far enough to avoid the hue and cry. Somewhere he felt safe. Somewhere he could plan.

But he had no idea where that might be. The man might be wounded. He would need sleep and food, somewhere to dry out his shoes and hose if he'd run along the stream. A fire. No one had spotted smoke, though, no one had smelt it.

Finally he whistled them all in. They were wasting their time here.

'Back to Chesterfield,' he told them with a weary heart. 'We'll eat, and meet again at the church porch in an hour.'

The fruitless search had leached the blood lust out of their hearts. Now whatever they did would be a hard slog until they found a hint of Roland to hearten them. He walked in front, still going through all the possibilities in his mind and coming up with precious few.

'John,' Walter called on Saltergate, but he held up a hand and walked on. Food could wait a few minutes; he needed to see if de Harville was still alive.

The man's wife was in the hall, staring out of the window as her son played in the garden with his nurse. A bailiff stood guard, leaning his back against a tree.

'How is he, Mistress?'

'Still with us, praise God.' The dark circles under her eyes were testament to the anguish and the sleepless hours.

'May the Lord let him recover.'

'That's in His hands, Master.' She looked him up and down, the dirt, the cuts from brambles on his hands and face. 'Has the hue and cry found the man?'

'No,' he admitted. 'We're going back out as soon as the men have eaten.'

'Then you should go and rest while you can.'

'What did the wise woman tell you, Mistress? Will he live?'

'No one seems willing to say.' A brief, sorrowful smile crossed her face. Her hair was hidden under a crisp wimple and she wore a simple gown of silk the colour of a summer sky.

'When people don't offer opinions that's always a sign things are bad. Don't you agree?'

'I don't know.' But inside he knew she was right.

The woman seemed to gather herself. 'No matter. It will be whatever God wills. All I can do is pray and see they treat him well. And wish you luck, of course.'

'Thank you.'

• • •

At home they crowded around for details, although Walter had already told them everything. He barely had time to eat and gulp down a mug of ale between answers. Then he returned to the church with Walter.

Fewer had come out this afternoon but he'd expected that. Men were too easily discouraged when success didn't come quickly, he'd learned. They found other things to do. But he still had ten of them, enough to split into two groups. He sent one with Walter over the river to look in the area where they'd discovered de Harville after Roland had taken him.

'What about the rest of us, master?'

'You're with me.' They'd search around Malcolm's house near Unstone. In truth, he knew that wherever they looked they were grasping at straws. He had no idea where Roland could be and the man was clever enough to stay ten paces ahead of them. At least they were doing something to try and find him.

There was no point in trailing through the woods; they were loud enough to rouse a herd of boar. Quicker to march along the road. The ground was dry and they kicked up a cloud of dust. The sun was hot; by the time they came close to the building he was sweating.

'You and you, go round to the back and wait for my call.'
They left without complaint. If Roland was here and came
out fighting they'd have no chance, but they were willing and
ready.

John gave them time, then nodded to the others and began
to walk. He took out his knife, feeling the dryness in his throat
and the fear in his heart. In a swift moment, he drew in breath
and kicked at the door. It gave, swinging wide, and he gave a
piercing whistle, the sign.

They roared, yelling, shouting, ready for battle. But there
was no enemy. If Roland had ever come here, he'd long
since gone. As the men wandered about, muttering and
grumbling, John sought any sign that the man had stopped
here.

The ashes of a fire, still with faint signs of heat. That was
enough.

'Go and ask people in the other houses if they saw anyone
here near dawn,' he ordered. If only he'd considered the
possibility earlier they might have stayed hard behind him.
But hindsight never paid the bills. It had happened; they
needed to make do with what they had. Unstone lay north of
Chesterfield. If Roland had continued he'd be in Sheffield by
now and they had little chance of ever finding him.

A villager had seen a stranger walking quickly along the
road four hours earlier, someone who kept looking back over
his shoulder. Roland. It had to be, although there was no
description.

They could search all day and the next and they'd never
catch him. The men began the march back to Chesterfield.
Quieter this time, dispirited, knowing they'd failed. But there
had never been much hope of catching Roland. He was
quick, he was smart, and he was as cunning as Reynard.

But questions kept nagging at him as he walked along the road. Why had Roland and Malcolm stayed in Chesterfield? What unfinished business did they have here and who was it with? What was the thing that could damn them and had they ever found it?

No answers. He had no need to find them. He'd done all he could by leading the hue and cry. He felt as if he'd let de Harville down, but there was no shame in not finding Roland. He'd go to Brother Edmund and have him send letters around the country to detain Roland for murder and return him to Chesterfield. It would do no good if he had the protection of a powerful lord but his duty would be complete.

The men went to the alehouse on Low Pavement. John gave this thanks, took his leave and returned to the coroner's house. He could sense the hush around it, a pall of sorrow, even before he knocked on the door.

Brother Edmund was alone in the hall, his head bent in prayer.

'Brother?'

The monk raised his head, a sad trail of tears on his cheek. 'He died an hour ago, Master. His wife is up in the solar with him.'

John crossed himself and said a prayer for the dead. To commend his soul to God. De Harville had never been a likeable man, but he deserved better. He'd died trying to complete his duty. Surely that had to mean something?

'I need you to send some letters.' He explained what he wanted. It was even more important now, with the coroner's death.

'Yes, Master.' He seemed relieved to have some task beyond grieving. 'Will they send me back to the abbey, do you think?'

'I imagine they will,' John said gently. 'Why, have you acquired a taste for Chesterfield?'

'It's a pleasant place,' Edmund said, then the stir of guilt crossed his face. 'I'm sorry. I shouldn't have said that. Not now.'

'We all have to live, Brother, as long as the good Lord lets us.' He paused. 'The coroner's son will need a tutor. Brother Robert taught his father. It's a thought for the future, perhaps.'

'Yes.'

He left the family to mourn. The news of de Harville's death had echoed around the town. He saw it in the shocked eyes of people on the High Street, on Saltergate. For one day, at least, the plague had receded to nothing.

His family was eating supper, Walter wolfing down the food, his head lowered over the bowl. Katherine looked at her husband, sadness in her eyes.

'How is his wife?' she asked.

'I didn't see her.'

'The poor woman. Poor boy, too,' Martha said, and what could he do but agree? The coroner knew the risks of what he was doing. It was his job and he'd tried to do it in the best way he could. If nothing else, there was honour in his death. But what use was honour when your flesh was feeding the bones, your family was bereft, and a killer walked free? None that he could see.

'No sign of this Roland?' Katherine asked as she placed a bowl of pottage in front of her husband.

'A sign, perhaps, but it doesn't do us any good.' He ate but he barely tasted the food. Men lived, men died, he told himself. Some ended this life violently. 'Life will change here. There'll be a new coroner.'

'Pray God it's one who leaves you alone.' Katherine softened her voice. 'I know I shouldn't speak ill of the dead, but he used you, John, whenever it suited him. You've almost died because of him.'

'I know.' He could feel the tiny pinpricks of a knife on his neck and smell the foul breath in his face. 'I know,' he repeated. 'Tomorrow it's back to work. I suppose the choir bench will be the town's memorial to de Harville now.'

In a curious way he'd miss the man. He was demanding, he was pig-headed and arrogant – but somewhere, deep in his heart, there had been a rod of honesty.

CHAPTER TWENTY-ONE

He approached the bench solemnly. Even more than before, he felt the responsibility of making it lie heavy on his shoulders. One side was complete. He eyed it again, smoothing a little here and there before measuring for the mortise holes and drawing them on the wood in charcoal.

'These need to be exact,' he reminded Alan, although the boy hardly needed it. Each job he undertook was the most important he'd ever done. He took great care every single time. It made John proud to watch him.

They made swift progress. By dinner Alan was working on the tenons, the tongues from the bench that would fit in the holes he'd made. Slow, cautious work, but he kept at it with hardly a break as John carved the outline of the other end. There was still a long way to go, but already he could picture the bench standing near the altar, polished to a deep sheen.

'Come on,' he said finally. 'I'm ready to eat.'

The cookshop was full of gossip and speculation. Some said that de Harville's killer was really a demon who'd made his escape to hell. Others joked that the hue and cry couldn't find a blind man in an empty field.

He chewed a pie that was hot enough to burn the roof of his mouth. It was just talk, he told himself, men passing the time, but still it angered him. Alan's hand on his arm made him look down. What's wrong? the fingers wondered. John took a breath and smiled.

'Nothing,' he answered. 'Not really.' How could you explain that to a child? 'It doesn't matter.'

Back at work his mood slowly brightened. He could let the wood talk and fill his blood with its words, washing out everything he'd heard over dinner. The men who'd spoken hadn't been on the chase; they knew nothing.

He finished an elaborate curlicue and it was done. John stood back, inspecting his own work. Every plane and angle looked right, just as they should be. He placed one end over the other, lining up the edges to compare them. Two small changes so they matched each other perfectly. Then he marked where the tenons would be and sat back on his heels.

'Your job now,' he told Alan with a smile. 'I can just watch you.'

Before the end of the day he'd finished. In the morning the lad could craft the mortises. Then they'd fit all the pieces together and hope the joints were tight. If not, he'd add a small shim here and there. Once that was complete, the polishing could begin. Long, wearying, but necessary for the piece to be worthy of a church like this.

Alan oiled the tools, rubbing patiently with the cloth and applying the whetstone to the chisels. John knelt by the steps to the altar and said a prayer for de Harville. Maybe it would help speed him through Purgatory.

No new cases of plague; that was the word as he escorted Alan back to his house. A blessing, he knew, but his mind was still too full of the coroner's death. John had only been here a few years, he was still a stranger in the eyes of many, but he understood that this marked the end of an era. De Harville's family had held some power around Chesterfield from a time before anyone could remember. But the son was too young to walk in his father's footsteps yet.

The murder of a man appointed by the Crown, who carried the King's writ, was a crime against the country. What happened from here would show just how much protection Roland had. By rights he should be declared an outlaw, there for any man to kill, with a price on his head and shunned by everyone. But if the lord behind him had the ear of King Edward that might conveniently be forgotten. Chesterfield meant little in London, after all. And de Harville was a very minor official, so easily overlooked and left to oblivion.

He was still thinking about it all as he turned the corner on to Saltergate. Brother Edmund was striding quickly towards him with a look of grim determination.

'Brother,' John said. 'God wish you well.'

'And you.' He stopped. 'I was just at your house. I wanted you to know that the funeral will be tomorrow morning. The priest from Clay Cross is arriving tonight to be ready.'

'We'll be there.'

'I hope the whole town will be. He served bravely and honestly.' Edmund shook his head. 'I must go, I need to pass the news.'

'Brother?' John asked, and the young man cocked his head. 'How are his wife and son?'

The monk was quiet for a long moment. Then he said, 'Broken.'

• • •

It was a sad, sober supper. No one was in the mood for idle chatter. Walter ate then left again without saying a word. John glanced at his wife but she simply shrugged and pursed her lips. No knowing where he'd gone. Martha entertained the girls with a story, but even that was hushed; no squeals of excitement, no hands clapping with pleasure.

CHAPTER TWENTY-TWO

The weather mocked the day. A clear sky as blue as it could be, the sun balmy and warm. It seemed wrong for the occasion.

As the bell began to toll they left the house. John carried Juliana, the girl squirming in his arms to try and take in the numbers of people arriving at the church. Every soul in Chesterfield, it seemed, and plenty from the land beyond. There were many he didn't know.

They squeezed into a space close to the porch. Katherine fanned herself as the heat grew during the service. The priest was unstinting in his praise of de Harville's qualities. His mercy and compassion, his wisdom and patience; things John had never seen. But let it be.

Juliana's face was hot, blotches blooming on her skin. He raised an eyebrow at his wife and carried the girl outside where the air felt cooler and refreshing. He let her down slowly, then watched as she ran a few short paces, turned and laughed.

It was what he needed, a sense of life to be lived among all the death. He squatted and she toddled back to him, arms outstretched. He picked her up again and began to carry her around the churchyard, stopping in the shade of the oak tree where the wood for the bench lay.

Setting her down again, she began to stroke it, tentatively tracing the outline of the end pieces with her tiny fingers.

Maybe she had his feel for wood, he thought with a smile. A pity for her if she did; she'd never be able to do anything with it.

Gently, he took her by the hand and guided her away. They would walk around the church. Do it slowly enough, with plenty of stops, and the service might be over.

The grave had been dug, a deep, dark hole in the ground that faced to the east. Come Judgement Day de Harville would be able to rise with all the rest of them and walk to his fate.

John rounded the corner. No weekday market today, just the drone of the curate's voice from the church. Juliana took a few paces and tumbled over a stone on to the grass. He hurried to pick her up and soothe her before the tears began. As he scooped her into his arms he glanced across at the wall.

The face was only there for a moment before it vanished. But he saw the scar, pale against weathered skin, and he knew exactly who it was.

Roland.

With his daughter in his arms he couldn't give chase. There was no one else out here, just a magpie that chattered wildly in the trees. Inside the church the curate's voice rose.

There was only one thing John could do. He dashed back into the nave, handed Juliana back to Katherine, and shouted, 'Hue and cry! The killer's outside!'

Men poured out of the church, gathering by the porch. The women followed, curious and chattering; the service was over.

It hurt to do this at a solemn moment, but it was the only way to try and catch Roland. John explained quickly, then the men were on their way, clambering over the wall and spreading out.

How much of a start did the man have? Two minutes? Three? It couldn't be more than that. The hue and cry vanished in a welter of shouting as he stood in the churchyard and watched. He was still there when the coroner's wife appeared, her skin white and her cheeks stained with tears.

'Mistress,' he said. 'I'm sorry. But there was no other way…'

'If they find him, it's all worthwhile.' She placed a hand on his shoulder. 'You did what my husband would have done. There's no shame in that.' With a brief nod she returned to the church.

'You should go with them, husband,' Katherine said. He looked at her. There was no rancour in her voice, only a look of concern.

'Yes,' he agreed. His knife was in his sheath and he touched the hilt like a talisman as he kissed her.

Walter was at his side as he set off at a run. Roland would do the unexpected, that was the only certain thing. The men had all rushed off to the north-east. He'd have gone in a completely different direction. Where? He stopped and tried to guess.

South, between the river and the lazar hospital. It was ground that the man seemed to know, that he favoured. He walked quickly, asking everyone he saw if they'd noticed anyone. People shook their heads. But Roland would avoid people; he'd try to pass unnoticed, scurrying and hiding. That would slow him a little.

'Where are we going, John?'

'Honestly, I don't know. He could be anywhere. What do you think?'

The lad looked serious, frowning as he pinched his lips together. 'Where we found the coroner,' he said. 'Or where they took you.'

That was plenty of ground to cover, too much for two people. Roland could evade them without even working up a sweat. An idea came to him.

'Would you be willing to come back to the leper colony?'

'Yes.' Walter seemed surprised at the question. 'But why? He won't be there.'

• • •

'I can't, my son,' the priest told him. 'They have to remain behind these walls.'

'Father,' John said urgently, 'we're searching for a killer. Every moment we spend talking he could be slipping away. All I want are those who are willing to help. The ones who want to. It's God's work.'

The priest sighed. 'The people in the town won't like it.'

'Now the coroner's dead there's no real authority in Chesterfield,' he argued. 'And we won't even be close to the town.' He hectored and pleaded, aware of sand trickling through the hourglass, until the priest finally gave way.

It was then he heard a shuffle of feet behind him and turned.

'We're ready, Master,' the sexless voice croaked, face hidden by the cowl. 'Just tell us what you need.'

'Alison?' he asked, to be answered by a small nod. 'Are you sure?'

'Aye,' she said. 'We're certain enough.'

There were five of them waiting. He couldn't see a single face under the hoods. But they listened carefully and began their slow, painful walk down to the lane. With seven in all they stood a chance of finding Roland – if he was even here. If he was like most men, the sight of a leper would scare him. Men who panicked made mistakes.

'Come on,' he said to Walter. 'We'd better join them.'

He tried not to think what he'd do if he found the man. It was safer to push that to the back of his mind. Instead they trod along the track to the clearing where he'd been held. Nothing. No sign that any person had been here recently. The same with the place where the coroner had been tied. The ropes that had bound him still lay at the bottom of the tree.

He cupped his hands and took a drink from the river, splashing water over his face and hair. His feet ached in their boots. John glanced at Walter; the lad was as impassive as ever, his expression showing nothing.

They plunged on. Another mile, but there was nothing to indicate a man had come this way. Some animal tracks, a dog perhaps, or a wild boar, but that was all.

'We'll go back,' he said.

'We should cut across the fields and find the lepers,' Walter said. 'They might have seen something.'

It made sense. They would be slow, none of them able to walk properly; they couldn't have come too far. He judged the way, across the common open ground where a handful of scrawny cattle grazed, and around the edges of fields that the plough hadn't touched. The quickest course was through a wood, with tall oak and elm and ash giving shade. They hadn't searched here. Before they entered, John held up his hand.

'Be very careful,' he whispered.

He stepped carefully, trying to avoid even the snap of a twig. His head moved from side to side, alert for movement and danger, the knife in his hand and ready.

But all he saw was a sparrow that flew up suddenly, and a red squirrel that flitted from branch to branch.

It wasn't too difficult to spot the lepers, moving slowly in their habits. They looked like a group of wraiths spread across the fields. It was a vision to terrify most men, like death walking among them.

They hadn't come far; that they'd been willing to come at all seemed like a small miracle to him.

'Did you spot anything?' John asked after they eventually gathered around him. None had. Perhaps Roland hadn't come this way after all; there were too many possibilities. He'd tossed the dice and lost.

He stood and watched as the lepers awkwardly made their way back to the colony that was their home. He only saw them as they were now, not the people they'd once been, loving, hoping, with dreams and ambitions and families. God had taken all that away from them, a death as certain as the plague, but one which took so much longer to arrive.

'What do we do now?' Walter asked.

'We go home,' he said with a sigh. 'There's nothing more out here.'

• • •

Men from the hue and cry were gathered outside the church. Someone had persuaded the alewife to donate a small barrel and they were drinking deep. John noticed the grave, filled in now, bare, dark earth against the brilliant green of the grass.

No one had seen Roland. He'd skittered out of sight and away. But he was still somewhere close; John was certain of that. Something had drawn him back here when he should have been far away. He still had something to do in Chesterfield.

What, though? Who was he after? Find that man and he could find Roland. He looked around the faces. Carefree, laughing. They'd done their duty, they had a tale to tell and some ale for their efforts. And if they didn't catch anyone, what did it really matter in the end? They'd never really expected to succeed.

As he entered the house on Saltergate and passed beyond the screens he saw the expectation on the faces. Katherine and Dame Martha looking so hopeful. All he could do was shake his head.

'No sign of him.' There was no point in searching further. The only way they'd catch Roland now was pure luck. He ate his dinner in silence, watching as Walter bolted his food and held out his bowl for more.

Luck against skill. That wasn't any sort of fight he wanted.

In the afternoon he collected Alan. They worked together in the churchyard, well shaded by the tree. John kept glancing over his shoulder, constantly feeling that someone was watching him. But there was no one. He made a sign to keep off the evil eye and returned to the job.

Everything assembled well; only one joint needed a shim to keep it tight. That was very fair work and he rewarded Alan with a broad smile. The bench would look glorious once they'd finished, a fitting memorial to the coroner.

In pieces, it seemed like very little, no more than cuts of wood. Together, it became more than the sum of its parts. It was something new, useful, maybe even beautiful. That was the magic of wood, the way a pair of hands could transform it.

Polishing was a tedious task, nothing to compare with the shaping and the building. It was no more than movement. Mixing the polish, applying it, leaving it to dry, then rubbing it down again. Layer after layer until finally the surface was hard and shining, fit to use, fit for display. But it would take several days before that could happen. Then the final fitting and gluing and moving the bench into the church.

He knew better than to look ahead. He'd learned that lesson long ago. You grabbed each day and tried to hold it close. The plague might take them all before it happened, although there had been no new cases that day. But he had his hopes, his dreams. He wanted to live a long happy life, to see Juliana grown, and keep all his family around him.

His arm ached from rubbing. Alan was tired, he could see it in the boy's eyes. Very carefully, he covered their work, leaving it room to breathe and dry. They'd have more of the same in the morning.

As he walked home, the feeling that he was being watched wouldn't vanish. But even when he stopped suddenly and turned, there was no one. Only a few souls about their business and the long light of a June dusk.

The shutters were closed in the coroner's house; a home in mourning. And what would they do now? Would the family stay in Chesterfield? Was there anything here for them now, beyond painful memories?

Idle thoughts and none of his business. He walked along the High Street, shifting the bag of tools on his shoulder. A voice called his name. The rasping voice he'd heard once before, the sound from the shadows.

CHAPTER TWENTY-THREE

It was coming from the same small yard between two houses where he'd heard it the last time. John drew his knife and slipped between the buildings.

'What do you want?'

'I gave you good advice before, didn't I?'

He hesitated. 'You did. But why won't you say who you are?'

A soft chuckle, like someone tossing pebbles down a well. The man stayed hidden, but this time John was more alert, trying to form an impression of him. Tall, broad perhaps. That voice had depth, it seemed to resonate from his chest.

'Does it really matter who I am?'

'Of course it does.'

'Only to you, then. No one else will care. Do you still want Roland?'

'He has to face justice. He's murdered. He killed de Harville.'

'If you want your justice, there's only one way to get it.'

'Catch him.'

'Kill him,' the man announced. 'If you send him off for the law, nothing will happen. In your heart you know that.'

'How can you be sure? He killed the King's coroner.'

'Believe me. I *know*. Believe me on this.'

'Why are you telling me?'

The man gave a short, harsh laugh like a fox's bark. 'Who else would I tell? Who else would listen?'

This was going nowhere. John didn't want to play games, to be led in circles by someone who wouldn't even show himself.

'If it's that important, why not kill Roland yourself?'

'I'd never get that close. Who do you think he's looking for?'

Of course. It made perfect sense now. He should have realised it before.

'Who are you?' John asked.

'Nobody you know. Nobody you need to know.'

'Why does he want to kill you?'

'Because he's been well paid to settle old scores. And he's never been one to leave a job undone.'

'Then what do you want from me?'

'Somebody has to kill Roland.'

'No,' John told him. 'You won't say who you are, you won't let me see you. You haven't even said what's at the root of all this.'

'Do you really want to know?' the voice rasped.

A stupid question. Too many had died. John had come close to it himself. Of course he wanted the reason behind it.

'Yes.'

'Then listen,' the man commanded. 'It was five years ago. There were four of us. We all felt like young men then, immortal and brave, and we believed in the lord we served. He was a favourite of the King. We were up on the border with Scotland. He'd sent us to sweep away the Reivers who kept coming down; our lord owned land there. But you might as well try to stop a river. But there was another lord who didn't feel as bound to the King. He talked about rebellion. Maybe they were just angry words, I don't know. It's too late to matter now. We spotted him out hawking with some of his followers one day. We kept watch on them, out of sight

252

and unnoticed. Then he rode off on his own. Foolish in that part of the country. Perhaps he had the arrogance of rank. We saw our chance, killed him, and we were away before anyone could catch us.'

'But someone found out.'

'We drank and we boasted. And just after that, our lord fell out of favour. The son of the man we killed discovered our names. We knew he'd want his revenge. We disappeared. We had to. Two years ago this son became an important man at court and his rise became our death warrant. He hired a mercenary.'

'Roland.'

'Roland,' the raw voice agreed. 'We had friends who could give some protection. You must have already guessed that. We stayed in quiet contact; it could be a way to save our lives. And then Roland found Crispin.'

'Blood demanded blood.'

'Yes. And you understand why just catching Roland will do nothing. He'll be pardoned and freed in a day. Then he'll come back to take his revenge on you, too.'

'It's a good tale, Master.' It fitted with all the rumours Dame Martha and de Harville had remembered. 'But none of it is my business. I wish you well with Roland. A long life and God's peace.' He began to turn away.

'He might choose to kill you anyway. Who are you? Just a carpenter, you're nothing.'

'Then why would he bother?' John asked. Being nothing could sometimes serve as a shield. 'You're the one he wants. After he kills you, he'll leave. You said he's a mercenary, an assassin. He'll do the work and claim his pay.'

'Is that what you believe? How many others has he murdered here, him and that man who travelled with him? Your coroner, your bailiffs. One more death would mean very little to him. Go and think about it if you wish.'

That was all. The man had said his piece.

John walked home in silence.

• • •

'A good afternoon, husband?' Katherine asked.

'Yes,' he replied after a moment. The first thing he'd done was pick up Juliana and carry her around the house. He needed some life, some joy to banish all the death from his head. 'A few more days.'

'And no more cases of plague,' she told him with a smile. 'There haven't been any since de Harville's death.'

That was coincidence. It had to be. Here they were in high summer with its heat and sun, days of sweat and work, and the pestilence had left them? Or maybe God had granted them a miracle. He didn't know. He couldn't trust that it had vanished yet.

Martha saw his doubt.

'Have faith, John. It's moved mountains before. That's what the Bible says.'

He let his wriggling daughter down to the floor and watched her run towards the girls as they played in the corner. Each step firmer and stronger than the last. A few more years and she'd be tall like them. A few more after that and she'd become a young woman.

He heard a gravelly voice echo in his mind.

'Yes,' he agreed. 'Let's pray it's true.'

• • •

Another morning and more polishing. A first coat for some of the pieces, rubbing and more of the wax for others. There was nothing to this, just mindless work. But it was all a part of the whole, and as his arms ached he tried not to lose sight of the glory in it all, even in the smallest, mundane details.

Alan laboured hard, his arm making short, stolid strokes as he rubbed the wood down between coats. He was mastering his craft well.

'Do you still have that money saved for more tools?'

A little, the hands said. Of course he did. He wasn't going to spend it on anything else.

'Good. Then we'll definitely go to the market on Saturday and look for that hammer.'

The boy's eyes widened with surprise and pleasure. Did he mean it?

'Of course I do.' There might be a bargain, or someone willing to take a little off the price in exchange for some work. John looked at his own tools. How had his father been able to afford them? He'd been too young to think of that question when the man died. And maybe it didn't matter now.

The cookshop was quieter today. The only gossip was wonder at the end of the pestilence. Men were wary, but hope glistened in their eyes. He ate and drank his ale, half-listening to the words floating around him.

He'd just drained the last few drops when a man came running. Every eye turned to watch.

'A body,' he called out. 'There's a body.'

Without thinking, people crossed themselves.

'Is it plague?' John asked. 'Where is it?'

'It's in a shroud.'

'Where?'

'Out along Holywell Street. In a ditch.'

No coroner in Chesterfield any more. No one to view the dead and pronounce. Without that, they shouldn't be buried. But in the summer heat the bodies would stink and putrefy in days.

He ought to go. If only to see the face; everything else he knew or guessed. But this way he'd know who talked to him and told him about Roland. A face outside the shadows now. Beyond life.

For a moment John didn't move. He gazed in the mug for a few dregs that might remain, then set it down.

'You go back to work,' he told Alan. 'I'll be there later.'

• • •

A small crowd had gathered. Bailiffs guarded the corpse. Their swords were drawn and they wore the cuts and bruises from Roland like badges.

John walked past them. Someone had dragged the shrouded body out of the ditch so it lay at the side of the highway. He pulled out his knife, took a breath, and slit the winding sheet open.

The man had a wizened, ugly face, pitted and scarred by the years. Long hair hung to his back, turning from dark brown to grey. He had the powerful shoulders of a fighter, broad hands now crossed over his chest.

He'd never seen the man before, but he knew him. This was the one who'd kept in the shadows and told his tale. He'd known Roland would find him eventually. He carried no fresh wounds, but John knew what he'd find even before he rolled the body on to its side. The small bloom of blood from the nalbinding needle on his back.

He'd wanted to pass on the burden of justice. But it wasn't a load John could carry, not one he was willing to take. He already had enough with his own family, with people he loved. God would take Roland when He was ready and the man would spend his eternity in Hell. That was judgement enough.

'You might as well put him in the ground before the smell becomes too bad,' he told the bailiffs and walked away.

• • •

Polishing, rubbing. That was how the afternoon passed. But his mind couldn't stay on the work. It kept slipping away to the man left in the ditch. John had no authority. He was a carpenter, he was nothing; the man had said so himself. He could issue no orders, make no proclamations. He didn't want to. This time the dead could bury the dead. It wasn't his business.

The house was in uproar when he returned to Saltergate. Chests had been dragged into the hall. He heard Katherine up in the solar giving instructions to the girls.

'What's happened?' he asked Dame Martha as she came out of the buttery with a jug of ale for the table.

'William's widow left my old house today,' she answered. There was dust on her gown and smudging her wimple. 'We've been over there cleaning. Your wife talked to the carter. He's moving everything tomorrow.'

'Tomorrow?' He'd thought he had more time.

'Why wait?' She stood, hands on her hips, assessing him with her old eyes. 'What about you? You must have heard the news.'

'I did, and I saw the body. It's not my business any longer,' he told her, and was rewarded with a smile.

'No,' she agreed, 'it's not, and Katherine will be pleased to hear it. Anyway, you have plenty to do. Walter, too, as soon as he comes home.'

No rest for the wicked, even as they tried to be good. Katherine greeted him with a wary look that only turned soft after he shook his head.

• • •

Supper was quick, bread and cheese; there was too much to do. John and Walter carried more chests down the stairs. Martha and the girls packed up the kitchen. Finally all that remained were the beds; they'd have to wait until morning.

'Hugh promised he'd come early,' Katherine said. 'It's going to take a few trips.'

He looked at everything waiting neatly for the next day. How could they have so much? But he knew the answer. This had always been Katherine's home, her mother's before her. It was the accumulation of generations, all the lives and memories she wanted to keep close and pass on to Juliana.

Their daughter was happy, tottering around, touching everything, discovering it all. He licked his finger and wiped some dirt from her nose, enjoying the excitement in her eyes. Something was happening and she didn't know what. They'd have difficulty getting her to sleep, he was certain.

Finally, though, she was down, eyes closing as she tumbled into her rest. He was exhausted too, muscles aching from all the lifting and carrying. More of it tomorrow, too. Much more.

He was the first awake, dressing and moving softly to find bread and cheese and ale. There was an hour before Hugh would arrive; it was barely dawn. John unlocked the door and stepped out into the day. Already warm. By noon the heat would be shimmering off the dust.

He walked across the market square until he reached Alan's house.

'Not today,' he told the lad and saw disappointment weigh down his face before the fingers began to move. Could he go and carry on working? He knew everything that needed to be done, the polishing and the rubbing.

He was so earnest, so eager, that it was impossible to refuse. The boy wanted to know that he was trusted to do a good job.

'If your mother allows it,' he said.

She was willing. 'If you think he can do it, Master. He can't come to any harm in the churchyard.'

'You know what to do,' John said. 'I should be ready tomorrow. You'll be the one who makes all the money today.'

All of it? the fingers asked. John nodded.

'Of course, you'll be earning it.'

'You're very generous, Master,' Alan's mother said.

'I have an apprentice who deserves what he's paid.'

• • •

As soon as Hugh arrived, John began lifting the chests. It was just as well he'd done the work on the cart, he thought, with all this load. Then the short trip to Knifesmithgate, where Martha was waiting, and he was unloading again as she told him where to put everything.

'How can you do this every day?' he asked Hugh as they hauled down the last of the chests. 'I'm surprised your back doesn't break.'

The man laughed. 'It's like anything else. You get used to it.'

Walter took charge for the next trip, as John took the beds apart and carried them down the stairs. Sweet Jesu, moving a house was work; he'd rather have been with Alan in the churchyard. At least there was no talk of more plague cases. Maybe God had truly given them their miracle.

But finally it was over. The house on Saltergate was empty save for dust and the one on Knifesmithgate was chaos. He knew his first task: putting the beds back together. He'd barely finished when he heard the knock on the door. A neighbour to welcome them?

He began to clean the tools and Katherine called, 'John, you'd better come down here. Now.'

CHAPTER TWENTY-FOUR

'What is it? Can't you find something?' He came down the steps brushing dust out of his hair. Then he saw Alan's mother.

'Is something wrong? Is he hurt?'

The woman had been crying. She was shaking, Katherine's arm around her shoulders. The words juddered out of her.

'I went to take him some dinner, Master. He'd rushed out without anything, he was so eager to start. He wasn't there. I've been looking for him all afternoon.'

'Maybe he went off to play and forgot the time.' But even as he said it, he knew the words weren't true. Alan was a boy who'd keep at his work until evening.

'Not without this.' The woman held up the boy's satchel. 'He wouldn't go anywhere without this.'

'Walter,' he called. 'Come on.' He took hold of the woman's hands. A hot day and they felt like ice. 'We'll bring him home.'

As soon as they were outside he began talking to everyone on the street. Had they seen Alan? Blank stares or shakes of the head. In ten minutes he'd assembled a group of men ready to search. They knew what a missing child meant. He sent some to go through the town, others down to scour the riverbank and the water.

'What about us, John?' Walter asked as the others left.

'We're going hunting.'

Alan wasn't missing. He'd been taken. His mother was right; the satchel would never leave his side. He'd learned that lesson well. Yesterday Roland had killed a man. Today Alan had vanished. This was no coincidence. He knew exactly what it meant. Roland wanted him and Alan was the bait. Where would he take him? A moment's thought and he knew.

'With me,' he told Walter.

They crossed the bridge over the Hipper and followed the road by the leper colony before following the track that led through the fields to the woods. They'd barely taken a few paces when he stopped.

'Do you have your slingshot?'

'Yes, John.'

'Collect a few stones and circle around to the far side of the wood. Stay out of sight but be ready.'

'Who's in there?'

'Roland. I believe he is, anyway.' And hoped he was. 'How long will it take you?'

Walter assessed the distance. 'Ten minutes.'

'Off you go, then.' He watched the lad vanish into the undergrowth with barely a sound.

He didn't want to involve Walter, but he had no choice. If he went against Roland on his own he'd be dead in a blink. This way he had a chance, however faint.

The minutes passed. John looked around. There were footprints in the dust. A man's and a boy's. They'd come this way; he was sure of it now.

He didn't try to be quiet. It would be far better if Roland expected him; he might not be looking for anyone else. Evening was falling and the shadows were long. As he walked into the wood the birds seemed to grow silent and the bushes and trees rose around him.

There was still the long twilight. Midsummer all too soon. And would he be alive for that? With God's good grace…

The path twisted until he was at the edge of the clearing. Roland stood in the centre with Alan sitting at his feet. The boy looked up, pleading. All John could do was give him the smallest of nods and hope he could keep the vow to his mother.

'I expected you before now, Carpenter.' Roland's voice rang out, haughty and mocking.

'I'm here. You can let the boy go. It's me you want, isn't it?'

'It is. Time to cut off the last loose end before I leave. At least the boy can't speak. He can't tell anyone about me. I don't know why you use him.'

'Then you'll never find out, will you?' He took a pace forward, feeling the sweat on his palm as he gripped the knife. 'You can let him go now.'

Roland grabbed Alan's hood and pulled him to his feet. He had his other hand at the boy's back.

'Can you guess what I'm holding, Carpenter?'

'Your nalbinding needle. It's a clever way to kill.'

'You'll find out for yourself soon enough. Come closer.'

One pace. A second.

'Drop your knife.'

'When you let the boy go.' He hoped Walter was close enough to use the slingshot and was as good an aim as he'd been before.

The man shook his head. 'You do as I say.' He jerked on Alan's hood again, lifting him on to the tips of his toes.

Very slowly, John extended his arm and opened his palm. Now, he thought. *Now.*

A buzzing sound seemed to stop time around them. Then came the soft hum of the stone whispering through the air. It caught Roland on the point of his shoulder, enough to make him jerk back and let go of Alan.

'Run!' John shouted but Alan was frozen to the spot. Another stone. It battered the man in the middle on his back and he dropped the needle. 'Run!' John yelled again, and this time the boy obeyed. 'Run back to town.'

More stones, one after another, each one finding its target until Roland was ducking and running for the shelter of the trees.

'You can stop now,' John shouted, and a few moments later Walter emerged.

'Did I do it right, John?'

'You did. You saved Alan's life. And mine. Again.' He stooped and picked up the needle. It was as long as his hand and thinner than his smallest finger. The point had been honed to a beautiful, deadly sharpness. It would pierce a man's skin with hardly any pressure.

It was the perfect weapon to kill up close, so easily hidden up a sleeve, ready to slip into a man's hand. He put it in his scrip.

'We should go looking for him,' Walter said.

But night was closing in. Roland would have his lair somewhere, too well hidden for them to find in the darkness.

'Not now,' he answered. But it wasn't over yet.

• • •

Alan was home long before John knocked on the door. He must have run the whole way, terrified.

'How is he?'

'Scared out of his wits, Master,' the boy's mother told him. 'What happened?'

How could he begin to tell her the truth so she might understand it?

'Does he have any injuries?'

'No.' She set her face. 'Someone took him. He told me that. Was it this man everyone's been looking for?'

'Yes, it was. He was using Alan to get me.'

'And did you catch him?' she asked hopefully.

'He escaped.'

She stared at him for a long time.

'I'm sorry, Master. But as long as he's out there I can't let Alan work with you. I know you've been very good to him, but this…' He could see she didn't own the words to express what she was feeling. 'We've escaped the plague, thanks be to God, and I won't lose him to this. I'm sorry.'

'I understand.' He'd do exactly the same for his child.

• • •

It was full velvet night as he walked back through the town. John kept his knife in his hand. Roland might be close; the man was bold enough.

At first he almost walked past the house, too used to the old home on Saltergate. He recalled just in time.

Katherine and Martha were still awake. Walter had told them his part of the tale and gone off to bed.

Things were still awry in the hall, piles of this and that gathered on the floor and the settle. He poured a mug of ale and drank as Katherine looked at him. She knew the truth as plainly as if he'd told her.

'You're a good man, John,' Martha said. 'There are plenty who wouldn't have gone after the boy.'

'I had to.'

'That's what I mean.' She smiled and all the deep lines crinkled on her face.

Katherine reached out, took his hand and squeezed it gently. To most people, it was done. Alan was home. But they understood that the ending still had to be written.

• • •

Later he stood by Juliana's bed.

'She wore herself out,' Katherine whispered in his ear. Around them, everyone else was resting, the air filled with the snuffles of night. A tiny sliver of light came through a crack between the shutters. He'd gone round and barred all the doors and windows. Chesterfield was safe enough, but he would take no chances with his family. Until Roland was dead he'd stay on his guard.

• • •

He could see Alan had worked hard the day before. He missed the boy's company and the sight of him so eager for another day's labour. For now, though, he was on his own. Polishing, rubbing down. Mindless tasks that let his thoughts drift.

But that was dangerous. He needed to be aware every moment. His hand moved to the knife, easing it in and out of the sheath.

John took each task methodically. He'd forgotten what it was like to do the jobs alone. Even though Alan couldn't say a word, his hands spoke loudly, and his presence, his willingness to learn, made everything go more quickly.

By the late afternoon he'd done all he could. The final coat of polish glistened on the wood. Tomorrow he'd warm the glue over a small fire and fit the pieces together. One day for it all to dry and then it would be ready to go into the church. He turned his head, craning to look up to the top of the spire. This would do justice to the building, he knew that. And to the memory of the coroner.

Carefully, he wiped all the tools with an oiled rag, slipping them one by one into the old leather satchel before he stood and hoisted it on to his shoulder. Going home with his muscles sore and aching, it could have been the end of any day.

But it wasn't. Roland was still out there and he was going to demand his reckoning. Sooner, rather than later. The man had taken Alan; he wouldn't hesitate to go after John's family. He couldn't keep them all safe, not every moment of every day. There could only be one answer: he had to go to Roland. It wouldn't be difficult. The man would be watching somehow, waiting for his chance.

But John would do it on his terms. Man to man he had no chance. But there were ways to give himself an advantage of sorts, to even things.

First, though, he had to talk to Katherine.

• • •

'Do you believe he'd really do that?' she asked.

'I do.' They were sitting in the garden, the sun on their faces. John cradled a mug of ale, staring down at the ground. 'I brought all this on us by working for the coroner.'

'It doesn't matter now, does it? You can't change anything. Are you sure he hasn't just gone? It sounded as if you and Walter ran him off.'

'Only for a short time. He won't stop until he gets what he wants.'

'Husband, he wants you dead.'

He tried to grin, but it was a weak effort. 'No one's managed that yet.'

'Don't,' she told him sharply. 'Fate's too easily tempted. What are you going to do?'

He told her, watching her lovely face darken.

'Will it work?'

'I don't know,' he admitted. 'But it's the only thing I can think of.' He took her by the hand. 'Come on. I want to see Juliana and the others before I go.'

She couldn't hide the tears; she didn't even try. At the door she clung tight to him, as if her love might protect him from harm. Dame Martha said nothing, staring at the new rushes on the floor and frowning.

He closed the door behind himself with a heavy heart. Still early in the evening, with the cries and shouts and footsteps of people on their way home. He still had a few hours of light.

He had no choice. This was something he had to do, or Roland would never give up. He had to keep his family safe. John took the nalbinding needle from his scrip and slid it up his sleeve, then gripped the knife in his right hand as he walked down Soutergate towards the bridge.

This wasn't how he wanted things to be. All he'd ever desired was a quiet life, working with wood, raising his family. But the coroner… no matter now. De Harville was dead and in his grave. Nothing could change it now.

Faces came into his mind. His father, the people he'd known here and there. The girl he thought he'd loved in York who'd proved so faithless. Brother Robert. Dame Martha. Walter. Juliana. Jeanette. Eleanor. Katherine.

As he moved past the houses, leaving the town behind, there were only the sounds of the country. Animals, birds. The call of a shepherd to his dog. The road was empty, cart tracks in the dust. The lazar house seemed far away. But everything appeared to be an insurmountable distance.

He was listening closely for any noise, scarcely daring to breathe. Roland might attack anywhere, at any time. But he believed that the man would want his battle. He'd relish the chance to humiliate and savour his victory. And if that was what he chose, so be it.

Thoughts and distance. One seemed to consume the other. He'd been staring at the leper colony on the horizon and suddenly he was walking by the wall. There was someone sitting by the gate, a bowl on the ground for alms.

'Pity on us, please, Master,' the rasping voice said. But there was a familiar note to it.

'Alison?' he asked.

'It is, Master. You shouldn't come here too often.' Today she seemed to have a little more difficulty speaking; the words gathered and clogged in her mouth.

'Maybe not. But here I am anyway, seeking another favour.'

'If it's people to go with you, the priest won't allow it again. I think he's terrified of what folk will think if they see us. We rely on their charity.'

'I see.' He'd been depending on this, to have an army of wraiths at his side. It seemed the only way to defeat Roland.

'I'm sorry, Master.'

'It doesn't matter.' He started to turn away.

'You look like a man surrounded by death.'

John smiled. 'You see that clear enough.' He looked back. 'How did you know?'

The laugh was close to a crone's cackle. 'I've walked with it for so long that it's like a friend to me now. I just wish it would come and claim me.'

'How old are you?'

'Thirty years, Master. The last five of them in here. I had a husband and three children once. They all died of the plague last month, not that I'd ever let them visit me here. Better that they believed I was already dead.'

'I'm sorry.'

'God raised Adam from the mud, isn't that what they say? And that's where our bodies go in the end. It comes to everyone and we go back to the ground.' Her voice had grown hoarse as she spoke. 'Why are you meeting Death?'

'Because it's all I can do now.' He told her. Maybe he simply needed someone to listen, someone who might understand. Maybe he was trying to postpone the moment. Slowly, awkwardly, Alison tried to stand, grasping at the wall to push herself upright. He moved forward to take her other arm but she pushed him away.

'Safer not to touch me,' she said. She steadied herself, then stopped to take a few breaths. 'Where is he, do you think?'

'By now I expect he'll be in the clearing where you found me. That's where he was yesterday. He'll have been watching me.'

'He might have run off.'

'No,' John said. 'Not him. Not until this is over.'

'Then we should go and meet him, Master.'

'Why? Why would you do this for me?' He was grateful, but he needed to know.

'Because you showed me a kindness before. You treat me like a person, the way I was before any of this. And because evil shouldn't walk the earth.'

'There's no guarantee we'll win. He might kill me. And then he'd kill you.'

'Perhaps it would be a blessing if he did. I'm already dead to the world, Master. I've been ready for a long time.'

'Then I accept.'

They walked without speaking. A slow pace, all her feet could manage. She knew the ground around here; it was where they collected the wood for their fires. Alison gestured to a path that cut across some common ground. The cows had been taken in for their evening milking.

Soon enough the woods surrounded them and the world became hushed. He let her lead, but as he sensed the clearing in the distance John tugged at her sleeve.

'I can't let you go in there without a weapon,' he whispered and let the needle slip from his sleeve. He held it by the tip. Her misshapen, ugly hand appeared, more claw than anything human, and closed around it.

'This is what he uses to kill,' John told her. Hidden inside her cowl, she nodded. 'Now let me go first. This is my fight.'

'No, Master. You wanted me with you. We go side by side or not at all.'

He smiled. She had spirit, she had fight. What had Alison been like when she was a young woman, he wondered? He'd never know now. But he was glad she was here with him. One deep breath and then a step…

• • •

Roland turned at the sound.

'Scared to face me alone, Carpenter? Yesterday it was a boy with a sling and today it's a leper.' He laughed.

Let him talk. The longer he spoke, the more unnerved he was. Slowly, John edged away from Alison. Enough distance and Roland would have to split his attention between the two of them.

'Which one do I kill first? You or… that?'

John's palms were slick with sweat. He could feel drops running down his back inside his shirt. On the way here he'd been filled with fear, wanting to turn back and knowing he couldn't, that it had to be this way.

Now it had gone. There was simply the moment. Watching Roland and taking one pace, then another, until he stood across the clearing from Alison. Now Roland looked one way, then the other, and the smile on his face seemed false and frozen.

'Well, John the Carpenter, do you think you can best me?'
He took the dagger from his belt and pushed the tip into the
ground. 'Come for me. You have the advantage.'

And where else did the man have a blade? In his boot?
There would be another, he was willing to wager, probably
more than one. But John stood still and said nothing.

Alison took half a step forward and Roland turned sharply
to face her. As soon as his back was turned, John did the same.
He couldn't see the woman's face, hidden deep in the shadow.
He didn't need to.

'Which first?' Roland asked. 'You, or you? Or the pair of you
together?' His voice had the odd, shrill note of worry. Victory
wasn't going to come as easily as he imagined. A bird fluttered
away through the branches and the man turned quickly.

Another half pace from Alison. He followed suit. They were
still too far for Roland to reach. John swallowed. His throat
was dry, as if he'd never had a drink in his life. Slowly, he raised
the knife, ready, and Roland's lips curled into a smile.

'So it's you and me, John the Carpenter. You'd have done
better staying with your tools.' His body was tense, ready. But
he'd taken his attention from Alison, brushed her from his
mind as no more than a nuisance.

A mistake.

John didn't understand how she did it. He never saw, his
gaze focused on Roland. But she seemed to soar through
the air. She covered the distance in one leap until she was on
his back and the man was screaming and twisting. Roland
tried to reach for the dagger he'd hidden inside his jerkin.
And then John moved, running. He felt his knife sink into
flesh, again and again until the body slumped under him.
Roland fell to the floor, Alison on top of him. Gently, John
reached under her arms and pulled her away, praying she was
still alive.

The nalbinding needle was still in her hand, clutched between twisted fingers. Blood covered the front of her dark habit, and the handle of a knife stuck from her thin chest. He pulled back the cowl and looked at what remained of her face. Her lips were pulled back in a rictus grin. Eyes empty, lifeless. Tenderly, he lowered her to the ground. Her body seemed to weigh nothing at all.

He cut the strings of Roland's scrip and pushed it into his belt. He was dead, too, a tiny blossom of blood on the front of his shirt, over his heart. She'd been the one to kill him.

John went to cut branches and vines, lashing them together to make a hurdle. It wasn't even or strong, but that didn't matter. All he needed to do was return her body to the lazar hospital. As he worked he started to hear the birds singing their twilight songs, as if the wood had come alive again without him even knowing it.

How had she done it? The most she'd been able to manage was a slow, hesitant walk. How had she found the strength to leap like that? It was as if something had given her the power for one last thing.

He couldn't mourn her. She was ready to die. She wanted it. That was why she'd come with him. But she deserved to be buried and remembered with honour. Alison had taken one small evil out of the world.

He laid her body on the hurdle and began to pull it along the track to the leper colony. Roland could stay where he was. The animals could devour him. Let his soul rot.

• • •

John knocked on the gate until someone finally drew back the bolt, holding up a rushlight in the creeping darkness. The priest.

'My son?' he asked in confusion.

'I've brought Alison home to you, Father.'

The priest bent, holding the light over her. He crossed himself. 'What happened?'

'It's safer that you never know. But she died doing something good. She was a brave woman.'

'God save her soul.'

'He will, Father. I have no doubt of that.' He took all the money from Roland's scrip and tipped it into the priest's hand. 'Give her a good funeral, Father, and use the rest here.'

'This is a very fair sum, my son.'

'Then spend it on the people here, Father.' He looked down at Alison for the last time. She'd finally found the peace she desired.

• • •

The walk to Chesterfield felt long. He ached to his bones, a weariness that rose up inside. A sliver of moon hung in the sky, the star bright against the blackness. At the bridge over the Hipper he opened Roland's scrip again. Just papers, writing on folded sheets of vellum that he couldn't read. He tossed them down into the water and watched them float away on the current.

He didn't want to know who had been behind all the killings. Ignorance was safer. Let every trace of Roland vanish. He held on to the leather scrip for a moment then dropped it into the river.

CHAPTER TWENTY-FIVE

Katherine was waiting for him. But he knew she'd have waited until the Judgement Call. He closed the door and leaned against it, exhausted. Then she had her arms around him, holding him close, not letting him go.

He clung to her. At the far end of the hall he saw Martha standing in the doorway of the room that was now hers. She smiled, then disappeared as if she'd never been there.

Finally he was ready to sit, looking around this new, unfamiliar place before settling on the bench by the table. A rushlight burned smokily.

'It's over now,' he said.

Katherine put her hand over his. 'There won't be anything more?' she asked. 'You're certain?'

'I'm positive.'

Roland had performed his duty. The men he had to kill were dead; those who employed him would be satisfied. And if he never returned, so be it. He doubted that they'd care. All trace of him would be gone. By morning there'd be nothing left in the clearing. If he had a camp somewhere, nature would grow over it. His name would be forgotten.

'Thank God for it all,' she said. 'And another day without plague.'

'We're free now,' John told her.

'Yes.' She leaned forward and kissed him.

No more coroner to arrive on his doorstep with his demands. Whoever took de Harville's place would have his own ways, his own men. Now John could fade back to working with wood and making his living with his true skill. That was all he'd ever wanted when he arrived in Chesterfield. He'd gained much more than he'd ever expected along the way, that was true. But the ugly parts, the deaths, he could leave those behind.

'I need to sleep.'

• • •

He stood by Juliana's small bed, watching Katherine as she undressed. Unbuckling her girdle, pulling off the old gown until all that remained was her shift. She combed her long hair, pulling down as it tumbled long over her shoulders.

John rested the tips of his fingers on his daughter's chest, happy as he felt it move up and down with the rhythm of her breathing. He was a lucky man to have all this.

Katherine slipped under the sheet and patted the bolster.

'Come and sleep, husband,' she said.

He took off his jerkin and tunic, letting them fall to the ground. The belt joined them before he untied his braies and pushed down the hose. And finally the sweetness of bed, with his arms around his wife.

• • •

Alan's mother stared at him.

'It's safe now,' he told her. 'There won't be any more trouble.'

She opened her mouth to speak, then closed it again and nodded. The boy ran out, the satchel slapping against his small body.

It was a good summer morning, still with the soft early scent in the air. The heat would come later, but by then they'd be finished with their work.

In the churchyard he let Alan inspect the bench. He ran his hand over it, feeling the smoothness and all the hours that had gone into its creation. Finally the boy stood back, grinning, and nodded his approval. John ran a cloth over the wood.

Walter should arrive soon and together they'd carry it into the church. He'd measured carefully, he knew how it would fit.

Alan's fingers began to speak. Is he dead? Did you kill him?

'Yes,' John answered with a sigh. 'You can put him out of your mind now.' He didn't want to talk about it, simply allow it to slide away into the past. But the boy had suffered; he deserved to know. Another question came.

'Yes,' he said. 'I promise. He can never hurt anyone again.'

He was glad when Walter arrived. Perhaps he'd have questions, too, or he might just leave it all be. For now, the lad was here for his height and his muscles.

It took time. First to the porch, where they rested, then halfway down the nave. Finally he nudged it into place and ran a rag over the wood one last time to remove any finger marks.

This was something to be proud of. It would still be here long after he was dead and nobody recalled his name. But who made a thing wasn't important. It was the act of doing and the creation itself that mattered.

'I need to leave for a little while,' he told Alan, and saw the worry on the boy's face. 'I'll be back. Just stay here. It's cool inside and you're safe. Completely safe.'

• • •

'Mistress, Roland is dead.'

She was wearing a crisp wimple and a plain gown. The dark shadows formed smudges under her eyes. He'd talked his way past the servant, then asked Brother Edmund to fetch her.

'Thank God for that.' But there was no pleasure in her gaze. 'Did you…'

'Yes,' John answered, but she didn't prompt him for more details. None of it would bring her husband back. 'I know it's a bad time.'

'I don't know if there will ever be a time that feels good,' she said. 'I'm taking my son and we're going to live with my brother and his wife.'

'I understand. But please, there's something I'd like you to see. Your husband commissioned it from me.'

She cocked her head to one side. 'What is it? He never mentioned anything to me.'

'You'll have to come and see it at the church.'

They walked side by side, not talking. People from the town came up to offer their condolences. She nodded her head at each of them but she didn't speak. John opened the heavy church door and let her pass, giving her time to adjust to the soft light after the brightness outside.

'Here, Mistress.'

She gazed at it, then at him and Alan by his side.

'You made this?' she asked.

'At your husband's command.' He knew he needed to gild the truth a little. 'He wanted to give thanks to God for sparing us all.'

She ran her hand over the curve at the end of the bench, then the flatness of the seat.

'You've done his memory proud,' she said finally. 'Both of you. Thank you. Did he pay you?'

'No, Mistress.'

'Then I will.'

'Thank you.' He placed a hand on the boy's head. 'Alan did much of the work.'

'Then I thank you, too.'

He blushed to the roots of his hair.

'You served him well,' she told John. 'I'll always be grateful for that.' She stroked the bench again. 'This is beautiful work. I'll see you're rewarded for it.'

• • •

How long before he came to think of the house on Knifesmithgate as home? He'd lodged there when he first came to Chesterfield, when it had belonged to Dame Martha. Now the room that had been his was hers and he was master of this place, as if the world had tipped upside down.

The women were still finding nooks and crannies for everything, Juliana tottering around behind her mother, amused by her new surroundings. But there was a jug of ale and a loaf of bread in the buttery and the sun was warm and comforting in the garden.

This was a time to look ahead, to see the future for them all here. All the girls growing in joy and laughter. Walter passing that cusp of manhood. He and Katherine could become old together, God willing.

But never forget the past. He was here, he was alive when he should have been dead. Perhaps there was a reason for it. Alison had sacrificed herself. She'd given herself death, the thing she craved, and in doing so she'd saved him. He knew no prayers of his could ever thank her enough.

November 1364

The year was dying, the leaves all gone from the trees. Mornings were crisp and sharp, the first frosts hardening the earth. There would be little more work until the weather cleared for spring. Just some small jobs in houses, and things that became too urgent.

That was fine. He had money in the coffer to see them through winter, and there were things he wanted to do at the old house on Saltergate. Alan would go there with him. Let the boy keep earning a little and practising his craft. He had a proper set of tools in his satchel now. The coroner's wife had been generous in her payment for the bench and John had split it evenly with him on condition that he used it for tools; they'd selected them together at the Saturday market.

Their new home had more space. It had grandeur. Yet every time he entered it took a moment to realise this was his, that he'd become a man of circumstance and property in town. Maybe he'd become used to the idea in time. But it was hard to believe that only four years earlier all he'd owned were his tools and a few clothes.

On an October afternoon, Martha had another spell away from the world. Katherine had sent Eleanor running off to find him. By the time John arrived, the old woman was back, chattering and smiling as if nothing had happened. There would be more, they understood that. And one day she might not return. But that was the future.

And the past… that was something to leave behind. No one had ever appeared to ask about Roland, and he was certain they never would. His victims lay in the churchyard, buried with the plague dead.

There had been no more cases of the pestilence since de Harville's death. It had vanished as suddenly as it arrived. He talked to travellers who claimed it had raged until autumn in other places, but Chesterfield had been safe.

Some said it was a miracle. He wasn't so sure. But whatever the ways of God, he was grateful.

The town had a new coroner, an older, sullen man who'd yet to make his mark here. John was happy to keep his distance and he'd received no call to help. At last he had his quiet life.

Juliana walked steadily towards him. No toddling now. Each stride was firm and purposeful. With a wide grin she extended her arms. He knew what she wanted and lifted her into his arms.

'You're heavy now,' he told her, bouncing the girl up and down on his arm as she giggled in delight.

He felt a touch on his shoulder and turned. Katherine stood there, smiling at the two of them.

'It's just as well you enjoy that. There'll be two of them to carry in a few months,' she told him with a smile, holding one hand over her belly.

He kissed her gently as their daughter laughed with pleasure.

ABOUT THE AUTHOR

CHRIS NICKSON is a popular music journalist and crime novelist whose fiction has been named best of the year in 2011 by *Library Journal* and in 2017 by Booklist. Specialising in historical crime, Chris is the author of three series for The Mystery Press: the Dan Markham series set in 1950s Leeds; the Lottie Armstrong series set during the war years, and, of course, his medieval mystery series set in fourteenth-century Chesterfield.

Also by the Author

The Crooked Spire
The Saltergate Psalter

★

Dark Briggate Blues: A Dan Markham Mystery
The New Eastgate Swing: A Dan Markham Mystery

★

Modern Crimes: A WPC Lottie Armstrong Mystery
The Year of the Gun: A WAPC Lottie Armstrong Mystery

www.chrisnickson.co.uk